Gusliar Wonders

MACMILLAN'S
BEST OF SOVIET SCIENCE FICTION

ARKADY AND BORIS STRUGATSKY
Roadside Picnic/Tale of the Troika
Prisoners of Power
Definitely Maybe
Noon: 22nd Century
Far Rainbow/The Second Invasion from Mars
Beetle in the Anthill
Space Apprentice
Escape Attempt

KIRILL BULYCHEV
Half a Life

MIKHAIL EMTSEV AND EREMEI PARNOV
World Soul

DMITRI BILENKIN
The Uncertainty Principle

VLADIMIR SAVCHENKO
Self-Discovery

MACMILLAN
New Soviet Science Fiction

ALEXANDER BELIAEV
Professor Dowell's Head

VADIM SHEFNER
The Unman/Kovrigin's Chronicles

VICTOR KOLUPAEV
Hermit's Swing

ALEXEI TOLSTOY
Aelita

VLADIMIR GAKOV, ED.
World's Spring

GENRIKH ALTOV AND VALENTINA ZHURAVLYOVA
Ballad of the Stars

GUSLIAR WONDERS

Kirill Bulychev

TRANSLATED FROM THE RUSSIAN BY *Roger DeGaris*

Macmillan Publishing Co., Inc.
NEW YORK

Collier Macmillan Publishers
LONDON

Macmillan Publishing Co., Inc.
866 Third Avenue, New York, N.Y. 10022
Collier Macmillan Canada, Inc.

Library of Congress Cataloging in Publication Data

Bulychev, Kir.
    Gusliar wonders.

    Translation of: Chudesa v Gusliaro.
    I. Title.
PG3479.4.U56C513   1983   891.73'44   83-981
ISBN 0-02-518010-X

---

10   9   8   7   6   5   4   3   2   1

Printed in the United States of America

Contents

The Dedication of Ananda's Temple

To a passenger on an approaching ship, our station, so vast, with its pipelike corridors, the globes of its laboratories and fuel storage, the tangle of cables and gravity pad, would be just a green speck on the radar screen. But in the three weeks I had been on the station I still had not seen all the labs and had not met all the inhabitants.

"Are you sleeping, professor?"

I recognized Sylvia Ho's voice. "No. I'm thinking. I put out the light because that makes it easier to think."

"Can you really make it a point to think? I walk and think, eat and think, talk and think."

"Before, I never really noticed whether or not I was thinking. Only recently, in my seventh decade, did I realize that thinking was worth being singled out as an independent process."

"You're putting me on, professor. But I just popped in for a minute—the captain asked me to remind you that the screen will be turned on in half an hour."

"Thank you. I'm coming."

I sat up in bed and barely managed to grab onto the grip in time. Since the morning, we had had weightlessness. Before experiments with the screen, rotation ceased—the station was positioned with an accuracy of a micron. I hate weightlessness. It provides a very few minutes of childish amazement at the possibilities of one's own body. Then it soon bores you, wears you down, causes a slight nauseous feeling, and makes it hard to sleep.

"Are you sleeping, professor?"

"No. Is that you, Taik?"

"You haven't forgotten that we're turning on the screen in half an hour?"

"I'm coming, I'm coming."

I groped around under my bed for my magnet-soled shoes. They slip over the floor too easily and demand a definite effort to pull them loose. The old-timers here look like speed skaters. I resemble a beginner on the ice for the first time.

"Professor, are you sleeping?"

"Thanks. I remember. I know that we're turning on the screen in half an hour."

"I was going past and decided to warn you. Today's your big day, professor."

I sat for a minute, listening to the delicate rustles that penetrated the station. These sounds, no matter how low they seemed, were a remarkable evidence of life, contrasting with the hopeless emptiness of space. A pot clanged in the galley, a robot whirred, the air in an air-conditioning duct rustled, a piece of lab equipment hummed like a mosquito, a kitten squealed. There were eight of them, I believe. Maybe more. They would flutter through doorways, their fur bristling, float before your eyes, and struggle to get their claws into something solid.

"Have you come, professor? Today's your day."

That was the Russian physicist. The physicists had done their job, and now they had to wait and worry like the rest of us.

"It's a big day for all of us," I answered. "And most of all for Sylvia."

Sylvia was sitting next to the wall opposite the screen, with a pad on her angular knees. She was smiling at me in gratitude, timidly. Have no fear, my little mouse, no one's going to chase you away. Today is really our day. For the time being, Sylvia and I are the only specialists for whom the screen will be working. The others designed it, assembled it, tuned it, and retuned it. We would watch. Sylvia was an anthropologist, I am a historian.

"Are you hot, professor?" Taik asked. He was squatting in front of an opened panel on the control panel.

"Open a window," the Russian physicist said.

"You'd catch a cold," the captain answered. "Today's your big day, professor. If the physicists haven't misled us."

The captain settled down into an armchair right in front of the screen. The screen was huge, the length of the entire wall, black, and therefore bottomlessly deep.

The Russian physicist took a miniature chess set out of his pocket but did not hold it tightly. The box opened, and the pieces blew out in a fan, like sparrows saving themselves from a falcon.

"Fifteen minutes," Richard Tempest said.

Everyone was calm, perhaps too calm. Silently, like speed skaters, some engineers entered the lab, cast spells over the control panel, talked softly, briefly, and for the most part incomprehensibly. Gradually the lab filled with spectators. It became crowded. One of the young people took off his shoes and sat on the wall, right under the ceiling, hanging from a grip.

"Sit down here, a little closer," the captain said. "And where's Sylvia?"

Parasvati gave me his seat. Squeezing the arms of the chair, I felt more secure.

"I still can't believe it," Sylvia said, glancing at Taik. He bent over a microphone, and dictated some figures to the bridge. Then he straightened up, inspected us like a commander before a battle, looked at the screen, and said, "Light."

"Let there be light," the physicist whispered. He had not picked up the chess pieces.

The lights in the lab dimmed, and the many-colored dials on the panel shone more brightly.

"Start," the bridge commanded.

A bright cloud appeared on the black ellipse of the screen. It grew in its depths, flared up and came close, spreading out to the edges. Green sparks raced through it. This went on for a minute and then the screen suddenly turned sky-blue, and reddish-brown-and-white spots appeared in the bottom half, as though the picture was out of focus.

"It's working," Parasvati said. "A hell of a lot better than yesterday."

"You call that better?" one of the spectators asked disappointedly.

"Ah!" Sylvia said. A magician had torn the veil from the screen, and brought the picture into sharp focus. Before our eyes stood an ordinary Earth landscape, so real and well-sculpted, as though the screen were a window on a neighboring world, a world flooded by hot sunlight, saturated by dust and a fresh breeze. A dark-blue, broad strip turned into the sky. On the ochre sand, houses took shape, and deep ruts in the narrow roads, and an occasional palm.

"Everything's OK," Taik said. "We're in the right spot."

"Is that correct?" the captain asked.

"Just a minute," I answered.

It was noon. A fine dust whirled above the ground that had been torn up and trampled by water buffalo. Enmeshed in a bamboo forest and covered by reed mats, a building was under construction. It was the logical center of the scene we were observing. Numerous teams of oxen and water buffalo stretched toward it, loaded with yellow brick. Lines of almost naked people, balancing on thin poles, ascended upward against the sky. On top, stonecutters were working. In the left part of the screen one could see a veranda, the pillars of which were abundantly adorned with delicate carvings. In front of the veranda two spear-carrying warriors were dozing.

"Well, professor?"

Everyone in the lab was waiting for my answer.

"It's Pagan," I said. "The end of the eleventh century."

"Hurray!" someone said softly.

"We made it?" a loudspeaker asked. The officer on duty on the bridge had become excited.

"Hurray!" the physicist answered him. "Three cheers for us!"

"And let's toss the professor in the air," Taik suggested.

"I have nothing to do with it; you could show the picture to ten different historians, and they'd all say the same thing."

"But the professor said it first."

They needed to relieve the tension. Better me than Sylvia. I just tried to avoid hitting any equipment, although there was no real need to—I floated slowly and solidly, like a balloon. My tormentors also were torn free from the floor and flew up after me, so in the semidarkness of the lab, lit by the sun of a distant world, a many-armed, many-headed monster moved. A good thing the people on the other side of the screen could not see us—they would have died of fright.

"Look!" Sylvia said, having managed to hide in a corner and escape the universal triumph. "Look! A man!"

A wrinkled, withered old man was carrying a clay pot, hugging it to his chest. He walked so close and was so clearly and distinctly visible that you could count the wrinkles on his face. It even seemed surprising that he could not see us. He paused for a moment, turned in our direction, took a deep breath, and continued on his way. His glance instantly interrupted the excited merriment. People floated down like autumn leaves.

"He wanted to tell us to mind our own business, but didn't know what language we spoke."

"A shame the movie doesn't have sound."

"But can the professor understand what they're talking about?"

"Only with difficulty. Almost a thousand years have passed."

"What a decisive capability!"

"Professor, tell us about them."

"You won't be bored?"

"Not at all."

"Tell us, professor."

"I don't know how to begin," I said. I do not like to be the center of attention. Even more so since I could not rid myself of the feeling that I was in reality a usurper. A pretender to the throne. The important thing was not history but the fact that people had finally learned to look back at the past.

Interference ran over the screen like black lightning, and the ground trembled.

"Increase power," the captain told Taik.

"It's already going," Taik said. "Another three or four minutes, no longer."

"Tell us about it, professor."

"It was a great civilization. Its possessions stretched from the Himalayas and the mountains of southern Auna to the Bay of Bengal. It existed for two hundred fifty years, and its capital was the city of Pagan. The building in the forest is the temple of Ananda, the first of Pagan's gigantic temples, constructed during the reign of King Kyanzitta. This temple, like many other temples and pagodas—about five thousand of them— stands in the center of Burma, on the banks of the Irawaddy River."

"Still standing?"

"Yes."

The old man with his pot was crossing the screen again. He looked tired and hot. Looking at him, I realized that it was hot in the lab too. And then suddenly the screen dimmed. The last thing we saw was a young girl running up to the old man and taking the pot. Black bolts of lightning blotted out the ancient city and it was impossible to make out the girl's face.

The artificial dead light of the flat ceiling flared on. The captain said, getting up from his chair carefully, "The session is over."

"Could it be that there was really nothing? That we just thought we saw it?" Parasvati asked.

"It's all been recorded," Taik said. "Do you want an instant replay?"

The people lingered. It did resemble a movie theater where a film had just been shown, an unbelievably imaginative, strange, and unexpected film.

"Taik, tell the bridge to begin rotation. Until the morning." The captain helped me to the door.

"It's remarkable," I said to him.

"And you, professor, refused to come here."

"Oh, so you know about that?"

"Yes."

"I'm a conservative. It's hard to believe in chronoscopy."

I really did refuse several times to fly to the station. I tried convincing the president of my college to pick someone younger, less occupied, quicker on the uptake. "All right," I said to him. "Let us suppose that that chronoscope does have something to it. Let us also suppose that under certain circumstances it is possible to find a point in space whose own time is one thousand years behind Earth's. But what can we see at such a distance?" The president was patient and courteous. The same as he had been twenty years before when he took his orals on Burmese history. He had always had a polite condescension toward the person he was talking to, whether one of his teachers or a professor under his jurisdiction. "No," he answered. "You are not right, professor. You can maintain with equal success that a steam locomotive will not move because it does not have a horse harnessed up inside. No one would have spent years on building the station if chronoscopy were a myth. If physicists calculate that the screen at the station can look back to Burma in its eleventh century, then that is what will happen." The president smoothed down some nonexistent hair on his bald spot and looked at me reproachfully: I have lived on Earth so long and still had doubts about the omnipotence of science. Then he said in a different tone, a tone demanding a kind smile: "In any case, we want to see the best Burmese history at the station. You, professor, are the best historian of Burma—and I am speaking not only as president but as your former student. And if the prestige of the university means anything to you . . ." There his voice almost disappeared and hé offered me a glass of orange juice. Drinking the juice, I thought, Why not? I'd never been further than the moon.

At first the station appeared as a green speck on the radar screen, gradually grew into a tangle of pipes, globes, and cables. I was greeted by strangers' handshakes, mostly young ones, lightly dressed for the heat. The station was like Rangoon on a May night: wet from the nearly monsoon clouds, stifling from the sun's rays, which got lost in the tamarinds' foliage and heated the blue air.

"Our heating unit is on the blink," Taik said, a young man whose long eyelashes cast a shadow on his prominent cheekbones. "Yesterday it was only fifty degrees. But we manage."

The captain accompanied me to my cabin. "I'm glad you've arrived," he said. "It gives our work some meaning."

"Why?"

"You're a busy person. And if you could drop everything and come here, that means that chronoscopy is worth taking seriously."

The captain was joking. He believed in chronoscopy, he believed that the screen would work and wanted me to believe as well.

Since then three weeks passed, and in my person the fans of the screen (there were no nonfans present) acquired a passionate neophyte. Three times in three weeks the screen shone, filled with colorful clouds, presented us with transitory, incomprehensible images, but that was all. And then, finally, we saw Pagan.

At seven in the evening sleeptime we gathered in the lab. One sitting a day. Twenty-seven minutes and a few seconds. Then the picture faded out.

My original proposal that the veranda with the carved columns belonged to the palace of King Kyanzitta was confirmed the next day when during the middle of the session dust rose in the distance and out of the dust clouds horsemen flew out and pranced around at the foot of the stairs. The guards stood up straight, raised their spears. An elephant with bronze-covered tusks approached the veranda. On its back, under a golden umbrella, a not-old man was sitting, with large features. I recognized him; he resembled a statue I had seen countless times in the half-dark central hall of the temple of Ananda. The artist was truthful, depicting the king as he had. Now there was no doubt that the king's mother really was, as the annalists maintained, an Indian.

"So," I said, "I was right. The annalists have to be believed even in the details—which cannot be explained as later political considerations."

"Who is that?" Taik asked.

"King Kyanzitta," I said with surprise. "It's perfectly clear."

"Professor, you're tremendous," the captain said. "Of course it's King Kyanzitta, whom we've all known since childhood."

The king was followed doggedly by the high priest, a person also well known from the chronicles, Shin Arahan, a wrinkled elder. The priest did not follow the king into the palace but set about giving the architect some invaluable instructions, even drawing arches in the dust with his staff.

That day we also saw the overseers beat with bamboo canes workers who had committed some kind of error. The sight was horrible; it seemed that human screams pierced centuries and billions of kilometers before entering the lab. Within two minutes the whole station knew about what happened and the lab was filled with physicists, electronics engineers, and assemblers, and their judgment was so severe that I felt ashamed for medieval Burma, and perhaps that is why, when the screen went off, I said, "Of course, if we saw the Crusades or Ivan the Terrible, none of you would become indignant."

"Don't be upset, professor," the captain answered, speaking for everyone. "It has been a hell of a lot worse than that. It's not worth descending a thousand years into the past just to see things like that. But we just happened to see Burma. And we cannot go into the screen and grab the overseers by the arm."

The next day, brown spots of blood were visible on the sand, where the corporal punishment had been performed. Toward the end of the session a wind started and covered them with dust.

My distant ancestors' life was hard, dirty, and cruel. The golden age of the chronicles and legends did not stand up to the test of reality. And the temple of Ananda seemed all the more remarkable: masterfully perfect, light, noble, destined to celebrate the greatness of the Pagan state down through the ages. It soared proudly above the suffering of the common people and became a monument to them, who had, despite everything, not lived their allotted years on Earth in vain.

The old man who had carried water the first day had a daughter. Everyone at the station knew the daughter, and the restless physicists have come to see her, and made bets about whether she would show up.

The daughter (or maybe the granddaughter) was of average height, slender, and supple like a river reed. Her black hair was gathered in a bun at the back of her head and adorned with tiny white flowers. Her skin was the color of teak wood, her eyes like mountain lakes. Don't try to reproach me with romantic exaggeration—that is precisely the way I remember her, precisely those comparisons came to mind when I first had a good look at her. And if I, an old man, speak of the girl in such an exalted style, you can imagine the reaction of the young people. Only Sylvia was dissatisfied. She looked at Taik. But he was looking at the Pagan girl.

I accidentally overheard a conversation between Sylvia and Taik.

"Everything we see is like a performance," Sylvia said. "Do you feel it, Taik?"

"You mean that it's all invented?"

"Almost. It doesn't exist."

"But they're real. And we don't know what will happen to them tomorrow."

"No, we know. The professor knows. Those people died almost a thousand years ago. Only the temple remains."

"No, they're real. From here in the station, we see them— alive."

"They died a thousand years ago."

"See how she's smiling."

"She will never see you."

"But I see her."

"But she died a thousand years ago! You can't fall in love with a nonexistent person."

"What nonsense, Sylvia. What makes you say that I've fallen in love?"

"Otherwise you wouldn't defend her."

"I'm not defending her."

"You'd like her to be today."

"I would."

"Crazy . . ."

I sat in my chair, unnoticed by them. I smiled when Sylvia ran away down the corridor, clasping a folder of drawings and photographs of the inhabitants of the Pagan era to her chest. Taik went back to the control panel and started rummaging around with the circuits, whistling a sad tune. He was like a person in love with Nefertiti—a beautiful moment from the distant past fixed in stone.

Three days later another event occurred that excited the whole station, for the station took to heart everything that happened in Pagan. Khmer ambassadors arrived. It might be difficult for a person unfamiliar with Burmese history to understand my excitement when I identified the long-haired, richly dressed, travel-exhausted men as Khmers. They slid down from kneeling elephants, raking their heels over the wrinkly gray sides, and servants opened golden umbrellas over them, a sign of authority and power. Yes, they were Khmers, whose empire bordered Pagan. And it was possible that that very day, or the next, a long argument among historians would be settled: Did Pagan pay tribute to Angkor, or was the chronicle of Dhammayan Yazavin correct in asserting that the Khmer kings recognized the power of Pagan?

The envoys proceeded into the depths of the palace. They were followed by men carrying boxes with gifts, bowls of betel, trays with fruit. The palace began bustling, surrounded by a crowd of curiosity seekers, and through the dust they raised one could see workers hastily knock down the scaffolding from the temple of Ananda—apparently, they wanted to show it to the esteemed guests.

That night I had to take a sleeping pill. Sleep wouldn't come to me. Time stood still. At any moment the envoys could leave and escape my observation. For me and for history the minor details that I alone could understand could allow me to determine the real relationship between the Burmese and the Khmer—ancient rivals and great builders.

And once again the screen lit up. Curiosity seekers were still crowded in front of the palace, and there were quite a few of them. Consequently, I said to myself, feeling relieved, consequently the envoys hadn't left.

From the well, carrying a filled jug, our familiar girl was walking. She set the jug on a step of the veranda and started a conversation with a guard. Customs in Pagan were simple, and the guard did not chase the girl away. He talked with her about something quite excitedly. Then a monk in the blue robes of the forest brotherhood joined them and glanced over the railing into the palace, and the second guard shouted something funny to him. A fat and oiled person, one of the palace retainers, stepped out onto the veranda, picked up the jug, and took a drink.

Taik forgot about his control panel. He was watching the girl. I snuck a glance in the other direction, where Sylvia was sitting. She was pretending to be lost in her notes.

One of the Khmer envoys slowly and triumphantly, like an actor in bad theater, appeared from behind the edge of the screen and stopped near the railing, staring distractedly at the white temple. He was followed by Shin Arahan, the high priest, who was tapping gently with his staff. He asked the Khmer something, and the physicist sitting next to me guessed his question: "How do you like our temple?"

The Khmer answered, and the physicist translated once more: "The temple is all right. We have better."

Taik stared at the girl. The girl stared at the Khmer, who was for her an exotic specimen of an alien, incomprehensible world. The Khmer, apparently, sensed her glance and, turning to Shin Arahan, smiled and said something. The physicist immediately translated: "Your girls are better than your temples."

Someone in back giggled. Taik frowned. Shin Arahan nodded and also looked at the girl. She became confused and took several steps backward. The guards broke out laughing. So did the Khmer. He was trying to convince Arahan, pointing a ring-laden finger at the girl, but the high priest smiled politely and, apparently, did not give the necessary answer.

" 'Give her to me,' the honored guest demanded," the physicist said.

"Shut up," Sylvia interrupted.

"Yes, do shut up," Parasvati supported her. "What will we do without her?"

"He's old," Sylvia said.

Taik was not listening to them. He was watching the screen. Later he told me that he was fighting the whole time against the desire to turn off the screen, as though that could change something, interrupt the chain of events. But it was only later that he told me.

The Khmer walked away, clearly dissatisfied. I said, "It's completely evident that Pagan was not a vassal of the Khmers. Otherwise Shin Arahan would not have dared to refuse the envoy. He was a great diplomat. If, of course, the Khmer was really asking for the girl as a gift."

"It would have turned out good. . . ." Parasvati said.

And he was right to have doubts. Shin Arahan stood for a minute on the veranda, lost in thought, rocking back and forth slightly, his eyes hidden in a net of wrinkles. It seemed he saw no one around him. But when the girl crept up to the terrace to take her jug, Shin Arahan suddenly awoke, shouted to the guards, turned and walked quickly away from the veranda. The guards walked over to the petrified girl from both sides, and one of them poked her in the back with the handle of his spear. The girl submissively walked in front of them across the square, and a crowd of elders silently cleared a path for her. The session was over.

This time, no one left the lab. When the lights went on I discovered that everyone was looking at me as though I could explain what had happened and, most important, convince them that nothing would happen to the girl. So I said, "The most favorable explanation is that Shin Arahan ordered the girl be taken out of sight of the Khmer. Perhaps he knows her father, perhaps he took pity on her."

"And the least favorable?"

"The least favorable—I don't know. There are always more bad interpretations than good ones. Perhaps the high priest decided to surprise the Khmer and give him a gift before his departure. Perhaps the girl somehow offended the Khmer and is to be punished. . . ."

"But she didn't say anything."

"We know very little about the customs of the time."

That evening Taik came to see me in my cabin.

"I'm going crazy, professor," he said.

"How can I help you?" I asked him. "Try to understand that it is an illusion, a documentary film that has been preserved in some marvelous way—and we are the first to see it."

"I can't believe that. I feel like turning the screen off. As though that way she would be able to escape. In the darkness."

Taik left to check the equipment, to make sure that tomorrow's showing would not be disturbed by an accidental break-down. But the next day nothing special happened.

True, we did see the old man. He was loitering in the dust in front of the palace stairs, pleading with the guards to let him in, but this time they were stern and not talkative. Apparently, the girl was still in danger. The last of the scaffolding was removed from the temple and the surface was polished. At the foot of the stairs a small but deep hole was dug, and mats were spread from the palace to the main entrance. Soldiers with short curved swords drove away the curious, to prevent them from stepping on the path.

The important events were to come the next day.

Human beings are curious creatures. Two days before only one problem had concerned me: What were the relations between Pagan and Angkor? Who paid tribute to whom? It was an important question for Burmese history, but of little interest to anyone other than myself. On the day of the last showing, on the day the temple of Ananda was dedicated—a majestic event, especially so because of the presence of foreign guests—I forgot completely about tribute, vassals, and kings. Like everyone else on the station I was worried about the girl, whose photograph now decorated every other cabin in the station. To see her smile again we would do anything, no matter how crazy it seemed. But we were powerless to do anything, crazy or not.

"Position," Taik said into the microphone. "Light. Session beginning."

"Position achieved," the bridge answered.

The light in the lab went out. On the screen was the square. The square was full of people. Only the path of mats leading to the temple was clear. Two lines of soldiers stood alongside it. Near the temple the crowd divided into bright patches. In dark blue robes were the *ari*—the forest brotherhood; in white garb the Brahmins; in orange and yellow the true Buddhists, the followers of Shin Arahan. Dust floated around the densely packed crowd and wrapped the scene in a light smoke.

The ceremonial procession came down from the veranda. First Shin Arahan set foot on the path, accompanied by his monks. Behind him under twelve golden umbrellas, King Kyanzitta. Then ministers, officials, envoys from Cambodia, from Arakan, from Ceylon . . . .

The engineers provided maximum enlargement, and so it seems that the frame of the screen moves inward, the temple grows, and we follow the king to the temple, marvelous and malevolent today. No one, not even I, an old fool, knows what is to happen. We wait.

We wait, while the king covers the distance to the temple. I looked at my watch. Ten minutes until the end of the session. Whatever will be, will be, I thought like a coward, but after we have left. And then I realized what I was afraid of, something I could not admit even to myself, something no one else could know.

There is a legend. It is repeated by many chroniclers. And many scholars believe it. On the day when a temple is dedicated, a hole is dug in front of it, and the most beautiful girl in the kingdom is buried in it alive.

And I see the king and the entire procession stop near the freshly dug hole—a grave. And I say, "Yes."

"What?" Taik asked. "What's going to happen?"

"I might be wrong."

"What's going to happen, professor?"

And so I told him about the legend. Before I could finish, the crowd parted and monks in yellow robes brought the girl, naked to the waist, tear-covered, beautiful as never before. I look at my watch. Four minutes to go. It could be over as soon as possible. We can change nothing. Taik keeps me from watching. He is standing right in front of the screen, as though he is trying to remember the moment forever so he can seek revenge: the monks' faces, the executioner's face—a large, dark-skinned man carrying a knife, who was walking toward the girl and turning halfway toward Shin Arahan, awaiting a signal.

"Taik, get away from the screen," someone behind me said. Taik was not listening. Shin Arahan nodded his head.

We were so close to the people in front of the temple that, it seemed, we heard their breathing and the girl's moan, which stopped abruptly as she gazed hypnotically at the shining knife. Then she screamed.

"Ay . . ." her shout resounded.

We turned around. All of us. Sylvia was standing in the doorway. She had come late. She had most likely not wanted to come but could not stand the solitude. Sylvia was covering her mouth with her hand and looking at the screen. We also looked there. But it was too late. We had lost our chance.

Taik had walked up against the screen, and had entered it. He was no longer in the room.

He was in Pagan. A thousand years ago and billions of kilometers away, in a crowd of monks, officials, soldiers, blue *aris,* and white Brahmins.

Mouths open wide in shouts; the executioner's hand, frozen in the air. The monks falling to the ground. Taik alongside the girl. He pushes away the bewildered executioner, snatches her up, and the girl, apparently in a faint, droops in his arms.

For an instant Taik stands motionless.

Only his eyes are alive. The pupils jump about, seeking a path to safety. He had already understood that he would not return, that he was alone in the distant past.

That is the way I remember him: a tall, broad-shouldered, ruddy young man in a silver jumpsuit and soft red ankle-high boots. On his chest, the golden spiral—the insignia of Time Service. He stood there, his feet wide apart, and the girl in his arms seemed weightless.

The scene was motionless. Only the dust rose slowly in the hot air.

And then the motionlessness exploded.

Taik ran along the mats, straight at us, but there was no screen in front of him; he saw only a dusty path, and beyond that a cliff over the Irawaddy. He disappeared below the bottom edge of the screen, and the soldiers, monks, and officials, regaining their wits, rushed after him.

The screen grows dim, black strips spread and it goes out.

And that is all. We never saw Taik again. Perhaps they were crushed when they jumped over the cliff. Perhaps they were caught and killed. Or she was killed and he sold into slavery. Perhaps they managed to run away and hide in the Chin Hills. Perhaps . . .

We could no longer receive Pagan. Something was not working in the communication system and it was several months before it was fixed.

Sylvia and I left on the first ship. The physicists stayed behind. They were arguing about the causes for the unusual event that they attempted to explain by formulas. I could not make head or tail of them. I'm an old historian, a partisan of conservative research methods.

On my desk there is a photograph of a girl with eyes like mountain lakes.

A Summer Morning

I had a slight cold. I was not really sick, just down with a slight cold. I woke up during the night from my own cough and could not go back to sleep.

Four o'clock. Outside it was getting light. In the park, past the buildings, a nightingale was laboring, and sparrows were interrupting it from the balcony. Feathery dawn clouds hung in the pearly sky, and everything around seemed painted in washed-out watercolors.

I felt like smoking. A sad state of affairs; as though I had slept myself out although I had had only three hours' sleep. I got up, went to the kitchen, and lit up, standing by the window.

Summer had arrived late. June, but the dandelions had not finished blooming. They raised their gray knitted hats right near the window, and poplar fuzz, seeming to come from the dandelions, floated up and hovered motionless in the air. The foliage was quite fresh—it rained every day.

Soon the sun would rise, driving away the watercolor tenderness, and imparting volume and weight to objects. Everything would become simpler.

A train stretched out silently along the forest at the horizon. From the distant marshaling yard I could hear the crisp voice of the dispatcher.

Where was the train going? I could make out the platforms and the reddish-brown freight cars, neat and tiny like a child's train set. It was easy to picture the train rumbling past sleeping suburban station platforms, the boards of which were still damp from the downpour during the night and where it smelled of damp leaves and a truck rustled on a nearby street carrying milk. It was strange that I pictured it all so clearly, even though I had never greeted dawn at a suburban station.

The train was already picking up speed, trying to wake up a *dacha* village that had become accustomed to the noise and slept on amid the suburban woods. The cows were being driven out to pasture, and the roosters accompanied them with desperate cries, as though bidding farewell forever.

I decided to go back to bed, but I broke out coughing again. I had to get a drink of water.

The faucet threw out a taut, stick-straight stream that smashed against the unwashed dishes, and the noise was variegated—at such a soundless time you catch the most delicate overtones before they are smothered, enslaved by the general, indistinct, monotonous noise of the daytime city.

But I did not feel like sleeping at all. And it was silly to stand in the middle of the kitchen in my underwear, admiring the view, while trying to persuade myself to go back to bed and miss the morning, forget it, not feel its caressing solitude.

I, trying not to make noise, not to hasten the arrival of day, got dressed. My shoes hit the wooden floor deafeningly, and the closet door shrieked when I opened it to get a clean shirt; the things in my apartment had not agreed to protect the morning, they were strangers to the ecological problem. I and my environment. It was no fault of theirs, they had no eyes to see the watercolor sky.

It was time to leave. And why not? Today was Sunday, my day, which I had intended, were it not for the fortunate accident, to spend senselessly, in a sham of work or rest and miss my dance with the clouds, the desperate competition between the nightingale and the sparrows, for whom its refined music was an empty amusement, while children had to be fed, worms caught, disputes with neighbors settled.

I was so filled with sympathy for the sparrows' problems

that I came to only in the hallway, quietly and carefully turning the key in the door.

Of course I did not use the elevator. It was not hard to picture how it would rattle and buzz, clambering up to the ninth floor, cursing its lack of lubrication and insolently slamming its doors, so that the entire world would know that it had to go to work at the crack of dawn.

I ran down the stairs and through the windows I could see the branches of a tall poplar that grew near the entrance, and through the branches I could see a long pink cloud. The smell of wet leaves, which flew in through a wide-open window, aroused a strange feeling in me—as though I had succeeded in something important, something I had been striving toward for a long time, as though the solution to an insoluble problem had come to me in my sleep, or a telephone call during the night had let me hear a long-awaited voice!

Whish, whish, whish—with broad strokes of the broom the janitor painted over the gray canvas of the asphalt with an invisible paint. That, too, was a dawn sound; during the day it does not happen.

I walked along the pavement, and my footsteps rang out like heartbeats.

Why don't people come out of their buildings at dawn to see the sun rise? Is it really necessary to be awakened accidentally? Doesn't anyone realize the extent of their loss? How marvelous to guess and to linger, to inhale every sigh of the breeze in the leaves, follow the martin's black lightning bolt with my eyes, to hear the buzz of a rare city bumblebee.

A truck was going down the street. Slowly, as though proud that it had thought to come out into the sun. A sprinkler truck. I felt like seeing the first rays of sun pierce the glittering fan of water, but I did not feel like following the truck, especially since the trolley was coming up to the stop. The completely empty first trolley, which came out on the tracks, especially to drive me through the city.

I took a seat near a window, and the trolley, gently setting off, immediately was hit by a stream of water, and the truck, viewed through the sheet of water pouring down the glass, seemed soft and flowing, like a Dali painting. And there was the smell of water in the trolley, as though it was traveling along the shore of a large lake.

A girl ran onto the trolley. She was happy that the trolley stopped for her and I was generous and did not argue with her when she shouted to the driver, "Thanks." After all, she did not know that it was my trolley—I had occupied it first.

The girl sat down across the aisle from me, and I saw her, as if through a magnifying glass. A wisp of dark hair curled over her ear, each hair shone in its own way, on her neck she had a small birthmark, and her eyebrows had been plucked too narrow, although I was not about to begrudge my traveling companion—she was beautiful, kind, and intelligent. She did not feel like sleeping at dawn. The girl sensed my watching her, and turned around quickly, and I smiled at her, to show how marvelous it was for us to share the same secret.

The trolley turned a corner widely—the whole avenue was at its disposal—toward Kiev Station and the driver announced that it was the last stop. I agreed with the driver—the second act of our day should take place in another setting—where precisely we would have to think up. Why shouldn't the girl prompt me on what to do next?

I was in no hurry to cross the square. I watched the girl run across its wide expanse, saw her red, pot-bellied bag shine in the station's shadow, dimly but not evilly. I could even say correctly that in her bag there was powder, lipstick, a notebook with a summary, a good book, a purse with money, a half-eaten piece of chocolate wrapped in tinfoil, a kerchief, an address book, a folding umbrella, an apple—a thousand things, and all of them necessary.

The sun's first rays reached the station's tower, lighting the clock. It was already five. Sparrow night was over. Now day would gather speed. But I was not sorry it had come. My journey continued. Two guys with a transistor radio came out of the station. Not esteeming morning's restraint, they tuned in several stations—another competition of the nightingale with the sparrow, only less justified and melodious.

I did not feel like going home. I wanted to be on an empty suburban platform. That is where I had not yet been but should be, to enrich and vary the morning. And what would the station be called? It was hardly surprising that I did not know yet. I would get out at one that pleased me. A holiday is a holiday.

But where was the girl? It was a shame that I had lost her. Although, most likely, our paths were similar—the subway was still closed, except for my special trolley, the others were in no hurry to get to work, and there was no one for them to carry, anyway.

But on the station platform I went to after buying a ticket in a machine with all the change I had in my pocket, there were people. Very businesslike, on the whole. Day-off toilers. Fishermen off late to a Sunday catch—didn't their wives let them go? A dacha husband with a voluminous shopping bag—undoubtedly he had sworn to his family that he would join them on Saturday but got held up and now was up and off as early as possible, impelled onward by a guilty conscience. Railroad workers going home from the night shift, a man carrying a television set, grandmothers in black dresses hurrying to their favorite suburban churches. A random assortment, and most of them without a good night's sleep.

And I caught sight of the girl again, as soon as I stepped into the railroad car still uncomfortably cool after being aired out overnight. She was sitting with her back to me, and I could see the curl over her ear and the red strap of her bag over her shoulder. I walked through the half-empty car to sit down across from her—not next to her—I didn't want to appear fresh. A man accidentally sits down opposite—we both had gone to the station and both ended up in the same car. Don't such things happen?

Well, let's get moving, I hurried the train. Just look, the next train is already leaving, and I could have taken it, but no, I trusted you, and you're taking your time.

An old man, maybe drunk, maybe asleep on his feet, staggered over to my bench and sat down next to me. And immediately fell asleep, leaning against me—it was more comfortable that way. I carefully moved out from under the old man and sat down on the other bench, not upset in the slightest by this minor event. The girl saw my struggle with my neighbor and smiled at me like an old acquaintance. I appreciated it. And the train finally pulled itself together, started with a jerk, and began crawling away from the city.

Over there, beyond a cluster of nine-story towers standing on a slope like brown mushrooms, was my research institute. Now it would be locked, and the watchman behind his glass door would be drowsing. A nice old man, convinced that we secretly fed on frogs, mice, sea urchins, and all the other creatures that came to us in such quantities as to make any other story unbelievable. The old man once asked me how they were, the frogs. Tasty? I answered that they were delicious, like children, which did not produce in him a desire to sample such a delicacy but did confirm his suspicions. For the old man we were flighty folk and if he had seen what we did, thoughtlessly cruel. Was a tiny step forward in understanding the brain worth the destruction of vast numbers of living beings? I cannot answer that question. I had not considered it until that very morning.

And here was the first platform—still city and no longer empty. From here I could see my apartment building—see it, but not quite distinguish it from the dozens of similar buildings on the horizon.

Finally, our train began to pick up speed. The herd I had seen from my apartment window had managed to reach the park and was now breakfasting hungrily in the morning coolness, trying to choose the freshest grass. A feeling sprang up in me of the indivisible unity of myself and the surrounding world, a consciousness that I was essential and inseparable from it; without me the world was not complete, imperfect, if only because it could not be reflected in me.

No, knowledge is not cruel, it is an organic part of each person. After all, the lion is not cruel when it kills an antelope to ensure the continuance of its species. The poor guinea pigs are sacrifices, too, not because of cruelty but because of an immense and innate desire to learn everything, to learn, to see, to understand the function of consciousness, the mechanism of our world, to understand, finally, how and why it happened that I got up this morning at dawn and felt this morning and the happiness of belonging to it.

The platforms at which the train braked or galloped by, barely slowing down, were empty. And no one entered the car and no one left it. The ten or fifteen persons who were spread out in the car without destroying its emptiness seemed to be awaiting a signal to leave it on the spot, to stand up all together and walk out, completing thereby their unstable and brief union with the train and forgetting about the journey that once, let's say five hundred years before, was exceptional, long, and worthy of tales and reminiscences.

The girl took a dog-eared book out of her red bag—people riding trains love to read long novels so that, like season tickets, they last a month. She was a puzzle, that girl. I could not figure out where she was going or why. But perhaps I am rejecting elementary explanations.

The train stopped at a damp platform lit by the slanted, still-cold sunlight. Suddenly I felt afraid—was this the place where I wanted to get off? Although, really, what difference did it make? I would get off the train with the girl and find out where she was going so early in the morning and why.

On the other hand, the old watchman was right to criticize us. We were brats who had received a toy train and to learn what made the wheels turn, we, without thinking, broke it into pieces, and then we had neither a train nor the truth. We believe that we cannot do without vivisection, although that is hardly a plus for us. What's the sense in creating a monument to a dog later—the dog is gone, and without it the world is a poorer place. But we cannot stop to consider all possible points of view—in that case we would stop, like Burden's ass, between two feedbins. It was better to hope that once we puzzled out the essence of thought, once we learned to read brains like a book, once we learned to hear thoughts, we would be able to help our little brothers. But would we help, or just hurry onward?

The girl would have to stand up just as the train was crawling into a town station, with concrete platforms and mesh-covered overpasses. I did not want to get off.

I stood up. Should I follow her? The girl would not be entering a picket fence of a little house sleeping amid blue, and no white dog would leap up when he recognized her.

"Good-bye," I said to the girl, but she did not hear me. She had already forgotten how we had ridden together through the pearly dawn.

The car was now almost empty. I stepped outside on the rear platform and lit up. Soon I would have to get off. If I spent another half-hour in the car I would lose my freedom to travel—I would turn into a tourist abroad, racing from store to store on his last day to find souvenirs for his relatives and beloved boss.

I got off at the next station.

I was right to do so.

It was precisely the one I had foreseen, wooden, wet from the rain and dew, with splashes of sun that fell onto the boards through the trees. The pines creaked in the wind, and the creak was the main sound after the rumble of the train's wheels had faded in the distance. A white peony lay on the platform—someone, in a hurry to catch the last train, dropped it and did not notice in the darkness. I did not pick it up, because it was beautiful just the way it was: on the gray boards black-green succulent leaves and the white jabot of the flower.

The path from the platform was sandy, absorbing moisture, crunchy, as though just beyond the pines lay dunes and the sea.

The dacha village was sleeping. White chickens were scratching the dirt in a flowerbed, destroying the gardener's efforts. A puppy on a much-too-heavy chain, inherited from a huge predecessor, ran up to the fence and yelped uncertainly, so that I would not suspect him of a reprehensible laziness. The chain clanked deafeningly. In the garden of the house next door an old man wearing military riding breeches, an undershirt, and a straw hat was standing, holding a watering can. I knew that this dreamed-of picture had haunted him all those years of military service: Early morning—he holding a watering can, gym shoes on bare feet—and the creak of pines. He had even hurried his troublesome, wandering soldier's life, to bring old age nearer. . . . But perhaps I was being unfair to him. Perhaps he was a great detective in the militia who raised roses while waiting for the next train to bring three majors, who would plead "Get us out of a jam, Ivan Porfitevich . . . there's been a mysterious crime in Malakhovka."

I walked further and further away from the station, peeking through fences, the most reliable criterion of the character and possessive state of the dacha owner: Where was the house I wanted to wake up in and hear the sounds I had lost somewhere in childhood—the buzzing of a bee, the clinking of cups on the veranda, and the creaking of the wellgate?

If happiness is an elusive condition of unknown cause that may or may not be connected with major events, or joyous occasions, I was happy.

And here was the house.

It badly needed repairs. The veranda was collapsing, the roof was caving in, an old apple tree rubbed against the house with its gnarled branches.

On the edge of the well there was a dented shining pail, and around the well, I could see a yellow layer of pine needles through the thin light-green grass.

I pushed the gate. It creaked, and the ancient fence, rotted near the ground, swayed. "Have to put in new posts," I thought. "That's the first thing—have to put in new posts."

Inside the house everyone was sleeping—no, the door to the veranda was open, and a light fragrant smoke—the scent reached the gate—was rising from the chimney.

"Excuse me," I would ask, "but do you have a room for rent?" Or I would say that I had lived here some thirty years before, as a boy. In any case, they wouldn't chase me away.

The lilac bushes, recently finished flowering, were wet from the dew, and I had to bend over to avoid getting a shower. A may-bug flew up clumsily from a bush, hit against my shoulder, and flew up like a rainbow-colored bullet. Lilac buds were still lying on the grass.

I walked up the squeaking gray steps onto the veranda and stopped in front of the door. "Anybody home?"

I said it softly, so as not to disturb anyone still sleeping, or myself, who had lain many years ago on an uncomfortable narrow bed seeing how the sunbeams illuminated the knots in the logs on the wall and the wisps of tow between them.

"Come in," a voice said.

A familiar person stepped out onto the porch. "We've been waiting for you," he said.

"Good morning," I said. "Excuse me."

"I said, we've been waiting for you."

"I woke up early, and didn't feel like sleeping, went out for a walk, got on the first train that came along and came here."

"Did you know where you were going?"

"I've never been here before. But it still seems to me that I lived here many years ago."

"Come inside. Take a look."

They had managed to move every last piece of our equipment here. It was remarkable how much apparatus they could fit into a small room. A bee was flying over the gray control panel, listening intently to the humming and buzzing back in answer—perhaps it sensed a kindred soul inside the machine.

"Why did you bring everything here?"

On the whole, I had nothing against the fact that I had turned up with my own kind, with familiar faces, fellow vivisectionists and frog-torturers. The coincidence did not surprise me, because life itself consists of coincidences, and today especially, coincidences seemed accepted and understandable.

"You haven't caught on yet?"

"I don't want to," I said. "You have a cup of tea for me?"

"Of course, let's all sit down and drink some tea. With sugar. We haven't slept all night."

"What's the occasion?"

"Your arrival."

"That's not an occasion for you. But for me."

"Who's arguing?"

The institute director put his soft, grandfatherly hand on my shoulder. He had walked up behind me, and I did not see him right away. About five people had gathered in the room. They were smiling like pranksters who had managed to sneak a frog into the teacher's briefcase and he, the poor duffer, was reaching into the briefcase right before summoning a flunk-out to the blackboard.

"How about it?" the director asked me. "Don't we deserve to be congratulated?"

"We?"

"You included. You haven't figured out why you turned up here?"

"Because I felt like it."

"Because we managed to tune into your biowaves and send a constant signal. You came here because we called you."

"A pity," I said.

They had been expecting a different reaction, a mixture of excitement and disbelief.

"Don't you believe us?"

I did. But I could not tell them about the dawn, the girl with the red handbag, the retired colonel, the creak of the pines, and the peony on the wet boards.

"Where are you going?"

"This is not the place for me to write my letter of resignation."

"Don't play games," the director said. "We could not warn you. The experiment would have been thrown off."

"That's not what I mean. I mean the guinea pigs."

"What guinea pigs?"

"And the sea urchins. I feel sorry for them. I'm changing jobs."

I left, leaving them in bewilderment. I undeservedly spoiled their celebration, although I was not trying to get revenge and was not even hurt. It was just that they could not understand me, and I wanted to preserve at least a tiny piece of my morning.

"Wait a minute!" someone shouted from the porch. "You yourself spent several years on the project. It's your work too. We thought you would be pleased!"

I said nothing.

At the station everything was still empty. It was still early, only six. To make the picture complete, the peony should have been trampled—a colorful detail for a sentimental tale. But the peony lay as before, warming in the sun, and the pines were rustling—nothing had changed. But I did not know whether to wait for the train or to return to the house and the old apple trees and pines—after all, they were sitting down to tea, laughing in a friendly manner, remembering how I walked up onto the porch and then ran away with a funny outrage they could not understand.

Vyachik, Don't Touch

1

His mother came to accompany Vyacheslav to the airport and behaved correctly. Vyachik had been afraid not of her tears, not of emotional outbursts, but of her instructions, which she had not given at home and might expound in front of the tourist group, in which everyone was sizing each other up, choosing partners or friends for the duration of the trip to England.

His mother was holding in her hand a rolled-up newspaper with the title in the Latin alphabet, for she always remembered that she must create the image of an efficient, contemporary, and intelligent woman. That was evident at first glance—the newspaper was laying it on thick.

Vyacheslav followed his mother's gaze. The women, in particular, were its victims. His mother pierced one of them, a thin auburn-haired woman, with her gaze.

"I thought," his mother pontificated, "of the frivolity with which intimate relationships among the youth today are entered into. I was forced to witness on the southern shore of the Crimea how a certain frenzy, typical of resorts, possessed superficially well-behaved girls. No, I'm no prude. . . ."

The auburn-haired girl had a straight part and reminded Vyachik of girls in watercolors of the early nineteenth century. The word "frenzy" just did not fit her.

"Are you listening to me?" his mother asked. "I hope you remembered your key. I might be at a lecture when you get back."

The sentence was pronounced too loudly, with a clear intent to produce an effect on the audience. The audience ignored it.

2

Lynda worked in a library and was thirteen years younger than Vyacheslav. At the beginning of the trip abroad she was embarrassed by the senior economist's timid signs of attention. Perhaps not the signs themselves, but the irony with which the surrounding people treated them.

Out of embarrassment, Lynda was dry and formal with Vyachik, until once in the bus a conversation started about a book by Garcia Marquez, and Vyachik became Lynda's ally in the argument. And soon she found two merits in Vyachik, ones that were at the top of her moral values: He was a good man, and he was well-read. Lynda stopped avoiding him.

And Vyachik was overcome by an unusual talkativeness. He wanted Lynda to know everything about him, beginning with his early childhood memories. He did not realize immediately that it happened because Lynda was the ideal listener, interested and sympathetic.

And nothing augured (it seemed to Lynda) any abrupt change in their even relationship.

One evening they were standing on the bank of the Thames. At their backs were the sad citizens of Calais, with one huge key to the city for all—the creation of the great sculptor Rodin. The Thames was narrow, just as they had expected, and on the opposite bank they saw the buildings on the postcards Vyachik had bought at the airport after they arrived.

"Are you married?" Vyachik asked, surprising himself.

"I reconsidered," Lynda said. "He was a nice person, but our interests were totally different."

Vyachik thought sadly that Lynda was still very young and could therefore make such categorical judgments. With maturity life became more complicated.

"You shouldn't have asked a question like that," Lynda said.
"Why?"

"It's interference into my personal life." Lynda suddenly
smiled and added, "Look, what a funny steamship! Ancient. I
haven't asked why you're not married."

"There's no secret to it," Vyachik said, admiring her strict,
distinct profile. "I've gotten used to living with my mother."

Lynda turned toward him, and her thin, high eyebrows
raised in amazement.

"You have to understand, my mother had no other life. She
divorced my father a long time ago. I am her only son, and
really the only person close to her."

"And what happens later?" Lynda's voice seemed to break
loose involuntarily. She did not want to seem to be interrogating Vyachik.

"Later?" Vyachik shrugged his shoulders. "I don't know."

"Do you know what I think?" Lynda said, after a short
pause. "You have probably never loved anyone with all your
heart. If that ever happens your mother will have to resign
herself to it."

"I doubt it," Vyachik said. "Mama never resigns herself."

The last night in London Vyachik began to write poetry. So
as not to awaken Zavadovsky, who was living in the same
room, Vyachik went into the bathroom, where he searched for
rhymes, seated on the enamel ledge and leaning against a hot
pipe. As luck would have it, Zavadovsky woke up during the
night and, half-asleep, burst into the bathroom. Vyachik's
pajama tops were unbuttoned, revealing a pillowlike belly and
chest that smoothly flowed into rounded shoulders. Vyachik
did not respond immediately. His fat fingers, like a mother
bird's wings when she protects her children from the hawk,
fluttered over the pad of paper.

Zavadovsky, despite his solemn promises, could not refrain,
and the next day shared his discovery with the others. After
lunch Maria Patrovna, an elderly woman who had it in for
Lynda, asked Vyachik to read his poems. Vyachik left the

table, not finishing his dessert, and Lynda, understanding what happened, quietly broke out crying and also left. Zavadovsky was sorry he had started the whole affair. Lynda found Vyachik in the hotel bar, where he had spent half his foreign currency on three glasses of whiskey.

This event changed their relationship. Not so much because of the fact itself of the senior economist's poetic affections, although Lynda was flattered, as much as the fact that Vyachik had suffered and been humiliated because of his feelings for her.

Vyachik suspected pity in Lynda's conduct, and Mama had always taught him to reject that feeling as shameful. But since, during the remaining weeks, the whole group, with several notable exceptions, acquired the custom of watching over them, and since it always turned out that they got seats next to each other on the bus or at the dinner table, Vyachik was swept, almost without resisting, into the rapid and sweet current of a strange timelessness.

3

They were strolling one evening through Liverpool, a city hardly predestined for romantic walks, a city shut up and occupied with its own business, and since other people had no business with them they felt a union of souls, rare even in people who have known each other closely over a long time.

And suddenly Vyachik felt the approach of the feeling.

He was not sure that he had guessed correctly, because at that moment so many varied feelings fused in him that his fingers began trembling. The signs coincided. The same condition of euphoria, of happy aloofness from concerns and a ticklish premonition that in a minute, an hour, a day, everything would be just as good. Or even better.

"I can do something now," Vyachik said solemnly.

Lynda did not answer, but stopped unexpectedly. They

stood in front of a store window in which an emaciated girl in a mink coat was bent over, admiring her elegant, skillfully painted plaster fingers. The sky over the street was green, and Vyachik suddenly felt that they were under water, and Lynda was a mermaid, sorrowful and defenseless.

"I know," Lynda said. "I understand what you mean."

"No, that's not what I mean." Vyachik wanted very much to be sure that Lynda understood him correctly. "I don't mean figuratively—it's a special feeling. Mama even wanted to take me to a psychiatrist."

Lynda raised her eyebrows. Vyachik became confused and unexpectedly asked, "Would you like a coat like that?"

"No," Lynda said, still staring at Vyachik. Her pupils reflected sparkles from the advertisement lights. Lynda reached out to his hand, and Vyachik froze, afraid to frighten her fingers away.

"You know," he said very softly. "It happens that way when I have an emotional lift." With his other hand Vyachik took off his glasses and put them into his shirt pocket. Lynda took away her hand.

"Why did you take your glasses off?" she asked.

"My glasses? Oh, yes." The glasses were returned to their previous place. "Why?"

"You looked as though you wanted to kiss me."

"Oh, no, not at all," Vyachik hastened to answer.

"I shouldn't have thought so," Lynda said sternly.

He had forgotten something. Something had been lost during these few minutes. And not only in him but in Lynda too. Lynda said, "It's late already. Time to go back to the hotel?"

Vyachik should have said no, because the question was uncertain and expressed no desire to return. But he nodded his head obediently, and they set off for the hotel.

"But why did you tell me about the psychiatrist?" Lynda suddenly asked after a silence of five minutes. And Vyachik, who thought that Lynda was angry at him for almost kissing her out on the street near the store window, was overjoyed by the question.

"Mama wants very much for me to be respectable," Vyachik said. "And when she found out I could handle things that way, she became frightened that it was not normal."

4

At that time, two years before, he had just passed his last doctoral candidate exam, and the weather was beautiful. Such a combination at times is enough for happiness. Vyachik was returning home and he understood that he was all-powerful. "I can fly," he said to himself as he turned into a lane. He even stretched out his arms, as though in preparation, but his arms cut the air and returned to his sides. No, he could not fly.

And then he saw the matchbox lying three paces ahead on the sidewalk. He stopped, because his new power was somehow connected with that matchbox. The box was white, with the word "Giant" written on it in red letters. Vyachik realized that he had to pick up the box from the sidewalk, but to walk over and bend down was too simple. Then he ordered the box off the road. The box did not want to obey. He had to strain and even take off his glasses, which interfered with his orders. The struggle with the box lasted about two minutes, and passersby looked on with amazement at a tall, stoop-shouldered man standing in the middle of the sidewalk, fixing his gaze at some point ahead of him and moving his torso involuntarily. The box was on the point of submitting, but just then a young boy walking by gave it a kick and it flew off to the side. Vyachik followed it with his eyes and at that moment he realized that, deprived of support, it was now in his power—he seized it in mid-flight and forced it to change direction and land in the trash container standing near a building wall.

"That's where it belongs," he said to the boy, but the boy did not hear him.

"Mama," he said as soon as he was home, "I've discovered that I have a rare quality."

"How was the exam?" his mother asked. "I've called the institute twice, but no one is around your department. A remarkably irresponsible attitude toward one's responsibilities."

"Everything went fine with the exam. But what do you think about moving objects at a distance?"

His mother kissed him on the forehead—he did not even have to bend over—he and his mother were the same height.

"The fundamental aspect of your specialty," she said, heading for the kitchen to warm up dinner. "Economics is the ability to control things at a distance. Power over society's productive forces. . . ."

"I can move objects by thought," Vyachik said. "Do you want me to show you?"

The excitement over the happy quality that made his heart tremble and demanded prompt action had not left him.

"Are you excited?" his mother asked. "Of course, you've used up a lot of nervous energy."

"On the street I saw a matchbox," Vyachik said. "Ten feet away. And I changed the direction of its flight."

"Vyachik!" his mother said. "Where is your tranquilizer?"

"Mama!"

"You know how your psychological condition concerns me. It was psychological changes that led to my break-up with your father."

Vyachik sighed. As far as Vyachik knew, everything was just fine with his father's psychological condition. His father had another family, two children. He sent Vyachik a card on all the holidays and presents on his birthday.

His happy state of mind gradually evaporated. His mother rustled around in the medicine cabinet, looking for the tranquilizer. Vyachik tried to lift the matchbox on the stove. It trembled, shook, but would not rise.

"Telekinesis has been condemned by science," his mother said, prying open the cellophane packet of medicine. "Take a pill and you'll feel better. Otherwise we'll have to show you to a psychiatrist."

Vyachik, of course, took the pill.

5

"And could you move something now?" Lynda asked. They had already returned to the hotel.

"I don't know," Vyachik said. "For it I have to have a special mood."

"And you don't now?"

"I had back at the store."

"And what happened?"

"I don't know. Something."

"Yes," Lynda agreed. "Something happened."

The following days they could not manage to get off by themselves, and the turbulence in his chest that so sweetly tormented Vyachik whenever he saw Lynda found no outlet. Before their departure their English colleagues gave a dinner in the group's honor. Maria Petrovna gave a twenty-minute speech of gratitude.

"Tomorrow," Vyachik said, "we will be in Moscow."

"Yes," Lynda said. "It's been a pleasure meeting you."

"Can we keep on seeing each other in Moscow?" Vyachik asked.

"Why should we? It's not really necessary."

"Why, you ask?" But Vyachik could not come up with a reason to keep on seeing each other.

That night Vyachik sat in his hotel room in total solitude, hiding away from his traveling companion who had set off to wander through the night city. He was thinking about the fact that for some people life could be over by thirty-five. Its transience or duration depended on random causes, which combine to form a general model of failure.

6

In the morning Vyachik and Zavadovsky almost overslept their departure and had to pack in a terrible rush. Vyachik's head and chest were empty, and the emptiness was so vast and resonant that Vyachik felt he could have been filled with grain like a grain elevator.

The whole group was already waiting in the bus, and the ladies greeted them with reproaches.

The seat next to Lynda was vacant, but Vyachik did not head there; instead, he sat up front near the driver. He tried to remember what the expression "Thus passes earthly glory" was in Latin, but couldn't.

Vyachik's isolated solitude was broken in the waiting area, because Lynda came up to him and announced, "I'm sorry that it happened like that. Please forgive me."

Lynda barely came up to his shoulder, and her voice kept cracking.

"I wailed like a baby last night," she said. "I'm a real crybaby."

"I didn't know," Vyachik said softly.

"Take my office phone number," she said. "If you want."

"Of course," Vyachik said. "When I have the photographs developed, I'll be sure to call you."

Boarding was announced.

They sat next to each other.

"I feel better now," Lynda confessed as the plane taxied out onto the runway.

"You don't realize," Vyachik said. "You don't realize that right now I can do anything for you."

The feeling seemed to rise up to his throat. Vyachik threw his head back to avoid choking on it.

Vyachik's power over objects, over the whole world, was so great that he could with one blow sink Westminster Abbey into the Thames or divert the flow of the Nile. And as if out of spite there was no object at hand that could be manipulated without fear of offending or hurting someone.

The plane halted, awaiting the signal to take off. The engines gave out a muffled roar, gathering strength to howl as the plane ran. Vyachik pictured the silver length of the machine, tipped by the aileron of the rudder. He carefully took it up and, lifting the plane slightly, turned it around an axis.

Someone gasped.

Lynda looked at Vyachik and saw that hard cheekbones had cut through his soft fleshy face. The tension that had overcome him was so great that Lynda's heart stopped beating.

"Vyachik," she whispered, putting a hand on his knee. "Vyachik, you don't have to. I believe you."

But Vyachik nonetheless turned the plane around 360 degrees, put it back down, and only then opened his eyes, smiled, and put a hand over Lynda's thin hand.

The flight was held up while they tried to determine what had happened to the plane. Lynda pretended to be mad at Vyachik, even though she was flattered that such an outrage was performed for her benefit.

"Just, while we're in the air—I beg you, don't," Lynda said.

"In the air, I, on the contrary, will not let the plane fall," Vyachik said with conviction. "With me they can fly even without the engine. I'll hold it up."

"Thanks," Lynda whispered.

During the flight to Moscow, Vyachik really did behave very properly. He permitted himself only a small misdemeanor: When the stewardess was handing out the lemonade, he made a glass flutter up from the tray and land in Lynda's hands. Fortunately, the stewardess was busy and not paying attention.

"Vyachik," Lynda said. "You promised."

7

His mother did not meet Vyachik at the airport. She was undoubtedly attending a conference and nobly suffering, torn between love and duty and placing duty a little higher than love. No one came to meet Lynda either, and Vyachik, grateful for the conference, took Lynda home, thereby extending the minutes of his silent happiness.

His mother was not at home. Only a note that listed the appetizer, the main course, and gave instructions for finding the dessert. The note contained the hope that the flight had gone uneventfully and that the trip to Great Britain had given her son much from a knowledge point of view. Vyachik smiled as he read: His mother could be touching at times. He put a yellow English briefcase on the table—a gift for his mother, his only purchase—and headed for the kitchen to take care of dinner. And then he realized that by using his abilities, he could revolutionize the tedious process of preparing meals.

Vyachik dragged an armchair into the kitchen, placing it near the door and settling down completely into it. A pity that Lynda was not there—she would have appreciated what he was intending to do. She had a real sense of humor, something his mother was lacking, even though she possessed other qualities in superabundance.

At first, Vyachik concentrated on thought action and, without leaving his chair, made the refrigerator door open. On the second shelf there should be a pot of soup. Let's put it on the stove. No, first we'll light the fire. It turned out to be a complicated business, one that required skill. First of all, the matches scattered out of the box Vyachik moved at a distance. He did not attempt to pick them all up, but selected one, the most beautiful, and struck it about twenty times, until it lit. That absorbed so much energy that Vyachik felt worn out. To renew his strength he pictured Lynda. Fortifying himself that way, Vyachik lit another match, but he had forgotten to turn the gas knob on the stove. On his next attempt he first turned on the gas, but by the time he managed to light a match, the kitchen was so full of gas that instead of putting his soup on the stove he had to open a window.

The gas burned, the refrigerator door was wide open, but the pot could not be seen from where Vyachik was controlling things. He mentally forced all objects on the second shelf of the refrigerator to move slowly toward the door, but before the white side of the pot appeared, a jar of sour cream fell to the floor, as well as two cucumbers, and—most annoying—an open bottle of sunflower-seed oil.

Folding his legs beneath him to avoid stepping in the mixture of sour cream and oil that was flowing toward his shoes like a stream, Vyachik put the soup on the stove. And yes, Mama had told him to add vermicelli to the soup. Where was the vermicelli? Usually it was on the top shelf over the stove. It took no effort to open the shelf. And there was the white package. Skillfully maneuvering the package, Vyachik made it tilt as it flew through the air and dump its contents into the pot. Unfortunately, only then did Vyachik realize that the package contained salt, not vermicelli. He had to put the salt back, although by this time the whole stove around the pot was covered by a silvery frost, and grains that had fallen into the fire were flaming up in dark-blue sparks. Pondering a moment whether it was worthwhile adding anything to the soup, since it was already too salty, Vyachik decided to finish what he had started. He found the package of vermicelli on the shelf but when he sprinkled it into the soup he missed, and most of it ended up on the floor.

This failure did not discourage Vyachik. He could sauté the cutlets. He took off the pot of soup in order to make room on the burner, almost upsetting the pot. But with a desperate effort Vyachik kept some soup in it and set it down in the sink. The mixed stream of oil, sour cream, vermicelli, and soup had already flowed under the chair and was creeping down the hall in a long tongue.

For some reason, Vyachik felt very happy. By an effort of mind he took the dish of cutlets out of the refrigerator and set it on the floor. From there he tried to toss them into the frying pan, not always successfully. One cutlet, for example, struck the wall and stuck to it. Two fell onto the stovetop. But the other three landed where they should, and Vyachik began looking in the refrigerator for butter, to make sure the cutlets did not stick.

"Vyachik," his mother said. She had been standing behind him for five minutes, but Vyachik, caught up in his creation, had not noticed her. "Vyachik, stop moving things."

"Mama," Vyachik said with joy, "did you see how I do it?"

"Unfortunately, yes," his mother said. She entered the kitchen, trying not to step into the puddle, and for some reason her first action was to scrape the cutlet off the tile around the stove. "Stop this nonsense immediately."

"Mama, that stuff is not important," Vyachik said. "We'll clean it up in five minutes. But now you can't object."

"Against what?"

"Against the existence of telekinesis."

"Yes, dear, I can object," his mother said. "By the way, thanks for the beautiful briefcase. I appreciate the fact that you think about me sometimes."

"Why 'sometimes'?" Vyachik dragged the chair out of the kitchen and got a rag.

"By the way," his mother said. "You are making a mistake."

"What do you mean, Mama?"

"I've already called Maria Petrovna."

"So soon?"

The kitchen served as an example of the deplorable fruits of childish misbehavior. Vyachik took note of it with some surprise, as though he himself had nothing to do with it.

"I feel greatly repelled by the cynicism with which that young person attempted to ensnare you."

"Mama, enough please! I'm not ten years old anymore."

"He's not ten years old anymore," his mother repeated sarcastically and pointed to the kitchen. "So he says."

"But did you see me do all this at a distance? Without moving from where I was sitting?"

"Any achievement of human intellect," his mother said, "has

significance only if it can be of use to humanity as a whole. I suppose that she really has turned your unstable head. . . ."

"But you saw!"

"I hope that you will never again attempt any such thing."

Vyachik threw up his hands and walked out of the kitchen. With sadness he thought about how all his arguments with his mother ended up with his throwing up his hands and walking away.

Going back to his room, Vyachik looked with enmity at the self-satisfied briefcase sitting on the desk. He ordered it to get off, but the briefcase, of course, did not obey. Vyachik squatted down by his suitcase, and pulled out a handful of film cartridges. After all, he promised Lynda.

"Mama," he shouted. "I'm going to get film developed."

"What's the hurry?"

"I took eight rolls in England."

"Architectural sights?"

"Everything. Architecture and people—"

"That's too much! On the day of your return from abroad! You're not going anywhere."

His mother had always encouraged Vyachik's passion for photography. But not now. She had every reason to believe that Vyachik was not excited about London's historic sights, but about the physiognomy of that young person. And that had to be nipped in the bud.

"I'm going," Vyachik said. And his mood immediately improved. In rebellion the beginning is the hardest part.

His mother did not answer, and her silence was more eloquent than an angry monologue.

On the stairway Vyachik was met by a neighbor, who, instead of saying hello, squeezed herself up against the wall. Vyachik did not notice her. He was smiling aloofly. In front of him, like a flock of birds, eight film cartridges flew through the air.

A Difficult Child

1

A conversation stuck in my memory. There was nothing special about it—I must have heard hundreds just like it. But at the time it suddenly occurred to me that an outsider would never guess what we were talking about.

My grandmother was sitting in the next room and complaining about life to her friend Elsa. I am favorably inclined to such conversations: It does Grandma good to get it off her chest. I was not listening especially closely, but my work was boring, mechanical, and several phrases stuck in my mind.

I was crawling over the floor with a tube in my hand and a scalpel in my mouth and was gluing in the lining in my bubble. The difference between a dilettante and a real sportsman-bubblist is that the dilettante throws out the outlining—it does not cost much. The professional glues the lining in with his own hands and fits the bubble to his shape so that the builder would no longer recognize it. The bubble's speed and maneuverability depend at times on such elusive trifles that you have to marvel. That's the way we all are—professionals. Once I was at a training camp, and bicyclists were training next door—a marvelous vestige of the dawn of the mechanical age. You should have seen how they cared for, remodeled, and drilled holes in their machines.

And then I heard my grandmother's voice: "Sometimes I lose heart. Yesterday he jumped on the top frame of the TV screen and ripped it off with such fury that I was afraid he would lose fingers."

"That's terrible," her friend agreed.

During her entire life things have been happening to my grandmother, and during her entire life Elsa has given Grandmother sympathy.

They talked a little more, I did not hear about what, and then Grandmother's voice once again reached my room: "I thought we would never get him out from behind the panel. The crack was tiny, but he had managed to climb through during the night, when everyone was sleeping."

"You must have been terribly upset."

"That's putting it mildly. We get up in the morning, and he's nowhere to be seen. Oleg"—that's my father—"almost lost his mind. And I went into the kitchen, and just as I pushed the buttons to code, Katerina had a premonition. She looked into the crack. It's a good thing I didn't have time to push the button. Later a technician told me that under the burner unit the temperature reaches two hundred fifty degrees."

"Did he crawl out?"

"Not at all. He was stuck—lying there and making a hissing sound. We had to have the burner unit taken apart. And the technician said—"

"But there must have been happy times as well," Elsa insisted.

"None at all!" Grandmother snapped. "But the most frightening thing is not knowing what trick he'll pull next."

"Dive into the garbage chute?" Elsa proposed as a working hypothesis.

"He's done that already. Katerina caught him by the hind legs. We have to keep everything locked up, hidden away. During the last six months I've aged ten years."

Grandmother's last words did not correspond to the truth. She looked tremendous. Her fight with Ker had given her life a certain pungency. The crown of martyrdom had rejuvenated her.

So then, as I listened to that unhurried conversation and as I crawled over the slippery lining with a scalpel in my teeth, I tried to imagine what my reaction would be if I knew nothing.

Suppose I were a stranger here, and had never seen Ker. How would I picture him? Like a kitten? A puppy? Or like a little devil in an old print?

I was not home when Dad brought Ker. I was held up at practice and therefore I was the last one to see him.

He was sitting on a table and looked to me like a hungry, frozen little monkey who had forgotten the liveliness and cleverness of the simian tribe. He had wrapped himself in a gray rag, with which he refused to part for any reason, and his enormous gray-blue eyes were evil-looking and suspicious. When he saw me he bared his teeth. Dad tried to pet him, but Ker brushed him aside with a long, fragile hand. Then he jumped off the table awkwardly and hobbled over to a corner.

"Look, Katerina, we have an addition to the family," Grandmother said sadly. She adored animals, but Ker was a terrible disappointment to her, as well as to me.

Only the day before we had been full of enthusiasm and were anticipating a joyous and touching encounter with an unfortunate orphan, whom we would pet, pamper, and patiently bring up. But here was the orphan sitting in a corner, hissing, and the tip of a not-fully-grown webbed wing was sticking out from under a gray rag.

Until I met him, I knew about as much about Ker as any other inhabitant of our planet. He and five other little ones like him had been found in a rescue capsule in orbit around the second planet in a system whose number I have of course forgotten. A settlement or base had existed on the planet but had perished of unknown causes. The ship had not had time to take off, but they were able to load their children into a rescue capsule and put it into orbit. Perhaps they were counting on help arriving, I don't know. But help did not arrive. The capsule's signals were picked up by the exploratory vessel *Vega*. The babies, when they were found, were barely alive. Then they were brought to Earth. And where else would you have them brought, since they were now homeless?

The *Vega*, of course, left a beacon in orbit, so that if rescuers had arrived they would learn where the babies had been evacuated.

At first it was thought that the babies should be raised in a special school. Then it was decided to split them up among families: The little ones needed constant attention and parental affection. And my father received permission to bring up one of the orphans. At the time I thought that some of my friends would burst from jealousy. Our family was almost ideal with regard to the family members' professions: Dad is a biologist, and a cosmobiologist at that; Mom is a doctor; and Grandma a well-known specialist in the theory of preschool education.

So we all started living together. If it could be called "together." I would not want to hurt Ker's feelings, but the lack of communication existing between us was similar to that between human beings and wild animals. Let us suppose you take an ermine into your house. An active, strong, and beautiful animal. You surround it with tenderness, feed it full with meat, make it a comfortable bed, but meanwhile you think that sooner or later—if not today then in a week, or a month— it will repay you with a return of affection. But it—today, and tomorrow, and the day after tomorrow—most calmly bites the hand that feeds it, keeps on stealing things, forming treasure stores of rotting meat under pillows, and just waits for a chance to run away, to return to the hunger and uncertainty of its forest existence. It is convinced that you are its enemy, that everything around it is the enemy, luring it into a trap to be eaten. Such is the analogy that could be made with Ker.

He did not want to understand anything. That does not mean that he really did not understand anything. He had the Russian language instilled in him, and we his language, so that if desired we could converse. But that goes without saying.

I remember that after about two weeks of such a life, in a moment of exasperation, when Ker had just torn a very important letter of mine into tiny bits and then eaten those bits, I said to him, "My fine friend, what's going on, are you provoking me to violence? It won't work. I don't hit babies."

He pretended not to understand a word, leapt up, and bit the finger that I was pointing at him in admonition. To be honest, I was always walking around with swollen, aching fingers, but in school and at practice no one wanted to believe that it was the work of my charming little orphan, so I told lies about a new pet skunk and told tales about Ker's gratitude and responsiveness.

He did not care at all about Grandma, destroying all her educational theories in one fell swoop. He paid no attention to Mom, but he did seem to be intimidated by Dad—but this only upset Dad.

Dad kept maintaining that our new baby was the equal of a ten-year-old in physical and intellectual development. He was growing more quickly than we, so that I met him when I was thirteen and he was ten. By the time I was seventeen we would be equal—if, of course, the physiologists were not mistaken.

There was no way he could be called stupid. The business with the observation diary is proof. The diary—that's an arbitrary designation. Ker, like the other children, was kept under constant observation. Cameras hidden in the walls kept constant record of his life. In addition, we agreed to jot down, in a big fat book—I don't know where Grandma could ever have dug it up—everything interesting, in our opinion, that happened with Ker. He did not know how to read. No one ever taught him, but somehow he guessed that people's periodic recourse to the fat book had a direct connection with him. Perhaps it was just that he connected the sequence of events—after all, children are very observant. All he had to do was get into trouble, and Grandma or I, Dad more rarely, would grab the book and begin making scratches in it. And then the book disappeared, and at first we had no idea that it was his work. He gave no sign. He kept biting the same old way, and refused Grandma's candies and her reprimands. In his eyes remained the same emptiness and anger at us, at all our earthly, amicably disposed world.

At that time I tried finding out from Dad how the other families who had taken a child were getting along. It turned out the same, to one degree or another. A female survivor was living with a professor of Cambridge University. She refused to recognize anyone.

We were visited by a psychiatrist, who confessed that "at the present stage we are powerless to find a path to their hearts" and then left. But Grandma upbraided him later: "Is that any way to talk about children?"

So, then, he was afraid of the book, apparently expecting some kind of trouble from it, and decided to burn it in the garden, and with this goal in mind, broke branches off the apple tree during the night, tore apart the lilac bush, put everything into a pile and lit it—but the green branches burned badly, something he did not know.

First the firemen came, then we woke up. I looked out the window and saw terrifying searchlights. The fire spotter had caught the scent of smoke and had come to save us. Ker ran back into the house, lay down in bed, all wet and covered with soot, pretending that nothing had happened. He had ruined the book completely but he was not satisfied, and in response to our reproachful looks he bared his teeth joyfully. His little teeth were sharp, vicious.

He could not fly. He would stick out his wings, looking like a bat and seeming to understand that in our eyes he was funny, even ridiculous. But he wanted to fly. He could sit by the window for hours watching birds—he felt closer to birds than to us. Once our cat caught a bat. As soon as Ker saw it he hurled himself on the cat, almost killing it. He took away the bat, but it had already been smothered. No one could take that bat away from him. Grandma was upset, cried in her room. He himself buried the bat somewhere. He must have decided that the bat was his distant relative. And after that, he kept plaguing the cat, hissing at it. Grandma ended up giving it to a niece, to keep it out of harm's way.

2

I found my old notes, my personal notes, just for myself, and was amazed—three years have gone by. I am already sixteen; our striped wonder—no one knows his age but he is almost an adult. He has grown some. But since I, too, have grown, and solidly, he still comes up only to my waist. Three years—that's a lot, a terrible lot, and what I was like three years ago, the things I did and thought, seem totally strange and silly, as though it had all happened to a different person. I was a smart and rather well-educated thirteen-year-old girl, but now . . . now I have different interests.

As far as Ker is concerned, it seems to me that he appeared in our house only a few days ago. I remember well the day and the first words that were said, and the first troubles.

The first time Ker spent a year with us. The whole year we made a song and dance over him. Later on Mom told me, "I feel quite embarrassed when I think of all the parental affection we took away from you for the sake of our little creature." I was not very bothered by it. I had enough parental affection, especially when you take into account that I am an independent person and can get along very nicely on half the average amount.

We all felt sad that our patience and attention were spent in vain. He would tear up a drawing of mine or do something else, and I would say, "So tell me, my big-eared friend, why do you hate me?" "Because," he would answer. He usually preferred doing without the assistance of intelligible speech. A sentence longer than two words was disgusting to him. Most frequently he limited himself to two expressions: "No" and "I don't want to." Then he added a new item to his vocabulary: "Go away." He did not want to study, either. In this we were completely helpless. And after a year he was suddenly taken away from us.

One day Dad came home and announced, "Ker is leaving tomorrow."

At that moment Ker was busy drawing squares in black paint on the gold upholstery of our couch. He did not know that the paint was washable and he was upset that no one was trying to stop him. Ker perked up an ear when he heard these words but did not stop drawing.

"Why?" Grandma asked in surprise. "Is he really doing so badly here with us?"

"Very badly," Dad said. "Here he always feels repressed."

Ker drew a broad black line down to the floor, froze in an uncomfortable position, listening carefully to what came next.

"We are so strange to him that I am afraid that we are inflicting traumas on him more than bringing him up."

"Where is he being sent?"

"A special lab—an isolated center where the conditions are close to their usual surroundings, or at least so the specialists hope. All the little ones are being sent there. They'll grow up together."

"But he's gotten used to us," I objected, without any great conviction.

"Used to us?" Dad asked in surprise.

Ker dropped his brush into the paint and skillfully splattered me from head to foot. As I was washing the paint off, Dad explained that the little guy had to live with his peers, that it was still not known when he would be able to return home, but that I should try to imagine whether I would like to spend years in isolation among Ker's relatives, and whether I'd prefer to live in a kindergarten with other children like me. I could not give a sensible answer, but Ker did not sleep all night, rummaged through the treasures he had acquired during the last year—he was a great scavenger, dragging everything off to his room: bottles, fragments of broken dishes, pebbles, old paper, twigs and branches that had struck him by their shape or texture. In the morning we discovered Ker downstairs, in the entrance hall. He did not want to eat breakfast. Collecting all his treasures together in a bag, he sat next to it, as though he were afraid of missing his train.

"No," Grandma said. She was the first to wake up and was very upset that Ker expressed absolutely no regrets over his departure. "You are not going anywhere like that. You'll have breakfast first, like everyone else."

"I don't want to," Ker croaked. He had no lips, and his mouth closed smoothly, so that you could not see even a crack. But when he opened it, it was like a frog's.

"Are you glad you're going?" I asked, picking up where Grandma left off. I attempted putting into the question all my hurt feelings at the unthankful little creature.

Ker stared at me and did not deign to answer.

He refused to have breakfast and waited for Dad near the doorway. We went outside with him to say good-bye, but he dove into the flyer and hid there. Grandma and I returned home, in a rotten mood. We felt like bawling, and Grandma kept castigating herself for not having found an approach to gain his confidence.

"Try to understand, Katerina," she said to me. "After all, in the final analysis, your father is right. Completely right. There are many of us, and only one of him. And what do we know about how his mother treated him? Perhaps he needs to have his head rubbed every morning."

"I saw you rubbing it, experimenting. He scratched you."

I was intransigent. Ker had insulted me. So good-bye and good riddance.

And that's the way it went all day: We were furious. In the evening Dad returned and told us how successfully everything had been arranged for the little ones, how everything had been calculated for their size, and the temperature, humidity, and so on had been computed for optimal values.

"But how did they greet him?" Grandma asked.

"Who?"

"The other little ones."

"How?" Dad shrugged his shoulders. "Calmly. Indifferently. Mama, don't try to apply our emotions to them. They glanced at him and went about their business."

That very night an extraordinary event occurred. Three of the six little ones ran away from their new home, demonstrating great inventiveness in the process. We were warned, because Ker might return home. But he did not. They were all caught near the space port, and how they managed to get that far is incomprehensible. During the night they traveled sixty kilometers. And they were still children.

The fugitives were brought back to the lab and told for the millionth time that no one, unfortunately, knew where their home was, and they, for the millionth time, paid no attention to the explanation and cajoling. As though they did not hear.

Then three or four days passed without incident. Not that we forgot about Ker—no, the house still contained a host of signs of his destructive activity, and on the morning of the fourth day, when I went up to Ker's old room, which Dad had decided to make a workshop, Ker was sleeping peacefully on the workbench, the bag with his treasures under his head.

"Oh!" I exclaimed. I felt very happy.

He opened his eyes and raised his fist at me—meaning, "Shut up and let me sleep."

"No way," I said. "You're a recidivist. Everyone wants the best for you, but you want the worst for everyone else."

Ker looked the picture of complete despair and buried his face in his bag, but I continued, "Now you'll have to be sent back to the lab where your friends are living, because people are worried about you."

I don't know what prompted my outburst. Perhaps, when he was told that he had to leave he packed his bag too quickly and wanted to get out as fast as possible?

Right then Ker leapt through the open window and by the

time I realized what was happening and raced after him, there was no sign of him.

Grandma came up to see what the noise was. She had been tormented by a premonition. Mom ran in, too, because the lab had already called and said that Ker and one other little one, who also lived not far from Moscow, had run away again.

The whole family looked for Ker, crawling through the garden—all its secluded nooks—but did not find him. Dad finally discovered him. Ker, it turned out, had returned unnoticed to his room and had already succeeded in destroying the workbench, which was uncomfortable to sleep on, indicating thereby that he wanted his old bed back.

After lengthy conversations with the lab we were granted permission to keep Ker, since that was what he himself wanted. And not long after the other little ones went back to their foster homes. Only two remained in the center. Apparently, as Grandma maintained, their Earth families had not provided the care that we—first and foremost Grandma herself—had been able to provide for our little terror. Grandma was being vain, of course, but evidently it is typical of grandmothers when it is a question of their grandchildren.

You might think that after all these adventures Ker would become calm and obedient and would start studying and would respect his elders. Not in the slightest. Everything continued almost the same as before. Not quite the same, since Grandma had now introduced a new threat into his repertory of punishments—to send him back to the center, which for some reason she called the "shelter." The threat worked. Another difference was that Ker had matured somewhat, and I noticed that he was stealing videotapes from me and playing them on his teaching machine at night. I cannot say how much he really understood, but he must have found it interesting.

On the whole, although he became a member of our family, and the very idea that he would ever leave seems strange, I don't feel that he is really one of us. Perhaps partially because he never forgave me my little revenge on the day when he ran away from the "shelter." To the other members of the family he was a loyal and obedient citizen; to me he was public enemy number one. And several times, when I had visitors, he broke into my room and behaved impudently and outrageously—purposely to make me furious. True, he did not succeed, but if my guests were not frightened by him but laughed, he would soon turn sour and crawl away to his room.

One more thing: This year Ker has learned to fly. At first he covered himself with bumps and bruises by jumping from trees and roofs but then he got the knack.

True, he did not fly very high or very fast. His wings grew long; they remind me of the wings of the very first airplanes. But they are very thin and fold against his back, like the spinal crest of some ancient dinosaurs. Sometimes he permits Grandma to scratch his wings—he stretches one out, and the sight, I must report, is totally unreal. Imagine my intellectual old lady sitting in an armchair, half-covered by a thin gray wing. At her feet a most real devil is comfortably settled down, his eyes narrowed with pleasure. Ker becomes embarrassed if anyone sees him in such a frivolous pose, hisses and pretends that he dropped by for a book or tape, and Grandma grumbles that no one lets her and Ker have the chance to have heart-to-heart conversations, although I swear that they never talk about anything. They remain silent and enjoy the simple process of contact.

The search for their real home has gotten nowhere. I can understand, although I find it sad, that perhaps these creatures will have to spend their whole life on Earth.

For three months now I have been on the Moscow all-star team. I considered myself a fair bubblist. A strange word—bubblist. I keep thinking that it must designate something fat and pink. And I am by no means fat and certainly not pink. When Ker learns to fly a little better, I'll find a way to take him up with me. Let him see that his enemy is also capable of something.

3

In life nothing can ever be foreseen. I have just taken out my old two-part notes, with a gap of three years between them. I am not concerned with whether I have changed or not, but with whether the very essences of events have changed. I reread my notes without intending to continue them—my adolescent graphomania has already left me—but I have begun to write almost imperceptibly to myself, plunging into the past, both the distant past and the most recent past.

Not that much time has passed, only a few months. Of course, if everything had gone as it should have, there would be nothing to write about. But Grandma got sick and died. It happened in a way that none of us noticed until it was over. Grandma was eternal, and if she was sick from time to time, we felt that it was in the nature of things. Grandma was often sick—she had a bad heart and would not consent to an operation. For some reason she was convinced that artificial valves for humans were contrary to nature.

Grandma died when no one was home. Ker that day had flown off to visit one of his fellows, who lived about a hundred kilometers from us, in the home of an unmarried woman professor. He did not fly with his wings but in a flyer—he did not enjoy curious stares and questions. He, of course, no longer bit people or hissed when he met a stranger but still tried to avoid meeting people. I was at a meet, and Mom and Dad were working. Ker returned home first and found Grandma dead. He, of course, did not think to call Emergency Aid, although that would not have helped—Grandma had died two hours before his return—but tried to drag her out of the building and put her in the flyer. Then Dad arrived home.

For several weeks after that all I could think about was Grandma's death. I could not keep my mind on anything. What do I mean? There were Grandma's things, her unread book, and in the closet, the dress she had sewn with such pomp for her seventieth birthday and never since worn. What an injustice that things have longer lives than people. I even

thought that there was sense in the Scythian custom that
committed to flames everything on earth belonging to a person, so that those close to him or her would not be reminded of
the deceased. They knew the value of oblivion. And perhaps it
was not the Scythians, and perhaps whoever it was was not
right. I fretted, stopped going to the Time Institute, where I
was working on an internship, gave up training, even though
the city championships were staring us in the face. Everyone
felt bad, but to our surprise it was the worst for Ker.

Whether he had never confronted death in his own world, or
just forgotten about it—he had been young—the most amazing thing was that he simply detested us all because of it. He
refused to communicate with anyone. He sat in his room,
refusing to set foot outside it. Only one time did he come
downstairs, walk into the library, put a chair up against the
bookcase, and pull out all the old children's books that had
once been mine and that Grandma had read to Ker during the
first year he lived with us. At that time I thought that he was
not listening to the stories, even that he was making fun of
Grandma. "In his world crocodiles don't walk down streets,
and he'll never be able to understand what absentmindedness
is," I would say, but Grandma would answer, "You've understood," and continue, "And now the absentminded man from
Pool Street . . ." Ker sat in the corner and pretended to be
examining the ceiling.

So then, he gathered all those books, took them to his room,
and set them near his bed. That was all he took. He did not go
to Grandma's funeral, perhaps he did not know what a funeral
is, or perhaps he just did not want to. And he never once went
to visit her grave. He had already grown stocky, like a ball. His
legs were short and crooked, and he spurned clothing in any
form, even in freezing weather. I do not think he reacted to
any changes of temperature. It has been only during the last
year that he has started wearing a baby's loose jacket, with the
opening toward the back. After Grandma died, he threw it out,
and I then realized that he had been wearing it just for her

sake. But perhaps I just thought that up because I needed to think that.

And he became a kind of lost soul, as though he had been deceived. He began looking very carefully at Mom—I think because he thought she looked like Grandma. He was afraid of losing her, too. Mom and I never discussed it, but she certainly understood, and her tone of voice during conversations with Ker (although Mom would say, "What conversations—he, as always, keeps quiet") became kind of conspiratorial, as though they knew something we the uninitiated could not.

He did not want anything to do with me.

About three months passed, and our life seemed to settle down into a rut. Ker more and more frequently disappeared on visits to his compatriot, who flew over to our place, too. They would go far from the house, into the forest, talking things over. I felt sorry for them.

Sometimes Ker would fly over to my practice sessions. He, apparently, enjoyed seeing us race in bubbles. Most often he remained in his flyer, watching me through the window, and I always felt his look. Once, for some unknown reason, he became worried about me, or so I would like to think, and took off in his flyer.

I really got it for that—it is thought that a flyer might damage a bubble, although it is purely theoretical. The instructor reprimanded me. He knew very well that I had nothing to do with it, but reprimanded me nonetheless, to take Ker in hand. Ker immediately flew away, without even considering that I, too, needed the flyer to return home. For a month he did not come to the aerodrome, but then he resumed his trips with me.

In July we set off for a meet in the Crimea. In Planernaya there are superb rising currents. Ker and I fine-tuned my bubble, checked every square millimeter. The stakes were high. If I finished in the top three, I would make the all-star team. Ker knew that.

When we unloaded our things in the valley in the morning I

stood there for a long time staring into the sky. I always love to watch flying bubbles. They looked like little balloons escaped from the hands of clumsy kids, and they shone like soap bubbles—and the people inside the bubbles were almost invisible.

The participants in the meet numbered about three hundred, no less. Some had come a great distance. Right overhead stretched a chain of bubbles belonging to the Kiev team. The guys had already told me about their bubbles back in Moscow; their spheres were bigger than ours and looked striped—red and yellow. From inside, they were transparent, but from the outside, colored.

The Kievians were very strong in group meets. Their spheres seem to hitch themselves together in flight, as though stuck together, changed formation in a flash to a chain, a circle, a cross. They scatter like beads from a necklace when the string breaks, but they find their neighbor once again flawlessly. I know how complex it is to work in figure flying—I myself was on the Moscow team for more than a year, until I switched to individual events.

Then I became infatuated with the Tajik slalomists. One after another their spheres would slide between the whimsically stretched ropes of the route, freeze for a moment, fall downward, and then float up in a spiral toward the sky. You even felt that if you squinted you would be able to make out the tiny threads by which an invisible puppeteer was pulling them. And right then I caught sight of the sky-blue bubble, known to everyone present, belonging to Rajandra Singh— the speed ace, last year's champion, and my main competition. Singh kept his cards hidden, floating leisurely over the field, as though he was flying to admire nature. I waved to him, although it was doubtful that he could recognize me from that height.

I went over to an acquaintance from the Leningrad team. He had just climbed into his bubble and had not had time to buckle himself in. The bubble looked like a transparent rag, a plastic bag.

"Give me a hand," the Leningrader said. Then he caught sight of Ker. They had never met before and he shuddered from surprise.

"Hey!" he said. "What's that?"

Ker was insulted, and frowned. He could not endure such familiarity. I gave the Leningrader a talking-to.

"Is that any way to act? You're treating him like a dog."

"I am not. Where's he from?"

"He's my brother," I said.

"Your blood brother?" the Leningrader said, not wanting to give in. He still had not caught on that I was in no mood to joke.

I watched Ker out of the corner of my eye, but my teammates had seen him—they knew him and were exploiting him shamelessly. It was better than tender emotion or amazement. I heard Sveta Sakhnina yell to him, "Ker, my dear, why are you so sad? Fly up about five meters and check the wind direction."

Ker obediently floated up into the sky and began to soar, higher and lower, and my Leningrader watched openmouthed. Then I said to him, "Climb in. How long do you expect me to wait?"

To tell the truth, I was proud of Ker and with each passing day became more convinced that he was beautiful in his own way, as any functionally designed body is.

The Leningrader, still amazed, climbed into his plastic bag. I fastened the top hatch and he began to inflate his bubble. He checked the propeller—it was working normally while idling—and signaled me to unhook the ballast. I took off the metal bar, and the bubble shot up into the air and hung above my head. The Leningrader was hanging inside the bubble like a spider in his web, and I noticed that his lashing was not very reliably arranged. The Leningrader was tilting the bubble, checking its maneuverability, and from behind the propeller turned into a glittering circle, and the bubble ascended, gaining altitude.

Ker dragged my bubble over to me, and I decided to test it. When I ascend, I never turn on the propeller until I reach a decent altitude. Evidently, no one except the very first aviators has ever experienced the remarkable sensation of flying in the sky with nothing beneath you. That is why in amateur bubbles a small nontransparent lining is put on the bottom—otherwise unexperienced people might feel they would fall from the heights.

From within the walls are almost not visible, and Ker and I had made the lashings that supported me in the middle of the bubble transparent as well. Therefore nothing prevented me from imagining that I was flying by myself, as in a dream.

Ker ascended with me, looking at me with angry eyes. I knew why—he cannot bear it when I ascend more than half a kilometer, since he cannot follow me and ceases feeling his own superiority.

I turned on the motor and quickly left Ker below me. The bubble obeyed me irreproachably. It was precisely at that moment that I understood that no one there could compete with me, that I would leave everyone behind, both in the speed events and in the slalom, where the course, marked out by ropes hung from balloons, was one of the most complex in the world. Beginning in the morning I would have to take my trial runs. Below me Ker was floating like a black dot, not wanting to land but unable to fly any higher.

But right then my dreams came crashing down. And all because of some crazy vacationer who appeared from behind a mountain in a flyer, headed straight at me. No one noticed him in time to make him land. Seeing so many bubbles floating in the air, he became frightened of colliding with one of them, headed his flyer sort of slantwise, to avoid the highest bubbles, floating effortlessly in air currents. I did not even have time to look behind me before he succeeded in tearing into my sphere. Something like that happens once every ten years. If I had been on a scheduled flight, if I had not been so independent when I took off, thinking I would just test the harness, I would have been wearing a parachute, and there would have been no real danger. Bubbles are the world's safest form of transportation; with two layers of plastic they are firm and elastic.

When the vacationer tore into me, he managed to hit the bubble with the flyer's only sharp part—the tail—and split the outer layer almost in half and make a good-sized hole in the inside layer. The gas started to leave so fast that the sphere wrinkled up before my very eyes and started downward. I turned on the gas supply full blast, but the results did not come up to my expectations: I might as well have tried to empty a sinking boat with a sieve.

Everything happened too fast. I did not even have time to become frightened. And my altitude was not all that high. The ground came rushing up to me, and I kept thinking of what I was supposed to do according to instructions in order not to crash. But I did not have enough time.

The guys who were watching from below just gasped when they saw that idiotic flyer destroy me, and the coach shouted to them to unfold a still uninflated bubble and to go up. But of course, they would not have had time—I was falling very fast.

Volodya Degrell, one of the few who realized what was happening, threw his bubble in such a way as to land underneath me right at the ground. He was taking a big risk, even though he is a great athlete, one of the ten best slalomists in Europe—he almost made it, but still almost. Only Ker made it in time.

He was fortunate (as was I), because he was circling beneath me, glancing up from time to time as though foreseeing something wrong. And then he saw me hanging in the sky in a bubble that was changing into a transparent rag with me at the center. He had to realize what was happening, but then he flew downward with such speed and when he reached me, only about fifty to seventy meters from the ground, caught me and began to flap his wings desperately to halt my fall.

As a result the two of us crashed against one of the Kiev team's bubbles, from which we bounced up and then fell into a canvas tarpaulin that the guys had stretched out. It was not that we escaped crashing. We crashed. But I got off with bruises, while Ker broke the fingers on his right hand and dislocated a knee.

They patched us together somehow, and everyone spoke to too great lengths about Ker, his resourcefulness, decisiveness. He endured the treatment bravely—he could not be given an anesthetic. It was terribly painful, but he endured. He seemed quite angry with me, hissed (as he had not for three years). Then I, even though everything inside me hurt, stretched out my hand and said, "If you want, bite me—if that will make you feel better."

But he turned away and did not look at me again, even though I crawled over to him as soon as I could get up, two days later, and did not leave his bedside.

That idiot vacationer came to apologize, and turned out to be a nice guy, an oceanologist. I even got to like him, but Ker looked at him so gloomily that the oceanologist soon left, embarrassed and broken-spirited.

We returned to Moscow, so I did not make the all-star team. I was even suspended for six months because I had gone up without a parachute.

I was already up and around, but Ker was still in bed. His fingers had healed poorly and all the luminaries of cosmobiology visited our home. Ker was visited by his compatriots. I often sat with him, and he, an adult now, would ask me in sign language when no one was watching to read him the children's books that Grandma had read to him.

But there do exist vicious circles. I had not been home when Ker arrived, and I was not home when it was learned that he had to leave.

As soon as I had recovered, it seemed senseless to sit around the house until the end of vacation. And Ker felt the same way. He had gotten a little stronger, walked around the house, and begun to study—he had decided, despite everything, to go to college. And I took a vacation. The most ordinary kind of canoe trip, for two weeks. Ker stayed in Moscow.

I remember that one night I was lying by the campfire, looking at the stars, and thinking, "Up there, on one of those stars, my Ker's folks live and do not know how far from home he has strayed and how he was forced to risk his life for his older sister, who is not really his sister and whom he, in better times, would not want to acknowledge." And I also thought how hard it must be for him to look at the same stars and think the same thoughts.

Then I heard another canoe landing at the shore—some other canoeists had arrived. I did not get up—I was not in the mood. Half-asleep, I half listened to what they were saying. Then I heard one of them, while sipping tea, pontificate, "Have you ever seen one of the wingers?"

"Who?" Irina, one of my friends, asked.

"The wingers. You know, several years ago they were found in space and brought back to Earth."

I pricked up my ears, knowing what he was talking about. True, I had never heard anyone call them wingers before, but all right—they had to have some kind of name or other.

"I do know—I've seen them," Irina said indifferently. She is a laid-back person and did not start explaining that she was actually quite familiar with one of the wingers, Ker.

"Well, I never have," the new arrival said. "We almost ended up in an embarrassing situation. About an hour and a half ago we were going down the river, when suddenly a giant bird swooped out of the clouds. . . ."

"More like a bat," a different voice corrected.

"Well then, a bat. And straight at us. A good thing we're not hunters and don't have any guns with us."

I leapt to my feet. Something had happened. Ker was looking for me.

"Katerina," Irina called, "did you hear that?"

"I'll take the canoe," I said.

"OK."

I looked for the paddle in the dark. Sergei came over and helped me get the canoe in the water.

"Should I come along?" he asked.

"No," I said. "It will be faster alone."

"You're wrong. Both of us can paddle."

I did not argue.

"And he circled us and flew on," a voice reached me.

We reached the first village at three o'clock in the morning. The post office had a telegram to me from Dad: "Fly home immediately. Ker is leaving."

It was precisely the everyday word "leaving" that struck me with its finality.

I woke up the ranger and pleaded with him to borrow his flyer. He gave in, and I flew home. Perhaps if I had thought to race straight to the space center, I would have made it in time.

No one was home. Only a message from Ker, dictated on the recorder, and the words seemed correct but indifferent: "I will return."

And that was all. Then I rushed to the videophone and dialed information. I was told that a special flight was leaving in six minutes. And I could no longer be included on it.

Even then I could have made it. As it turned out, the flight was delayed, almost half an hour, and my spare bubble would have gotten me to the space center sooner. But I, fool that I was, collapsed on the couch and started bawling. I felt terribly hurt at life, at myself, at Dad, who had not warned me, at Ker, who had not found me. At that time I did not know that the flight had been held up because of him: He had roamed all the tributaries of the Oka and returned home half-alive and had to be dragged aboard by his compatriots. Because everything was a matter of minutes: The ship traveling to their system was not an Earthship, and they had to be flying out to Pluto's orbit on a planetary vessel, to pick up the starship. And they learned about it too late, because the information about Ker's planet had come to Earth unexpectedly and the situation had not been immediately figured out.

After sobbing my heart out, I went up to Ker's room. Everything was as it had been. He did not take anything with him. Except three children's books. And he could not refuse the flight. Everyone has a home.

Tale of the Turnip

1

I brought Lucina a polyanka. At the sight of the present Lucy sat down on the couch and remained there motionless for a long time. Nothing is more pleasant than giving presents which make a person sit motionless. I sat down opposite her and watched her closely, filled with pride, and waited for her to come to herself so she could let me know what I would be doing during the next few days.

"A polyanka," Lucina said in her velvety voice. With her accent, the word sounded almost like polee-yanka. Elegant and tender.

"Do you know where the name comes from?" I asked.

"No. Probably from the Russian word *polyana*, a forest glade, because it is so beautiful and the patterns shift, like the flowers in a forest glade."

"Nothing like it. The butterfly is named after Theodore Polyanovsky."

"Yes?" Lucina said distractedly, stroking the most delicate nap of the polyanka with her long thin fingers. "That's interesting. Poleeyanovsky."

She was not at all interested. She had withdrawn again. I wanted to tell her about Polyanovsky, to prove to her that he was ugly, boring, and tedious, imprudent and even dumb. That what had set him apart from other mortals was a remarkable bulldog's tenacity, and a capacity for self-sacrifice in the name of the work at hand, even if it was completely without value to other mortals. Although who could judge what was most important in our mixed-up, complicated world? How good it was to live in the quiet, provincial twentieth century, when everything was clear, Newton was considered an authority, and Euclid was taught in the schools, when people moved with the speed of turtles in airplanes, and lazy trains still braked to a halt at tiny villages. Now only our grandmother can dream about the rippleless calm of those days, while we grandchildren, as one might expect of grandchildren, cannot wait for our grandmothers to finish their slow tales and run off, fly off. . . . Maybe I am getting old—why else would I feel drawn to the calm past?

2

Polyanovsky combined the quickness and decisiveness of our times with the persistent consistency of the last century. He is an ideal who fell out of time and miraculously lasted in space. Miraculously, but with what a skill!

The head of the mine, Rodriguez, called me to his office and said, "Lee, we have a guest, a guest we must help. Will you take him down into the mine?"

"It's late," I refused. "The mine's been closed since yesterday, and you know why better than I. The water will come any day."

"A special case, Lee," Rodriguez explained, shading his right eye. "Please meet my friend here."

Then I noticed a man sitting in the corner, hunched over and staring at the floor. My first impression was deceiving. He was only waiting for the right moment to hurl himself into the fray. He had already broken the inflexible Rodriguez and was intending to crush me.

"Hello," he greeted me, unfolding his mismatched limbs one by one. "My name is Polyanovsky, Theodore Fyodorovich. Have you heard of me?"

He had absolutely no doubt that I knew of him. But I hadn't. Which I promptly admitted.

"But I have heard of you," he said, with a touch of hurt in

his voice. "Rodriguez told me that you were the best scout in the mine, that you knew it like the back of your hand. And that right now you have nothing to do, isn't that right?"

"The boss would know best," I said.

"Now that I've seen you, I don't have any doubt about it," Theodore declared, in the tone of an examiner. "And I'm counting on you."

I turned to Rodriguez with a look of total bewilderment. I did not like our friend Theodore. I had a week off, and I was planning on a trip to the mountains.

"You can see," Theodore said, pointing his powerful nose at me, which was crowded on his too-narrow face, "I'm counting on you. You're my last hope. For some reason Rodriguez does not want to let me down into the mine alone."

"That's all we'd need," I said. "You'd never get out alive."

"I should warn you," Theodore then said, "that I'm going into the mine in any case. Even if I have to go alone. And if I do, the entire responsibility, I mean the moral responsibility, will be on your shoulders."

He took an enormous hand out of his pocket, unfolded a massive index finger to poke at Rodriguez. And at me.

"Excuse me, professor," Rodriguez said with an uncharacteristic piety. "If we had known about your arrival beforehand, we would have alerted you that under no circumstances would we give permission to descend at such a time of the year. Come back in three months. Then everything will be OK."

"Three months from now there won't be any reason, and you know that very well," Theodore said. "I have to be in the mine today or tomorrow."

"But the water is coming!" I exclaimed. I felt sorry for Rodriguez. It was not his fault. He had just called me so that someone else could confirm that it was impossible to go down into the mine.

"I'll manage in time," Theodore objected. "I've been in tighter spots before. You can't imagine. And I've always come back. After all, it's my job."

"All of us have our jobs," I said. Rodriguez fussed with some papers on his desk. The fight with Theodore was up to me.

"But if I don't go into the mine, the discovery won't be made."

"All the discoveries in our mine have already been made."

"Really? What do you know about entomology?

"Nothing."

"Then how can you maintain that everything has been discovered?"

He opened a folder that he had been holding under his arm. There, between two sheets of transparent plastic, I could see, like a great treasure, a piece of a butterfly wing. About the size of the palm of my hand, no larger. It was a deep blue, but I knew that all you had to do was turn it several degrees and it would look orange, and if you turned it a little more, it would turn green, then flare up in a scarlet gold.

"Do you know what this is?" Theodore asked.

I did not like his interrogating tone.

"I do," I answered. "Why shouldn't I? It's a butterfly, one we call a rainbow. And other names."

"Have you seen it yourself?"

"A hundred times."

"What do you know about it?"

"Nothing special. It lives in trees."

"Its size?"

"They fly high. Well, up to a half a meter in wing span."

"How many wings?"

"Two, four? I've never counted them."

"Eight," Rodriguez said, his eyes fixed on his papers. "And six pairs of legs. Once some children brought me one. I wanted to preserve it, take it home, but moths ate it."

"Could you catch me even just one specimen?" the professor asked.

"When? There aren't any now. When the trees grow, there will be butterflies. That's why I recommend your coming back in three months. Admire them to your heart's content. Only they stink to high heaven. Worse than sal ammoniac."

"That doesn't matter," Theodore said. "Whether they smell or not does not matter scientifically, if there is not a single specimen in any collection anywhere. If no one knows the creature's life cycle, if I am the only one with an idea about the subject . . ."

"So why stick your nose into the mine?"

"Haven't you ever thought about where your rainbows come from?"

"From the turnip. Where else?"

My affirmation plunged our visitor into complete confusion. "You think so? Are you guessing, or have you seen them?"

"Where else could they come from?" I asked.

"Then let's go into the mine. We'll find the cocoons there."

"And then?"

"Then? We'll raise rainbows on Earth. Do you know what the wings are made of? It's the most beautiful, most durable material—simply unbelievable!"

Rodriguez pulled the weather report for the next few days out of a pile of papers.

"Take a look," he said to Polyanovsky. "The temperature is already higher than normal. The sap has started to flow. Today at noon solar radiation will reach the critical level. You see, I've met you halfway, I called Lee and without telling him anything, offered to let him go down into the mine. His opinion is the same as mine. Therefore the matter is closed. Tomorrow you can take a look at the appearance of the shoots, a sight, I can say, that is unique enough to attract film crews and artists. Then you'll catch some butterflies, and we will help you with pleasure."

"Now I don't need butterflies. It's essential to find the early stages of metamorphosis. When the flight of the butterflies begins, it will be too late. Can't you understand that?"

"I understand everything, but I still won't let you into the mine," Rodriguez said with an air of finality. And he reached out for the intercom, because visitors really were expected at any minute and they had to be accommodated: Each one was certain that he was the guest of honor at the banquet.

"Cosmodrome?" Rodriguez asked. "The second one from Earth hasn't arrived yet?"

"I'll get into the mine. Don't think you can stop me. A lot stronger people than you have tried."

"And so?" Rodriguez, who also put himself in the class of strong people, asked.

"Nothing came of it."

Polyanovsky turned around sharply, and took an unbelievably long step that carried him out of the room.

"Are your quarters comfortable?" Rodriguez asked in a hospitable tone.

Polyanovsky did not answer. Rodriguez turned to me. "Watch him. He might really try to break in."

"There's a guard."

"Keep an eye out anyway."

I left. A cold dust hung over the bare gray valley, boring to the point of repulsion. There was frost in the hollows. Evening was approaching. The air held that kind of excitement, tension, that always precedes the explosion of spring. A wind was blowing over the valley, and the dust rose around the cube of the mine elevator, covered the approach paths, and collected in drifts around the ring of the drying plant. A greenish stripe appeared in the darkening sky—a ship was landing. It was two hundred kilometers to the cosmodrome. I wanted to go there very badly. I was drawn by the atmosphere of a space town, where there are many strange people, where there is a hubbub and noise, where news falls from the heavens. I went back to Rodriguez and offered to go to the cosmodrome to pick up our visitors. After all, someone would have to drive the crawler there.

I got back from the space town late. It was almost dark, and the moons—there are about thirty of them here—were taking turns popping up from behind the horizon and moving across the sky. I went to the mine, to see whether everything was

OK. At the top of a hill, near a future tree, I found the guys on the first shift. They were standing around a mound and arguing about whether there would be a sprout tomorrow. I said that the sprout would not come tomorrow and they believed me, since this is my fifth season here, and I count as a veteran. During the evening I did not see Theodore anywhere, but to tell the truth I had forgotten about him. So I went to bed.

I was not that interested in the sprout. I had seen it five times already. In the final analysis even the most entrancing sight, for which people will travel halfway across the galaxy, can become boring. For them it is a marvel—for me, it's just a job. I had meant to get away to the mountains. I knew a cave whose walls were covered with marvelous emerald crystals. I wanted to take a cluster to Lucina. It takes half a day to climb up the mountain, and then another day to go through the cave, no less.

I hit the sack about two o'clock in the morning. An hour later Rodriguez woke me up and asked me when I had seen Polyanovsky.

"He's not in his room. And nowhere in the area either."

"If he tries to get into the mine, he'll be sent back," I said. "Akhundov is there. He won't let him in."

"Still . . ."

I dressed and, cursing entomology, went over to the elevator to find out if Akhundov had seen Theodore.

Akhundov had not seen Theodore. For a very simple reason. Akhundov had been put out of action. Polyanovsky had apparently come upon him from behind, clamped an anesthetic-soaked cloth over his nose, and put him to sleep. It was our own fault. We had grown accustomed to the fact that all life on the planet appeared only during the summer, and until the sprouting started, there was nothing to be afraid of—who in his right mind would go into the mine? Akhundov had been sitting in front of the entrance, admiring the stars, not suspecting that anyone would commit such a crime.

I had to call Rodriguez and the doctor, to bring Akhundov back to consciousness.

Then Rodriguez said, "I just don't know what to do now," and looked at me.

"What's the latest report? Maybe he'll get out by himself."

"The report doesn't mean anything. You can hear it yourself. It's not your first season here."

I could hear it myself: Deep underground there was a rumble. The mine was gathering strength, the movement of sap had begun.

"In that case I'll go," I said.

"Who should I send with you?" Rodriguez asked.

"No one. It's simpler alone."

"Then I'll go with you."

"You don't have any experience. And while we get you ready, we'll be wasting time. I'm all set. I had been planning on going to the mountains, into a cave, so all I have to do is put on the suit and I can go."

"Please excuse me, Lee," Rodriguez said.

"It's my own fault," I said. "You asked me to keep an eye on him."

The door to the elevator had been forced open. I could not have done it.

I checked out my suit, took a spare tank and mask for Polyanovsky, rope, knives, and an ice axe. Rodriguez slapped me on the helmet. There were about two hours until dawn, and we were hoping that the water would not start, although we could not be certain. Rodriguez and Akhundov remained on the surface for communications. The doctor went to wake up Singh and get him over to the mine with a second suit, just in case.

I entered the elevator, and Rodriguez waved me on, to make sure I did not waste any time. I myself did not want to waste any time. I had never been in the mine when the water was flowing, and I didn't want to start now.

It was strange descending by myself—you always go down in a group. The walls of the main shaft glittered in the light of my helmet searchlight. The sap content in the mine was higher than usual. A cloying smell filled the air, the ordinary, not very pleasant smell that we all were permanently saturated with, it seemed. Even above the elevator's drone I could hear sighs and rustling, as though living beings were moving on the other side of the walls, demanding to be let out.

Below, in the central hall, I stopped for a minute, trying to decide which direction Polyanovsky had taken. The tunnel toward the west would hardly have attracted the entomologist. It was fully domesticated, broad and well-worn by footsteps. I did not know whether he had a searchlight. Most likely he did. He seemed a prudent man.

Water was trickling down the walls, and the floor of the central hall was covered with two inches of it. I lowered the visor on my helmet and turned on the radio.

"How are things?" Rodriguez asked.

"A lot of water," I grumbled. A large flatworm dropped from a wall and hurried toward the elevator, as though it was trying to escape on it. The flatworm splashed the water loudly, and I threatened it with my ice axe, so that it would behave more politely.

"Where are you going now?" Rodriguez asked.

"The new shaft. It goes downward, and our entomologist would probably conclude that he would get into the labyrinth of the mine more quickly that way. It would take him a lot deeper."

"And closer to the center," Rodriguez said. "Yesterday he conducted a major interrogation, and I like a fool showed him the plans. He let out that he wanted to look for his cocoons in the main vessels."

"That's all we need," I said with anger. "There it's all a big flood."

Meanwhile I had been walking down the new shaft, slipping along the sweet mass of ore, sometimes moving over to the links of the conveyor, where it had been left in place.

"Rodriguez, which crew left fifty meters of conveyor down here?"

"I know," Rodriguez said. "They argued that it was the periphery and there was no sense hauling heavy weights around. I permitted it. As an experiment."

"After an experiment like this you'll have to bring in a new conveyor all the way from Earth."

"OK," the boss said to justify himself. "I wanted to take the chance."

"They were just too lazy to drag the equipment out. That's what the experiment is."

I was in a nasty mood. Rodriguez understood why and did not respond to my grumbling.

All kinds of animal life hampered my walking. In the winter the inhabitants of the mine are sleeping or quietly digging passageways in the ore. But now . . . some of them had quite vicious dispositions and terrifying appearances. In my suit I was safe, but Theodore was almost naked. It seemed that there were mortally dangerous animals in the mine—last year a group of biologists had come, cut them up, examined them. But then I remembered that Akhundov had stepped on something and was laid up for a week, his leg as big as a log.

The drift turned to the left, and headed downward. It led to a large cavity in the center of the deposit. The cavity was natural, and we thought about how we could use it, but the main vessels passed not far from it, so we left it alone to be sure we didn't damage the deposit.

I walked along the drift, with water flowing over my helmet visor and I had to keep wiping it clear to keep it from thickening. The searchlight was unreliable—many patches of light were dazzling and interfered with my looking straight ahead.

Suddenly I thought, It's really stupid. Why don't we call things by their right names? When the first explorers came here, they named things more simply. The deposit was a turnip, for example. It was we miners who gave the official name: "deposit."

3

When they offered me the chance to come here, at first I thought of it as a real mine. When they explained, I refused flatly. But then I was overcome by curiosity, so I came anyway. And I am not sorry. You can get used to anything. A job is a job. And the planet itself appeals to me—a solid white spot. Although, of course, the mine is the principal attraction here. I, as I remember, tried explaining to Lucina what it all meant: "Imagine, my dear, a planet on which the seasons change twice as frequently as on Earth. Not far from the equator there is a broad plain surrounded by mountains. The climate there is oppressively continental—not a drop of moisture the whole winter. And temperatures that reach one hundred fifty degrees below zero. What do you think plants do during the winter?"

Lucina wrinkled her beautiful forehead.

"They must shed their leaves."

"That wouldn't help."

"I know," Lucina declared. She really wanted to be intelligent. "No hints. They dry up and hide their seeds in the ground."

"Let's make the problem trickier. Summers are short, less than a month. During that time the plant must complete its developmental cycle and produce new seeds."

"I know," Lucina interrupted. "They grow very fast."

"Now, I will unify all your theories and even add to them. Imagine a very large plant. So large that its roots can reach water that is located deep in the ground. These roots are not only pumps that bring water into the stem but also a storehouse where nutrients are kept. You get a turnip. Only a turnip half a kilometer in diameter."

"A half-kilometer!" Lucina exclaimed.

"Now," I continued, "the plant can calmly die out for the winter. Its central part lives hundreds of years, only in the ground. As soon as spring comes, it produces new sprouts, and the turnip supplies them with food and water. And our mine is inside the turnip. We dig our tunnels in it like worms. But we are intelligent worms, because we try not to damage the main vessels that carry water to the plant. Every three years we move on to a new plant. There are hundreds of them on the plain, although they are several kilometers apart from each other. There are young turnips, about the size of a three-story building, and old-timers—we found one more than a kilometer in diameter."

"Ugh, like worms," Lucina said, wrinkling her nose.

"When summer comes, predators descend to the plain, and in the summer others make their way to the surface. For them the turnip is just a winter shelter. We have, for example, unbelievably beautiful butterflies, whose wings can have a span of half a meter. We call them rainbows."

"I want one," Lucina said immediately.

"I'll try to get you one," I promised. "But the important thing for us is not the butterflies but our output. It's a dense mass, rich in sugar, vitamins, and proteins, which we can or dry on the location. We feed the whole planet and neighboring bases. We even export our turnip to Earth. It's also used for perfumes, and in pharmaceuticals—you've probably read—"

"Of course," Lucina hastened to interrupt. And I did not believe her.

4

And so I was walking down the narrow drift on precisely the day when no one could go down into the mine. Spring had begun. In a day, or even sooner, the turnip's vessels would begin pumping water and sap upward. During this period the mine was closed, and the equipment removed, and we went on vacation until the sprouts had stopped growing. This usually lasted two to three weeks. And that crazy entomologist, instead of waiting a month, had to go down alone, without a suit, in search of some kind of cocoons.

It turned out that I was headed in the right direction. I let Rodriguez know. "Juan, there's a racer here that's been dissected. He's been past."

A racer was terrifying in appearance. We often encountered them and had gotten used to them. The guys made knives and other souvenirs out of their shining stingers. Once I brought Lucina one of the knives. She threw it out immediately, as soon as she learned that it was the stinger of a caterpillar.

Polyanovsky could not have gone far. I was wearing special boots that did not slip very much on the slippery surface; I knew where I was going; and finally I was not looking for anything other than Polyanovsky—I was not studying caterpillars along the way.

Walking was becoming more and more difficult. Drops were falling from the ceiling, each of which would fill a glass with its sweet juice, and I started floundering. The walls of the drift were sagging under the pressure of the water. The turnip hummed, overjoyed with spring. And somewhere in the sticky abyss Polyanovsky was wandering, and with each passing minute saving him became more and more questionable.

Toward me crawled and ran larvae, flatworms, mangas, racers, leapers—all the inhabitants of the turnip who do not go outside during the summer but sit it out inside, living it up on the free eats. The fugitives were traveling in a solid stream, rushing to get away from the central shaft. They knew very well when it was time to hightail it. I shoved them aside with my boot. A large black and orange leopardlike manga raised its head and watched me go past in amazement, seeming to think: "Where's that idiot going? Our underground friends don't come back from there alive."

I counted on finding Theodore in the main cavity, but all I found were signs of his recent presence. On one of the walls he had made several slashes with a knife, as though prying something out. Then he apparently had moved toward a hole. And that he should never have done. I informed Rodriguez immediately.

"It looks bad—he's gone on."

"Oho!" Rodriguez said and was silent. I understood why he did not say anything. His duty as the director was to order me back. But he couldn't—that would mean the end of Polyanovsky.

The hole led into one of the turnip's nutrient vessels, vertical tunnels through which water traveled to the sprout. I had climbed them during dry periods, and they were then shafts in which it was always damp and hot, not tempting to return to. We carefully entered them on the map of the mine so as not to hit them with a drift. Below, in the depths, water was pumped up. Millions of various beasts were patiently waiting their turn to clamber out into the world. They swarmed in the black water in such quantities that the water itself seemed alive. And that was during the dry season. What was going on now was something I did not want to think about. But Rodriguez was silent, and that meant that despite everything I would have to go in.

"You decide," he said. "Your suit's reliable."

The bastard, I thought. Cowardice was bubbling up in me. And I could do nothing about it. Only I was sure that I would tell Lucina nothing about it.

And I went over to the hole.

I stuck my head in. Remember, I was in my suit, a rescue suit that offers almost complete protection. Polyanovsky set off on his travels in a regular jumpsuit. Water came up to the very edge of the opening, about ten meters away, no more. The shaft, six meters across, was filled with such a quantity of living beings that I wanted to blink. The creatures teemed in the water, covered the wall several layers deep, swarmed, celebrating their imminent liberation. Everything there was alive, crawling, chewing, and on the opposite side of the shaft, about five meters below the opening, huddling against the wall, Polyanovsky was hanging by his ice axe, covered with insects.

"Are you still alive?" I asked as I lit up my eccentric friend with my searchlight.

"Oh, so it's you," he answered matter-of-factly. "I'm going to fall soon. Could you help me?"

Help him? Helping him was impossible, of which fact I informed Rodriguez, and thereupon drove the first hook into the turnip's thick flesh and climbed out into the shaft. I was immediately swarmed over by the shaft's inhabitants. Although, fortunately, they accepted me as one of their own and did not show any animosity, they were still not about to give me any sitting room on the tunnel wall.

"Hold on!" I shouted to Polyanovsky, and I then had to shut my visor, because a playful leaper had decided to make friends with me and take up residence on my cheek. Then I remember driving in another hook as I pushed away a "spectator." With the third hook, I looked down and saw that the water had already climbed up to Polyanovsky's feet. Although he was a dedicated and selfless explorer, he lost control of himself. The water, as such, was invisible—it was a paste of living creatures. Polyanovsky attempted to pull up his feet, then fell with a splash into the jumble.

"I'm coming," I yelled for some reason to Rodriguez and, squinting with disgust, dove after Polyanovsky.

I caught him, tried to get my arms around him to pull his head to the surface, but at that moment the most terrifying thing happened: The flow began. The turnip roared as it turned on all its pumps, and the water came, picking up speed, upward. Of what happened after I don't remember very much.

5

At that time dawn had begun on the surface. And since many people in the space town knew that our turnip was one of the largest, about one hundred people had gathered around it, waiting impatiently for the first rays of the sun to peek from behind the horizon. Everyone knew that it would happen today.

As soon as it dawned, an enormous mound strewn with dry branches and a layer of dead leaves began to swell slowly—it was the dreadful and invincible movement of life. As if a giant who had slept a hundred years under the ground had decided to take a look outside and see what the uninvited Lilliputians were up to. And they just moved away from the hill and turned on their cameras. Rodriguez was not among them. Rodriguez was sitting at the elevator control panel and listening to the water in the turnip's veins growl.

A few minutes later the thunder of the bursting earth resounded and hurling branches and leaves, chunks of ore and stone, several meters away, the first sprout appeared out of the ground. Not appeared—tore through, like a sword piercing a curtain. We always say "sprout," and you might think that it is not large. But a sprout is a green finger slightly smaller than thirty meters in diameter. And it grows at a rate of three meters a second. For which so much water and nutrients are needed to bring it into the world. Within a minute it was no longer a sprout but a bunch of unfurling leaves one hundred fifty meters high. And these sprouts, some slightly smaller, some larger, more spreading or less, crept out over the whole plain, and as though by a wave of a magician's wand the barren gray earth turned into a lush, bright green forest. And immediately the forest's first inhabitants, breaking loose to the surface simultaneously with the sprout, began to build homes, gobble leaves, prey on their neighbors, drink the nectar of the unfolding flowers, and sparkle their wings under the sun.

And then the decisive moment in the fairy-tale spectacle arrived. At least that is what those present said. All of a sudden there was an obvious and significant swelling on the side of the mighty green trunk that was facing the spectators, as though the plant was planning to send a mighty shoot in that direction but for some reason did not. And then something in the green mass flashed. At first no one guessed that it was a knifeblade. When the opening was large enough two hands appeared at the edges, and they began to split the green bark. The sight, they say, was mystical, terrifying, and suggested thoughts of evil spirits breaking out of confinement to find freedom. Finally in the opening, from which a clear sap was flowing, a man in a suit appeared, smeared with sap and a green mass. The man tumbled out onto the young grass, pulling another man behind him, who was unconscious and blue from asphyxiation. Only then did the spectators sense that something was wrong and run over to them.

I still had enough strength to open my visor and demand that they call a doctor for Polyanovsky, because it would have been a bitter disappointment for me if after such a fun-filled journey through the turnip's veins he were to die. They understood me and gave him artificial respiration.

They say that when he came to—I did not see it, because I regained consciousness later—the first thing he asked was, "Where are my cocoons?" The people near him thought he had flipped out, but Polyanovsky pulled open the zippered pocket on his chest, opened the pocket, and there flew out, one after another, straightening their wings, five rainbows, which now, after becoming fashionable on Earth, are known as polyankas, after Polyanovsky, an entomologist dedicated to science. But my name has not been enshrined in the annals of entomology.

6

Of course, I told this story to Lucina ten times more briefly, otherwise she would not have listened to the end and would have considered me an envious *nudge*. However, brevity did not save me.

"He's a real man," she told me pensively. She was looking straight through me, through time and through billions of kilometers to where the inflexible Polyanovsky fought his way through the sweet turnip.

"Think what you're saying!" I said indignantly. "I'm the one who brought you the polyanka. And I was the one to pull Polyanovsky out of the mine."

"You, you—always you." In Lucina's voice was boredom. "I would like to meet him."

"Why?"

"You wouldn't understand."

It would have been better if I had brought her a cluster of emeralds.

If It Hadn't Been for Mikhail

1. *Marina*

Of course I'll tell you everything in the order it happened. There's no reason for me to hide anything, all the more since I've thought from the very beginning that it would have been better to stay home. But Raissa is so nice, you can't imagine what a wonderful woman she is, always ready to help, never refuses anyone anything, plus things are just interesting when you're with her. I only have a few friends, and as I get older they get fewer and fewer, but sometimes I tell myself that life has a meaning if people like Raissa still exist among us. I knew her husband before, but only superficially. I knew that she had a hard time with him. He had promise, had invented something interesting, and had a great future predicted for him but he became the most ordinary kind of engineer, no better than the others and maybe worse. Well, what? But Mikhail always remembered his hour of glory, and never forgave others for his failures. And least of all Raissa, who fed him, dressed him, took on work at home whenever he was let go by a research institute—because, you have to understand, his coworkers were jealous of him. There are people like him everywhere, and no one has an easy time with them, but it's hardest for the family. Do you understand? No, what I'm saying is relevant to the case, directly relevant, because if Mikhail had a different character, or if Raissa were different, or if I had acted differently. . . .

Well then, Raissa invited me to go along with them to hunt mushrooms. Everyone knows that I love to hunt mushrooms. Sometimes none of the others finds more than a dozen, but I'll never come back without a full basket. They have an artist friend, I don't remember his name, he seemed to stay in the background. We arrived, the weather was OK, although it looked like rain. We sat for a while with the artist, who lives by himself, and then he left to go back to Moscow and left us in the dacha. So far nothing had happened, but then Mikhail asked, "What time are you getting up?"

We were wiped out from the trip—we had worked all day and were tired, so we said we had no intention of hurrying and we'd get up when we got up. Mikhail said, "I'll get you up at six in the morning."

We asked him to put it off at least till eight. But he answered that if we just wanted to take a stroll in the woods, or play badminton, for that matter, we were perfectly free to do as we saw fit, but that he was getting up at six with or without us. Well, I could see that the man was wound up—several times during the evening he tried rebelling against us on various subjects but he did not succeed. Raissa immediately found a compromise, and he did not have enough ammunition to start a war. We avoided arguments, went to bed early, and Raissa woke me up at six; we got ready and prepared breakfast, but Mikhail, naturally, slept on without any intention of getting up. We asked him why it was we had to get up at the crack of dawn. He, without opening his eyes, began to pontificate: The weather was bad, and there were no mushrooms and besides, he had come to relax—in short, he repeated all our arguments from the night before.

We left the house at nine-thirty and headed for the forest. The weather was really unreliable, and halfway there Mikhail began arguing that there was going to be a thunderstorm and we'd get soaked, that we should hurry home, and whose stupid idea was it to go mushroom hunting in such terrible weather? There was no thunderstorm in sight—we might be getting a drizzle, and during a hot spell in the forest that can even be enjoyable—we weren't made of sugar, we wouldn't melt.

At that point the sun peeked out and then Mikhail started in with the idea that he was in danger of a heat stroke, and he didn't like the vegetation, and that any moment we'd be attacked by mosquitoes. So you can see the mood we were in when we entered the forest.

Once in the forest Mikhail immediately informed us that if there had ever been mushrooms, it must have been before the revolution and the population explosion. Now there were more people than mushrooms. But if in the field I was ready to turn around and return to Moscow, and only pity for Raissa held me back, why then in the forest I was independent. I said *au revoir* and went my own way. Raissa tried to follow me, but Mikhail staged a performance whose theme was that no one loved him and that everyone was leaving him to be devoured by the wolves and mosquitoes. As a result I was left alone and until noon gathered mushrooms to my heart's content.

What did you say? How did I find it? No one else would have. I was picking up a fir branch, looking into the bushes. I was looking for mushrooms and found a chunk of metal. The metal was sticking out of the ground about an inch, no more, as though at some time, perhaps a thousand years ago, it had fallen to earth and entered the depths. I was surprised that there was no rust. It glittered. I had a knife with me. I pushed the needles aside with my knife, shook the metal a little, and it came right out of the ground. What did it look like? I've already drawn it for you, described it in detail. All right, I'll repeat it. It was about five inches long, similar to a crystal, but something like gears stuck out on the side. It struck me as curious—not beautiful, just curious. Like an abstract sculpture. I thought that if I put it on the sideboard, it would look better than an old knickknack. It was heavy, but in proportion to its size. I returned to the glade where we had agreed to meet, and Mikhail was already ranting and raving: "Why did we ever have anything to do with here! We've lost half a day! Absolutely no mushrooms, I would have been better off staying home and resting." He kept on, all about me, but I did not respond, just showed them my basket of mushrooms. I could tell that Mikhail was about to accuse me of running over to the nearest market and buying them, but that he could not say, so he declared that the mushrooms weren't worth a damn—they were all toadstools, even the ones that looked like white mushrooms were satanic, but any fool could tell the difference. Raissa was close to tears, and she regretted having gotten me involved, but I was not that bothered. Right then Mikhail saw the chunk of metal and declared that it ought to be thrown away as fast as possible, and he just couldn't understand how people could litter the woods with metal, as though I were the one who had thrown it away, and he tore it out of my hands, and, saying that we were ruining nature, threw it into the bushes. I tried to preserve a sense of humor and answered that he was the one who was ruining nature. I wanted to display the piece of metal in my room, where it would bother no one. But here, in the bushes, a rabbit could run into it. With those words I pushed through the bushes, picked up the metal, and carried it with me. Mikhail grumbled, but his orders are not law for me.

Later, when we were headed back to the city on the train, Mikhail took another look at the metal and this time became interested. He began turning it around this way and that, noticing any axis of symmetry that did not seem quite right, and spotted something in the gear. He started cursing out engineers, who had never had the brains to think up even such a simple thing. But apparently someone had, but had not shared his idea with Mikhail. And then he just took the metal away from me, saying that he wanted to show it to his boss, because it was all a mess—they didn't give him a decent budget, and someone else was throwing money away. I answered that I was not about to give the thing up and was going to put it on my sideboard. Mikhail was almost in tears, and I would never have given it up if Raissa had not looked at me so imploringly that I just had to. He gave his word that he would definitely return it as soon as he had shown it to the boss; I never saw it again.

2. Raissa

I find it difficult to talk about my own husband. I know that he has many faults, but who among us doesn't? Mikhail is an overgrown child. He has had a hard life, and had to face injustice and incomprehension. I can assure you that he is an extremely talented engineer and perhaps my guilt is that I did not push him, did not appeal to his vanity, and even indulged him. Like a mother who knows it's wrong to spoil a child but does it anyway. So I have to take the blame for everything that happened.

What are you saying? Yes, of course I should have taken Marina's side back then on the train. But I was very tired: We had walked a lot in the forest, there weren't many mushrooms, and Mikhail was in a bad mood, so when I saw that he wanted to get that toy, I decided that even if it was spoiling him, it might help him with some engineering idea. Sometimes all he needed was the slightest shove, and his imagination would begin to work, and in that case it would benefit everyone. And with Marina the thing would sit on her sideboard without serving any useful purpose.

Marina did what I wanted; she's marvelous—an intelligent and kind woman. Even though she did not want to part with the metal, she gave it up for Mikhail.

At home Mikhail spent the whole evening sketching something on a piece of paper, saying that he was struck by the fantastic asymmetry of the metal. He examined it from every direction and made measurements. He said he was taking it somewhere, but I was skeptical about that, because Mikhail had more than once caught fire but later cooled off. And he did cool off toward the thing, about two days later. It remained on our table, and I said to Mikhail, "Let's return it to Marina.

She's already asked me about it." He, of course, blew his top, so I stopped arguing. The next morning I quietly took the metal out to the balcony and left it there. I reasoned that if I gave it back to Marina right away then Mikhail might realize and feel terribly hurt. But if he realized now, I would say that it's on the balcony. A few days would pass and he'd forget about it.

No, I didn't notice any difference in it then. Not in its weight, not in its size. The next day it rained hard and Mikhail looked out the window and saw it lying on the balcony. He got very angry. He brought it in, wiped it off, and told me that I was just not thinking about his future. Excuse me for talking this way about Mikhail but at the time I behaved without self-control and said that all those toys were a sham life, and that real life was passing us by. I was rude, a lot of things had built up inside me, and I attacked Mikhail unjustly. After our angry conversation I walked around dejected, and Mikhail was also gloomy and began to measure the metal again and make more drawings. Then, after I had fed him supper and he resumed talking to me, he suddenly claimed that I had switched rulers on him and given him an inaccurate one as a joke. I couldn't understand. An inaccurate ruler? All rulers are alike. No, he said, I had ruined all his measurements, where was his ruler? Well, I found it, once again he measured his metal, jotted something down, and went completely to pieces. I wanted to comfort him, and walked toward him, but he didn't want to talk to me any more, grumbled, then was gracious enough to show me the metal. "It," he said, "has grown." I looked, but couldn't see anything. I was not about to argue with him, I thought he was just overtired. Only later, when Mikhail went out in the evening, did I take the metal, examine it closely. It seemed to me that a second gear had appeared on its side, a little one, completely miniature, like a pea. Where do you want me to show it? On this drawing? It was right about here.

Then I committed another error. I told Mikhail that I thought it was time to show the metal to specialists. Suppose they had lost it and were now searching for it? I even tried appealing to his pride. "Your intuition," I said, "has suggested that there was something wrong about the metal. From the very first moment." "No," he said, "my intuition deceived me." And he ordered me not to bug him any more, because he himself would make the decision. I'd have taken measures myself, but I was up to my neck in other things. For the last time I told him that in his place I'd . . . and so forth. He blew his top and hurled the metal into the garbage. I stealthily retrieved it and carried it out to the balcony again, so I could return it to Marina.

Three or four days went by. I did not look at the metal even once. Did it rain? Yes, it rained the whole time. It was only on the fourth day that I went out on the balcony, in the evening, to take a look at the flowers. It had already gotten dark, and when I stumbled over the metal, I did not realize right away what had happened. It was lying there, big, complicated, with little wheels in a variety of positions, but when I bent over and tried to pick it up, I saw that it had broken the flowerbox. It was lying there, sparkling in the dust, and I was so frightened that I cried out to Mikhail to come running to help me. He came, but acted as though he was not surprised. He even said, "I predicted this." The devil caught my tongue: "You predicted that your metal would break the flowerbox?" He answered, quite seriously, "It's a self-reproducing automatic system that I suspect has been sent from other worlds to collect and store information." Maybe I haven't remembered his words exactly, but that is the meaning. Then I added oil to the fire: So it was collecting information in our garbage? He picked it up carefully, carried it silently back into the apartment, and put it right on the tablecloth, as though it were a crystal vase. I took another good look at it. Before it could be called a piece of metal, but now it was a whole machine. Even the wheel that had been the size of a pea was now the size of my fist, and no longer just one wheel, but a triple contraption that seemed to flow back and forth, and when you touched it, it would begin to turn. And I counted eight gears. There were little wires, and crystals—everything you could think of. I cannot say that I really believed it was an automatic system, but I was of course surprised and said, "Are you finally going to take this thing away?" He looked at me as though he was frightened and said, "You're crazy! This is my big chance!" He carried it over to the corner, to his desk, and began to make sketches, measure it, weigh it—like a boy with a new toy—you can't have it, and that's it! And what would you have me do? Call the police or the Academy of Sciences? We, you have to understand, have this piece of metal with little wheels that we found in the forest and it's growing on our balcony, and my husband thinks that the Martians have thrown it down to us to gather information.

That night he sat up late. I fell asleep, because it had been a hard day, but I was very worried and woke up during the night with an unpleasant premonition. I saw that Mikhail was sleeping, his head on his desk. But the machine was even larger, taking up almost the whole desktop. A jar with flowers lay on its side, squeezed by gears, and the water had spilled out of it but the floor and desk were dry. That's when I first felt that the machine was alive. Alive, intelligent, and evil. It wanted to drink and it would want to eat, too. I was terrified for Mikhail, and screamed out, "Mikhail! Is everything all right?" And Mikhail raised his head, blinked his eyes, not understanding where he was or what was going on. Then he said, "Go back to bed." I obeyed, but I did not sleep for long. I tossed and turned because I could see that Mikhail was suffering from an internal conflict.

In the morning I went to work, and Mikhail was still sleeping. I took a look at the machine. All around papers were heaped up—it was a terrible mess. They were all scribbled over with numbers, formulas, and sketches. One of the wheels was lying off to the side, by itself. Perhaps it had come off by itself. But then I saw that there was a file and a lot of metal trash. That meant that he had filed it off. I wanted to ask him but could not bring myself to wake him up. He would have to leave for work soon. I set the alarm clock for eight-thirty and left. All day I was in a bad mood. I even called up Mikhail at work. They said he wasn't there. Then I called home. Mikhail did not answer the phone for a very long time, and when he did his voice sounded nasty. I asked him how things were going. He answered, "Everything's fine—I'm busy." I asked, "Are you feeling bad?" "No, I feel OK." Then, like a fool I reproached him for filing the wheel off. You should have seen what happened then. "You," he said, "can't wake up all of Moscow and tell them I don't sleep nights, delving into the secrets of the machine on which my future depends. It is my only chance, my last chance to jump into immortality." "Immortality" was the exact word he used. "I," he said, "must today—right now—understand the functional meaning of the machine. It is a gift of the gods to me personally, a challenge to my pride and talent." And then he hung up.

I suffered through another two hours of work, then begged off and rushed home. Mikhail was very, very nervous. Who knew what he might do? I was sorry for him, and for the machine, although I know that there can be no comparison between a live and dear person and a piece of metal from who knows where. But I had a kind of strange feeling about it as though it were alive. I had to wait for the trolley, then I remembered that there was no food in the house, and ran over to the store. It was my own fault—when I arrived, Mikhail wasn't there, and the machine was in tiny pieces. I started bawling. There were fumes in the apartment—he had burned all his papers. He could not take the strain, was not up to his big chance. That is what I feared. Right then the door opened and my Mikhail appeared. He was drunk and didn't give a damn about anything. "What did you do?" I asked. And he was confused, since I had come home earlier than expected. "Why did you touch it?" he asked. But then he thought a little and handed me a different version. "This," he said, "is a form of

reason that is alien to us. Malicious. I am incapable of understanding it, and so is all humanity. We have to fight against it."
But I could see that he was talking out of his own impotence.

3. *Mikhail*

"I find this interrogation incomprehensible and I consider that you have no right. Well, all right, if you say so, it's not an interrogation but just a conversation—but we're hardly on equal terms. I do not consider myself guilty of anything at all. I based my actions on intelligent considerations. It was the work of an alien and enemy intelligence, and if I had not destroyed it with my own hands, the whole world might have been destroyed. What are my reasons for believing that? My experience. My experience as an engineer and inventor, my intuition, in the last analysis."

"You're not being logical, Mikhail. If you were so sure of your correctness what made you gather the pieces the next day and take them to the institute?"

"I killed the creature. But its parts might still be of use to science. The reason is evident."

"Did you do it at your wife's insistence?"

"By no means. My wife is not an educated woman, and she could not understand the motives for my actions. Why? Did she tell you so?"

"No, she didn't. I supposed that seeing the fruits of your research, she decided to take the remains somewhere, and you got frightened and did it yourself."

"So then, she did tell you."

"Was that what happened?"

"She has no principles."

"You supposed that you would be able to prove to others that you were worth more than they thought. And when you realized that the structure was beyond your comprehension, that you would not be able to get anything from it, you smashed it to pieces, to make sure it would not fall into the hands of someone who could understand it. You would not be needed."

"If you are going to threaten me, I'll just get up and walk out. I had no personal interest in the thing. I was defending humanity against an external threat. You can attribute any thoughts to me, but I'm not afraid of you, not you here, not the others elsewhere."

"All right. I, it is clear, will not be able to shake your self-confidence. Although I suspect that you really have none. But why did you burn all your notes and drawings? They might have helped us."

"Understanding is dangerous. The thing was a toy sent to us from afar to enslave humanity later."

"I'd prefer to think you're being sincere. But unfortunately I can't believe you. You would like to forget about it, the way you have forgotten your failures, shifting the responsibility onto others. But when you saw that your obedient wife was gathering the pieces and planning to take them to someone, you realized that this time you would not be able to get your way and rushed to us with your first version. Do you remember your first version?"

"I've always had only one version."

"Let me remind you. You came to us and stated that you found these pieces in the forest. The way they were. Then you got your story mixed up, and we did not believe you. You could not even name the place where it happened. Then your wife entered the scene."

"I didn't want to get those close to me mixed up in this affair."

"Doubtful."

4. Marina

"This is the forest. . . . Of course I remember. This is where Mikhail started acting up, saying that it was going to rain and that we had to hurry back. And there's the spot, by the bushes, where I set off alone. You think that it was an intelligent machine? Just think, how terrible it is—I was planning to put it on my sideboard as a decoration! And the whole business about Raissa leaving Mikhail, I sort of feel guilty—if I hadn't given him the metal, everything would have remained the way it was. Don't think that I feel sorry for Raissa. No, she should have divorced him long ago. It was no life. But still, it was a family.

"Now, go forward to the left, down that path. Usually I don't take paths, but that morning I saw right away that we were late, and mushroom pickers had already passed by, so I went deeper into the forest, about two hundred paces, and then started to look. Here I found my first mushroom, but tell me, do you also think that that thing was a threat to us? No? I didn't think so either. It was so pretty, so cute. But if it was a machine, why did it grow and eat? I know, Raissa told me, that it drank up the flowers' water. So then, Mikhail committed murder? I once read a science-fiction novel where the same problem arises—in no case can one shoot at the representative of an alien civilization, even if they do not resemble humans at all. Of course, Mikhail was totally wrong, and when we discussed the problem at work . . . Even if you did ask us not to talk about it, how could we not talk, since I was there, and Raissa, and all her problems, but even so practically no one believed us. When we discussed it, Temnikov—he's very well-educated—said that it was Mikhail's duty to establish contact with the being, not to panic and engage in destruction. I can't condemn Mikhail, that is, I do condemn him, but not that much, because I also would have been frightened and run away. . . . Where now? Let me think. To the right, as far as the ravine, then cross it. Good thing that I put on my rubber boots, it's wet down there. But you must have your ideas about it. What do you think, was it from another planet? And how did it fly here?"

"Marina, it is hard for us to come to any final conclusions. We suspect that this thing fell to Earth from space. But if we tell you, you'll run out and create a panic throughout Moscow, there's no holding you back."

"I won't say anything to anyone, you can rely on me. You know what the girls at the institute call me? Marina the grave, because no one keeps secrets better than I do. But how did it end up on Earth? Was it thrown off a spaceship? Yes. They're watching over us, I saw it in the movies. They fly down, build pyramids for us and statues on Easter Island. And do you know about the Baalbek terrace? It would be impossible to build it without extraterrestrial technology. At least admit that it was a scout who was to determine how advanced we were and whether we are worthy of being helped."

"We have to disillusion you, Marina. No one threw it down, and it doesn't seem possible for it to be a scout. It's a living organism."

"Metal?"

"No, not only metal. It has a complex composition."

"I always said that Mikhail was capable of murder. He had this strange look. But do you think that its comrades could be hiding right here in the forest and waiting for us? Are you armed?"

"Mikhail's looks were quite ordinary. There are much worse. It was just that he understood his impotence with regard to what he confronted. He could not endure it. And so he took his revenge."

"On the piece of metal?"

"Yes. On the metal. And on himself. And on everyone whom he considered his detractors. But that is a long story. Will we get there soon?"

"Yes. We're almost there. I have an excellent visual memory. Up ahead there will be a tiny fir, then the spot. But if you don't think his comrades are waiting for us, then why are we going into the forest? I looked around carefully, and there was only one of them. It was quite tiny."

"We believe you, Marina. But if our suspicions are correct, then we may see other ones like it."

"But didn't anyone notice when they fell? If they fell they'd have to get red-hot and have the appearance of meteorites. This isn't Siberia, but Moscow. Someone must have noticed. Especially if there were several meteorites."

"But suppose they weren't meteorites?"

"What then?"

"Microscopic spores."

Marina did not have time to find out what they meant. In front of her, amid the firs, something was glittering. They ran a few yards forward and reached a small glade surrounded by a dense grove of firs. In the glade there were three trees. The trees were made of metal and at first sight resembled Christmas trees, since they were thickly covered with parts in regular geometric forms: spheres, cogged gears. All the decorations moved in the wind, clinking against each other. The trees were rather large, taller than Marina. They stood there firmly, and their trunks split at the ground, as though they were standing on a tripod.

"Why didn't you tell me sooner!" Marina exclaimed, stopping at the edge of a small pool.

"We weren't sure," Professor Smirnov said.

"Are these their fruit?"

"No, most likely something like leaves. They use them to collect solar energy."

"So they arrived here as microscopic spores."

"Most likely."

"And what will their fruit be like?"

"That's the most interesting thing."

"It's a shame that Raissa isn't here. . . . Say, don't tell Mikhail for a while yet that you found them. Let him suffer since he destroyed the first seedling."

Professor Kozarin's Crown

When I got off the train, it was already dark. A fine, endless drizzle was falling. So it seemed that autumn had already arrived, even though it was still a long way to autumn. Or perhaps I wanted autumn to come as quickly as possible, so that I could forget upon the evening train, the platform, and the path through the forest. Ordinarily everything happens automatically. You sit in the first car on the subway because it's closest to the exit, you buy your ticket at the rear booth, in order to save twenty paces. You rush to the third car from the end, because it stops by the stairs leading to the asphalt path. You leave the path near the double pine, because if you walk in a straight line through the birch grove, you will save another one hundred twenty paces. Everything for the month has been measured out. The length of the path depends on how heavy your handbag is today.

The drizzle was falling, and when the train left and it had become quiet, I heard the raindrops hitting the leaves. The station was empty, as though the train had carried away every last person and I was left absolutely alone. I went down the stairs to the asphalt path and, as was my habit, walked around a puddle. I heard my own steps and thought that the steps were older than I. I must have been tired, and my life was not what I wanted.

I was returning so late because I had stopped off to see Valya's aunt about the dark-blue lamp for Koska, and it was the fourth drugstore before I found dogrose syrup and I had to buy three bottles of lemonade for Raissa Pavlovna, not to mention the sausage, cheese, and other food—a quarter-pound here, a half-pound there—and all of a sudden, I was carrying a twenty-pound bag, which I felt like depositing beneath the nearest pine and walking away.

I left the asphalt path and went straight across the birch grove. It was slippery. I had guessed my direction in the darkness and worried about tripping over a root.

I would have been willing to run around to different stores after work and then be jolted for almost an hour on the train, if there were any sense to it, but there wasn't, just as there was no sense in much of what I was doing. I sometimes think about how relative time is. We've been married a year and a half. And Koska will soon be seven months old, and he's beginning to make sense of things. And this year and a half, on one hand, began only yesterday, and I remember exactly how things were, and on the other hand, it has been the longest year and a half in my life. There was one life before, a second after. And the second life is coming to an end, because, evidently, a person dies more than once, and in order to live on and remain a human being you have to make a clean break, not drag things out, not dawdle. Begin over from the beginning.

Despite everything, I slipped and almost fell, barely saving the dark-blue lamp. My right shoe was soaked—I had intended to stop by the shoemaker's but, of course, there wasn't enough time. I entered the village, and the streetlights were already on, so I could walk faster. A white mutt raced along the picket fence, choking on its anger toward me. It was at least an emotion of some kind. The worst thing is when emotions disappear and people simply cease noticing you. No, everything stays within normal limits, appearances are preserved, you're fed, your buttons are sewn on, and you're even asked whether you forgot to stop in the repair shop. And you soon come down with a cold. The further course of thoughts is rather elementary. If I catch cold, then there will be no one to fill up the shopping bags in Moscow.

Kozarin's dacha is the second on the left, and behind the lilac bushes I could see a light on the terrace. Raissa Pavlovna was sitting there and laboring over her storehouse book, in which all her income and expenses are recorded. I never met a person who took each kopeck so seriously. And I was surprised at first that Valentina, so carefree and happy before, seemed to hit it off with her. Perhaps, she, too, would keep a storehouse book, with columns for every day and hour?

We rented the dacha because Valentina's aunt had found it. The dacha was old, creaking, and gray on the outside. Formerly, a Professor Kozarin had lived there, but he had died three years before, and the dacha went to his niece, Raissa, because the professor had no other relatives. Everything had once belonged to the professor. Raissa had thrown it all into the storeroom, as though she wanted to erase him from her memory. I don't know whether she had ever had a husband, but she certainly had no children. She didn't like Koska, who annoyed her, and if it weren't for her friendship with Valentina, Koska and I would have had our problems. The dacha was small: two rooms and a porch, not counting the kitchen and the storeroom. Raissa would have been happy to rent the whole thing, but she had to keep one room for herself—she had started a garden, which had to be cared for. We were not exactly the tenants Raissa would have wanted, but she had no choice—the dacha was far from the station and from Moscow, there were no stores or other signs of civilization around, and Raissa was asking an exorbitant price, as if for a villa in Nice, and as a result, like the finicky bride, ended up with no one. She had to agree to us.

I bent over the gate, threw back the bolt, and entered the yard, walking down the slippery path, bent over in hope of avoiding the lilac bushes and a cold shiver down the back of my neck. Raissa was sitting at the table, not, it is true, with her storehouse book, but with a guide to drugs, her favorite reading. In response to my hello she just said, "Out on a spree again?"

I felt like hurling her three bottles of lemonade at her like grenades, but I set them down in a row near her, and she said, absentmindedly, "Oh yes, thank you."

Her manner was that of the Queen of England thanking a servant who had brought ice cream. Then Valentina came in and was apparently happy that I had arrived. "I was getting worried."

She might have chosen a different greeting, and everything would have ended harmoniously, but I knew that she was not worried at all, but had been blissfully knitting or dozing off in a warm room, while I was hauling myself out here, and she was thinking that the summer would soon be over, and her confinement in the dacha, and she would finally meet her prince. Or maybe that was not what she was thinking. She lived a calm, almost vegetable existence, leaving it only under the influence of her hatred for me.

"I was living it up." I found it curious to watch her reaction. "Went out drinking with Semyonov, then I watched a hockey game."

Valentina smiled skeptically and flooded me with a wave of condescending scorn. She was not wearing eye makeup, and so her look seemed cold. And I stood there and practiced hating the slender fingers lying indifferently on the table, and the curl under her small ear. It was a hard lesson—a lot easier learning to hate yourself.

"You've lined, my dear," Valentina said. "Long lines?"

"I told you, I went out drinking with Semyonov."

How I wanted to make her lose control of herself, to make her show her true face, angry and indifferent.

"Remarkable," Raissa squeaked. "A young man from a good family—"

"My family is no concern of yours!"

And I immediately pictured her and Valentina tittering when Valentina had told her how my father tried to forbid me to marry her. He said, "You haven't earned a single kopeck all your life and now you want me to feed you and your wife?"

Later, looking backward, I realized that Valentina was counting on our apartment, on my father's high salary and comfortable life. When my father said all those things, she quickly changed tune. She skillfully masked her thoughts with a concern for my education: "You have to study. Your ideas about quitting school and going to work aren't right. It will be hard for us." She played her role beautifully. She had nothing to lose, only her dormitory bed. With her physical attributes she could have picked a better bed than mine. There were those willing. That I knew.

The first three or four months it did not seem that there was a wall between us. Valentina worked, I worked, we found a room, and I transferred to the evening division without a hitch. But then Koska entered the picture, and when Valentina left work and Koska materialized, things really got tough. For her, too. She was still counting on my reconciliation with my father, for my own good, she would explain, in order not to pay for a room and not to wait for the landlady to get sick and tired of the nightly performances that Koska was so good at and ask us to leave the premises. But I was firm. At that point I began to catch on to her game—which was a loss—but I kept on hoping all the same.

"I have nothing to do with your family," Raissa said, pursing her lips. "I mean that family."

In other words, she did have something to do with my— this—family. The usual sort of alliance of two hyenas against one hare.

"How's Koska?" I asked, so as not to get carried away.

"He's sleeping," Valentina said, biting her lips, just like Raissa. Valentina is easily subject to influences.

Raissa got up, gathered her bottles, and squeezing them against her stomach with her book, crept off to her room. She had rented the porch to us, and got her money for it, but preferred to spend time on it.

I peeked in our room at Koska. My son was sleeping, and I fixed his blanket. Koska did not look like anyone, and therefore those who thought they were being kind would say he was a chip off the old block, while Valentina's aunts and friends would repeat over and over: "Valentina, what a resemblance! Your nose! Your mouth! Your ears!"

They say that it's bad for a child to grow up without a father. It would be best if Valentina agreed to leave Koska with me after the divorce. I know that my mother would agree to take me back with my son. She loves him. She's one of the ones who considers him a chip off the old block. And Valentina doesn't need him—he's just the sad proof of a miscalculation. When she finally does find happiness, she'll have other children. That's all I need. I caught myself thinking about divorce as a *fait accompli.*

"Is your shoe soaked?" Valentina asked mockingly, coming in after me. "Didn't you make it to the shoemaker's?"

"Mmm," I mumbled, in order to avoid getting into a conversation. I was uptight, my nerves on edge. Now she would find a way to reproach me more painfully for our poverty.

She found it.

"You know, Kolya," she said, dissembling, "I can do without a new coat. My old one will still fit. You need shoes more."

I caught her glance. Her eyes were cold, mocking. Words rushed to my throat but got stuck there in a lump. I coughed and headed for the door. Valentina did not run after me, and I pictured very clearly how she stood there with her index finger touching her sharp chin, smiling mysteriously. The blow was below the belt.

It was already after ten, and although tomorrow would be Saturday, when I could take it easy, I decided to go to bed a little early. I was tired. I could go to bed on the porch, as always, and Valentina would stay inside with Koska, in case he had to be changed. But I would have to go inside for my sheets and pillow. And I didn't feel like it. I might explode. Consequently, I took out *The Corrosion of Metals*—an amusing topic for my mood—and started reading. Valentina soon peeked through the crack in the door and asked me in a whisper (Koska was sleeping lightly) if I was having tea. I hissed at her, and she hid behind the door. I realized that Valentina had something in mind, otherwise she would have come out on the porch and mewed for a while to get me in a calm state of mind. For the time being, until autumn, she still needed me. To bring groceries and help around the house.

It would soon be midnight. In the far room Raissa's bed squeaked: The landlady was going to bed, since she had to get up early to feed the chickens. My eyelids were sticking together. I couldn't remember a single line from *Corrosion*. I had corrosion of the soul, that I knew. And I knew that at age twenty-one I could start life over. Valentina had not gone to bed either. She was planning new humiliations for me, waiting until I could take it no longer and go in for my pillow. She'd wait a long time. I looked at my palm—it had blood on it, I must have killed a mosquito without realizing it. A light rain pattered on the roof, which was echoed by the even sound of streams of water flowing from the rainpipe into a barrel on the porch. I did not even have anything to cover myself with—my jacket, still not dry, was hanging in the kitchen, near the stove. Take the tablecloth off the table? Why not? I'd certainly give Raissa pleasure in the morning when she pokes her nose out on the porch and sees how I used the craftswork with four grinning tigers' faces on the corners. Just as I put an empty plate and a salad dish on the floor and grabbed a corner of the tablecloth, Valentina came to the door—I could hear her every step, especially at night. I just managed to open my book.

"Kolya," she said softly, "are you busy?"

"I'm working," I snapped. "Go to sleep."

I must have dozed off at the table—I suddenly woke up because the rain had stopped. It was very quiet, except for the sound of Valentina's steps on the other side of the door. How she hates me, I thought almost calmly. A large moth struck the glass window of the porch. I stepped soundlessly toward the couch and, without extinguishing the light, immediately fell asleep.

I woke up rather early, although Raissa was considerately conversing with her precious chickens right next to the porch. It was a sunny and windy morning, the trunks of the pines squeaked, and wasps buzzed in a corner of the porch. I did not realize immediately why I was sleeping the way I was, as though in a train station. The first few seconds I was in an excellent mood, but then quanta of the previous day's thoughts and words started to return, and I let my legs hang over the edge of the bed—I didn't want anyone to see me. The room was quiet, so I took a look inside. My family was sleeping. Only Koska was doing it unrebelliously. Valentina rolled up into a knot, her head hidden under the blanket—even in sleep she was avoiding my eyes.

I took a towel and my toothbrush and went out into the garden, to the wash basin fastened to a pine trunk. While I washed, Raissa silently snuck up behind me and said in a rustle, "Sweet dreams, my doves, you'll get no milk."

She did not say hello, so I was not about to. But there was good sense in her acerbic sentence. The peasant woman Xenia lived two houses down, and we got milk from her. Without saying a word I picked up a water can from the porch and went to the well. As I walked, I was surprised at myself. I was calm. And I could not realize immediately the reasons for my calmness. Only as I was returning did I realize what it was: It turned out that while I slept, I had come to a decision. As though I had solved a problem in my sleep that had eluded me for several days. Today I would talk to Valentina. And tell her everything. The conversation could be put off for years. There are families in which someone puts off the conversation. For a year, two, five, and then it is already too late.

Valentina was already up. She was clattering the dishes in the kitchen and hearing me walk up the steps to the porch, shouted, "Good thinking! That you guessed about the milk!"

Decoding these words was as simple as could be—Raissa had let her know that without her reminder I would have left the baby without milk.

At first I wanted to talk about the divorce at breakfast and even thought up my first words but I was afraid that Valentina would receive my words with total indifference—it's a skill she has—and just say, "Be my guest." I wanted her to feel what I felt, or even five percent of it. So I tried to behave normally during breakfast, and when Valentina told me that yesterday Koska had twisted off the head of his doll, I smiled obediently.

"Are you full?" she asked, finishing her coffee.

"Of course," I answered, and reached out for *The Corrosion of Metals*. She was hinting that I ate more than I earned. In addition, at any moment she could ask whether I had had a good night. I needed *The Corrosion of Metals* as a screen. I had to come up with a way to start the conversation.

"Kolya," Valentina said, "I have something serious to talk about with you. Just, please, don't get upset."

My heart seemed to burst, then fall. I had not supposed that Valentina would beat me to it. Had she found her new prince? Perhaps with the help of Raissa, her obliging older friend? Why didn't I speak up myself before breakfast!

"Yes," I said indifferently. I felt that my hair must be standing on end, my head was so full of thoughts.

"I promised Raissa," she said, "that I'd do something. We owe her a lot. Well, you know . . ."

I didn't know anything. I cringed, like a dog awaiting a blow, but what did Raissa have to do with it?

"You know that she has problems bending over and she wants to rent out the storeroom. If a window were put in, it would make a quite nice room."

"Well, let her rent it out," I answered automatically. They were obviously in collusion, but until I could get to the heart of things it was wisest not to resist. "Soon she'll be renting the attic, too. And the empty kennel."

"Raissa asked me to ask you to take out the professor's old journals and papers, and there are two trunks, and some other junk. She showed me."

I could have said that I had to study. I could have said that I had a right to rest at least one day a week. But I got confused. I had prepared for a different conversation.

"Whatever you say," I said.

"That's just great."

The storeroom smelled of cat droppings. The sun fought its way in through a small window under the ceiling, and the dust floated in its rays. The papers were tied in bundles, and the journals were heaped in piles in the corners and on the shelves.

Raissa appeared behind me and said, although no one had asked her, "I gave everything valuable to the institute. They came from the institute. I gave it away without compensation."

She liked the last expression, so she repeated, "Without compensation."

"For some of the books, a collector would have paid a pretty penny," I said.

She did not catch the irony and immediately agreed, as though she herself had been lamenting the fact. "There was a pile of books here, and some of them were old and valuable. The professor had a remarkable library."

Valentina put on a plastic apron and scarf. She went into the storeroom first, and a ray of light lit up her hair. Why didn't things work out between us? Why was it someone else who should admire her hair?

"Pile up the papers and journals by the kitchen," Raissa said.

Valentina did not answer. Apparently, she had been informed on the subject beforehand.

"I've already made arrangements with the secondhand dealer. He'll come for the stuff with his truck," Raissa informed me.

They had had no doubts that I would spend my Saturday at hard labor. My agreement was a mere formality.

Valentina bent over and handed me the first packet of journals. I carried them out into the garden and put them on the ground. The journals were in German; *Biophysische* dated ten years ago. I thought of how fast a person disappears from life.

How quickly everything is forgotten. These journals lay on the shelves next to the books, and a man named Kozarin, whom I have never seen, not even in photographs, walked up to the shelves, and the contents of the journals were imprinted in his brain. I opened one of the journals at random and saw exclamation points in the margins and several underlined passages. There was a steady feedback between Kozarin's life and the life of these articles. And most likely, these journals and the huge piles of paper scrawled over by Kozarin himself, had lost contact with people as soon as the professor himself ceased to exist. Soon the junk dealer would come and take them to be pulverized and recycled, and on the fresh paper new journals would be printed, each one of which would adhere to a person, grow together with him, and most probably die with him. Three years ago in this dacha there existed a closed world constructed by Kozarin over a period of many years. Now Valentina and I were clearing out the last remains of it, so that a new world—Raissa's impersonal and tidy little world—could reign triumphant. And I had the idea that I would have to, the next time I was in the library, look in the catalog to find out what Kozarin wrote, what he dreamed up, whether there was a thread that we were breaking here and that should reach out to other places and another time.

"Kolya," Valentina called, bringing me back to Earth, where not a single thread will be left behind me. "Where have you disappeared?"

Raissa was busy in the kitchen—keeping an eye out to make sure that I didn't steal any of the junk. I asked her as I went by, "What was Kozarin's specialty?"

"A professor," she answered naively.

"There are different kinds of professors. Chemists, physicists, historians."

"A physicist, I guess," Raissa said. But I did not believe her. It was just that the word "physicist" sounded more impressive to her.

Valentina had already dragged several bundles out of the

storeroom, and all I had to do was carry them through the kitchen. I kept glancing at Raissa out of the corner of my eye, and it seemed to me that she was moving her lips, counting the bundles so that she could later enter the totally useless figure into her account book.

We worked for about an hour. Once I had to stop and run in to Koska but on the whole he behaved himself nobly that morning, as though he foresaw the coming of the decisive moment and was trying to be equal to it.

Valentina swept out the dust, and we started in on the trunks. Of course, Raissa already had gone through them with a fine-tooth comb, and then dumped everything that did not appeal to her commercial or domestic interests into a jumble. Side by side in the trunks there lay old, hole-ridden shoes, broken cups, rags, books with the beginning and end missing—and most important, a mass of fragments of wire, nuts, screws, boxes with diodes, pieces of schematic diagrams, and, what was quite strange, two carefully made models of the human brain, scribbled all over and pierced here and there by needles.

"The professor had a hobby," I said. "But no one knows what."

Raissa, who had heard everything, immediately answered from the kitchen: "You can't imagine what a condition I found everything in. The dacha was absolutely not adapted to be lived in. Jars, test tubes, and wires. And many whole pieces of equipment but the man from the institute took them. A whole machine."

Then you were afraid, you were not sure what your rights were. After all, the whole dacha was an inheritance. Now you simply would give anything away. However, I did not state my opinion aloud.

We dragged the junk out to the street until the trunks were light enough to carry out through the kitchen. Outside, a mountain of junk was towering, and it looked pitiful—inside the storeroom it did not seem quite so pitiful. Then I took out the last bags and boxes, and Valentina took a damp rag to wipe away the dust, and I lingered in the garden, because I wanted to meditate on the transience of human existence. But nothing came of it, meditation did not appear on command. Instead, I remembered that the decisive moment was approaching and that I had almost forgotten about it, because I did not want to remember, and during the hour or two we spent cleaning out the Augean storeroom, Valentina was clever enough not to remind me of the sad reality.

I pulled a ring with projections—like a crown—out of the pile of junk, and I thought about how before, if I had found such a thing, I would have thought of something funny and would have crowned Valentina Queen of the May. Now she would not understand such jokes. Well, I could always crown myself king of the fools.

I went back to the porch, where I would have to start the conversation. And with the same words that Valentina used before: "I have something serious to discuss with you." I hate such conversations. They never do any good. But I was not hoping for anything good. Any minute Valentina would walk in.

I was frightened of her walking in, but then a life-saving thought came to me: I had to wash up. I threw the hoop on the couch and spent a long time rinsing myself off under the thin stream of water from the green washbasin on the pine. Then I saw that Valentina was rushing toward the washbasin with a towel in her hand, and I returned to the porch. Well, I said to myself, it's time. The reason it's all happened this way is that you've been spineless too long. Enough.

I heard the steps squeak under Valentina's feet. I could not find a place to put my hands. I took the hoop. Valentina came closer, and I took a step away.

"What's that you have?" she asked.

Suppose Raissa overhears, I thought. I can't say anything in front of Raissa.

That was a remarkable excuse to put off the conversation, but, as if on purpose, Raissa flashed past the terrace and headed for the gate. She undoubtedly was hurrying to speed up the junkman. There was no retreating.

"What is it?" Valentina repeated.

"The crown of the Queen of the May . . ." I said. "Or of King Solomon. It doesn't matter."

And I put the crown on my head, and my tongue began to pronounce the prepared and carefully rehearsed words: "Valentina, I have something serious to discuss with you."

At that moment I fell silent. I did not hear Valentina's answer, because I disappeared. It was a strange instantaneous feeling of vanishing. I preserved the feeling that inside me were images and thoughts, but none of them seemed to have any relation to me at all. It's impossible to describe it, and I swear that no human being ever experienced anything similar. With the probable exception of Kozarin.

Later I analyzed those unusual feelings of mine. The human brain contains billions of nerve cells, each of which has its own work to do. And among them there are many that do nothing but wait their time, for when the brain confronts so many new sensations the ordinary working cells just cannot handle them. So they, like detectives, rush to the rescue, seizing and throwing away various possibilities, trying out variant explanations, until they find the single correct way out that can be transmitted to the other cells. If that's not it, then why did my brain, after the first instant of panic, realize what was happening to me?

I saw, I knew, I heard—call it what you will—what was going on in Valentina's mind. If you think that I was reading her thoughts, you'd be wrong. I was not. I was inside Valentina's mind, and things that would require lengthy descriptions became my acquisition in an instant.

There was terror, because Nikolai (Kolya), who has been nervous ever since last night, could not settle down, finally decided on something terrible, something that could never be made right later on. And his words about a serious discussion and the fact that his hands were trembling when he put that hoop on his head. He's going to say, he's definitely going to say, that he can't go on living this way, that he's leaving. And he, of course, is right in his own way, because it was clear from the very beginning that he was going to be unhappy. After all, he could not see into the future. He couldn't then— more exactly, did not want to. When we had that discussion with his father and it became clear that his parents would not approve, that's when I should have left him, gone to work on some volunteer project. Then there wouldn't be the problems, all these terrible problems, for him. How has he held out all these months! He's been studying on top of everything else— gotten thin and frazzled. How could she dare to hang such a burden around the neck of a person she loved—herself and Koska. Oh, if he could wait just a little bit longer, in the autumn Koska could be put in a nursery and she could go out to work. But it was too late. Because Kolya's love for her had died, had died back in the spring or over the winter. There were his hands, ordinary hands, perhaps, not very strong but she could look at them for hours, learning every line on them, and dreaming of bending over and resting her head in them. But she couldn't because she was so guilty before him: She did not have the strength to refuse her selfish happiness. And all of life then seemed to be made of small and large wonders. It was a wonder to go with him to the movies and know that he'd buy toffees at the snack counter and give them to her one at a time, and each time his hand would linger on hers. It was a wonder to run into the next room in the dormitory and beg, in return for future considerations, Svetka's black dress, because Kolya had bought tickets for a concert by a French singer—and then to sit in line at the hairdresser's and look at her watch, and no time would be left and she might be late, although Kolya would not say a word. And there was the greatest wonder, about which she could not tell anyone in the dormitory or else it would melt away. Why hadn't she been able to save Kolya from himself? After all, he was proud, he would not go back on his word. But she was a woman. And a woman is always older than a man, when neither is twenty yet. His parents hadn't liked her. If she had been different—a student, a Muscovite, maybe things would have been different. He needed a different woman. How stupid it was to remember how she had tried to please his father by washing the windows, when she hadn't been asked, and it was all out of place and only succeeded in annoying him. And she saw that it was annoying him, but couldn't do anything to stop. And then Kolya lost everything. Dried up, like a brook during a drought. Only duty remained. Kolya was conscientious. He should have left long ago. He would help Koska—he was a good person. How tired she had become during the summer! Not only physically, that was not the same thing. She was tired of constantly holding herself back, to keep from exploding, from pleading for a life that could not be given. How hurt he was yesterday when she said that he ought to buy shoes, that her coat could wait. She should never have said it, it just seemed to escape. She really didn't need a coat, since she had an old one. Kolya had to be well-dressed. After all, he went out with friends, stopped by his parents. And no one should know about their money problems, that the dacha had gobbled up two months' money. It was a good thing she had been able to persuade her aunt, so Kolya didn't know how much it was really costing. But she had scraped together the extra hundred rubles they needed. Kolya still hadn't noticed that she had sold her boots and green jacket. That was nothing. She had no one to dress up for. But it was still constantly frightening that Kolya could think that she was reproaching him for his small salary. He might feel that way out of pride. But what if he did not have a specialty? Soon she'd go out to work, and he'd finish school, it was all nothing—but it was too late to think about it. He works and studies so hard. She knew that he didn't go out drinking with anyone and had lost almost all his friends. And yesterday he was up till midnight studying. She had a toothache, but the aspirin was on the porch. She was about to go out, but was afraid of bothering him. He was irritable, tired—it was better to suffer in silence. She most likely would not have felt this way before—it was all so simple—go out and get the pill, but for a long time she had been hanging over an abyss, and her arms were getting tired, and there was a river below. Her tooth ached, she tiptoed back and forth, took a look at Koska, that tiny Kolya, and she kept wanting Kolya to come in and put his hands on her shoulders. Although she knew he wouldn't. She tried knitting. She hated knitting but she had to pick up a little extra money somehow to help Kolya out. Raissa had arranged it for a friend. She was so greedy that she was probably keeping five rubles out of the twenty for her efforts. But with her everything was simple. She was an unpleasant person but did not pretend to be good. You could be frank with her. When she asked to help clean up the storeroom, she should have been told that it was not a gift. They could have struck an agreement, so that she and Kolya could take strawberries and other berries from her garden. For Koska, of course. It was very awkward going to Kolya. She got up before dawn, kissed him on the cheek, and even in his sleep he scowled. He was totally turned off by her, his whole body rebelled. She tried not to think about it, because up to the very last moment, until Kolya mentioned a serious discussion, she had hoped to hold out until autumn, as though that was the magic shore that had to be reached. And she herself understood that she was deceiving herself. A cup once broken can't be mended. And while he was working in the storeroom, it seemed to her that his hatred of her had passed for a while. She even felt like singing. But once again she was deceiving herself. Maybe she should take Koska and go, and send a letter later. "I will always love you, dear, but I don't want to be a burden." After all, she wouldn't be lost. But now it was already too late. He himself would chase her away. And be right to do so. My poor Kolya, my stubborn little boy. What's he thinking now?

I realized later that all of this lasted only a moment, well, possibly two or three seconds, because Valentina noticed that I was wavering, that I was elsewhere, and rushed to me, and I fell, and the crown rolled onto the couch.

I came to immediately, and Valentina's eyes were near; she was so frightened that she could not speak. Her lips were trembling. That is a literary expression, and I had never before actually seen a person's lips tremble. My head was spinning, but I still managed to sit on the floor, then stood up, leaning on her arm. She had thin, strong arms. I held her hand and thought that her fingers were rough from constant washing.

"Nothing special," I said. "It's passed. Honestly."

"You're worn out, sit a while, please."

Out of fear for me she lost her ability to control herself, she was ready to break into tears and to cuddle up against me. And although I no longer knew what she was thinking and would never again put on the crown (tomorrow I will take it to the institute), I continued to read her mind. And I was frightened that she would break out crying, that she would break down on the spot, and I couldn't let things go that far—for the next fifty years I had a clear task: Never, not a single time, to allow that silly child to bawl. Let others bawl their heads off. And then a harmful idea came to me—it happens when I feel good and am in an excellent mood. I said, not letting go of her hand, "As I said, I have something serious to discuss with you."

The fingers, whose rough pads were carefully touching my palms, immediately went limp, lifeless.

"Yes," she said in a child's voice.

"Your aunt is coming on Thursday?"

I watched her carefully, as though I had only yesterday met her. She did not dare raise her eyes.

"She promised."

"Let's persuade her to stay overnight. And I'll get tickets to a concert. Or to the movies. We haven't been anywhere together for ages."

"Make it the movies," she said, before she could have realized what I said.

And then she suddenly rushed at me, desperately grabbed the sleeves of my shirt, pressed her face into my chest, as though she were trying to hide, and started bawling buckets.

I stroked her shoulders, her hair, and mumbled rather incoherently, "What are you doing? Stop—Raissa will come . . . Don't . . ."

Flowers

Sometimes he permitted himself the luxury of not awakening immediately but of stretching out the sweet state of half-sleep for several minutes, and his first thoughts were calm, smiling, mixed in a strange way with the remnants of dreams in which he could do anything—even more than when awake. Then the sounds of the house uninsistently and gently invaded the drowsy visions. Muffled voices, the chatter of a bird outside in the yard, the clinking of cups in the dining room. . . . Sounds comprehensible and incomprehensible, but favorably disposed to him joined in a unique melody, invented that morning specially for him. All his worries were surmountable, all his problems soluble, as in school—only the thought that he might awaken in a silence, when no one needed or wanted his awakening, was intolerable.

The sheets, even though they had become warm during the night, were fresh and smooth. He had not twisted and turned during his sleep; he slept austerely, on his back, but still changed the bedding every night because he could not refuse himself the pleasure of seeing, as he lay down to sleep, the thin, straight folds, and to smell the light scent of cleanliness.

He rubbed his firm palm over his smooth, hard, sunken-in stomach. For three months he had been following a sensible diet. He had started after he had accidentally caught sight of himself in a mirror in an unguarded moment and realized that his stomach was sticking out. It was the third month he had been losing weight, like a jealous collector collecting lost pounds. Every few days another pound—it was a fine collection.

The door squeaked comfortably. His wife looked in. The most beautiful woman in the world, the most sensitive and attentive, whom he had loved for ten years already, which did not prevent him from loving other women with the same generosity and sincerity, and affairs with them only strengthened his certainty that he had not erred in choosing her as his wife. That certainty in the correctness of his choice, in his own perceptiveness, was pleasant. He smiled at his wife and she bent over his pillow to kiss him on the lips. He could smell her morning coffee and good French perfume, without doubt the one he had given her two days before.

"I'm getting up," he said, and stretched to drive off the remnants of morning languor.

"Breakfast is on the table," his wife said.

The omelette was remarkable. He had never had one so good. Yes, but it was time to go. Better now, right after breakfast. It was strange that in attempting to be a person's benefactor, you could not avoid a strange awkwardness, uncertainty about yourself.

He went to his study and lit up his first cigarette of the day, the morning one, the best tasting. Under his window the car was waiting, and the driver lazily but lovingly polished its shining side with a chamois cloth. A good car. Perhaps it would be better to do without this trip? Knowing him, and enjoying encountering resistance so that he could break it, he did not like situations in which someone else played the role of victim. That is why his friends and relatives were inclined to explain his achievements and not always good reputation by his intelligence, luck, and talent—but not cruelty, which seemed incompatible with his character.

But why did he think about resistance? He wanted to save a person from nothingness, and if he did not, others would take over, others who would not consider morality. Pavel, most likely, would want to join in with the victors, but would not take the first step out of pride. You cannot leave the shore only because the current is too fast. If you don't learn to swim, you'll die in a flood.

"Will you be home for dinner?" his wife asked.

"I'll try, my dear. Either way, I'll call."

He gave the chauffeur the address. He had received the address the night before, because it was better to take personal responsibility for such a serious conversation, rather than to take a risk by entrusting the matter to an efficient but insensitive assistant. And he would have been happy to do without Pavel. Any system that needs human knowledge, skill, and memory is heartless, since it tends to squeeze out of an individual everything he or she has and then move on as quickly as possible to the next victim. Only those remain afloat who associate themselves with system and nourish themselves on the same food as it does. But still, he consoled himself, what I am offering Pavel is the only way out for him. And let him decide himself which side of the road he wants to travel on.

"Here it is," the chauffeur said. "I'll go in and have a look?"

The chauffeur's surprise was understandable. Even the car seemed to shy away from the street of crooked, unpainted houses, dirty ditches with shaky, slippery boards thrown over them.

"I'll go myself."

The chauffeur climbed out of the car and opened the door for him. He walked up the path, then went up three steps; the middle one was split and about to collapse. The doorbell did not work. Not surprising, since it looked like the electricity had been turned off. In the window of the house next door he saw the white blurs of children's faces, but their attention was fixed on the car. He knocked, meanwhile calculating as a matter of habit what it would take to get the house in shape— painting, a new roof, a new fence. But it would be cheaper to build a new house. With that thought, he stepped into the narrow entryway, which smelled of naphthaline and something sour.

"It would be cheaper to tear this shanty down and build a new house," he said to Pavel. "Although, I hope, you'll be leaving here."

"You haven't changed," Pavel said.

"But you have. Later today I'll send a good barber over here."

"Thanks. Come on into the living room. How long has it been? Five years?"

"A little longer. Six years and three months."

The plywood ceiling was sagging in the middle of the room, as though made of canvas. On the dining table, next to an unwashed pot and three cups, was an ink-pot. His glance slid from the ink-pot to a little girl who froze, her pen aimed at him, and a deep blue drop slowly swelled on its tip, then crawled off. He cannot budge, hypnotized by the inevitability of its fall onto the page of an opened notebook and only when it finally broke loose and splattered against the white paper, throwing out thin little paws that fattened at the ends, could he once again hear Pavel's voice. "Go on now, go for a walk."

That was meant for the girl, his daughter. No, in Pavel's dossier, which he had skimmed the day before, there was no mention of children.

The girl picked up the notebook, holding it flat so that the ink spots would not run, backed around the man, and disappeared down the corridor.

"Your daughter?"

"No, the landlady's. But I say if I stay here I intend to adopt her."

"I hope you won't stay here."

"You came to express such a hope?"

"In part, yes."

"Have a seat."

"I'll stand."

"In a hurry?"

"As always."

"Then tell me, what's brought you here?"

"Can't you guess?"

"My guesses are not what interest you."

"They really do."

"You need me."

"Correct. And we are not the only ones who need you. Everyone needs you. When the Lord God created you, he did not suppose that you would want to spend your days on Earth in a hole like this."

"I am satisfied with life."

"That is not true. Look here, this is an official invitation. This says it all. How much you'll get and where you'll live. If you don't understand something, I'm prepared to explain it."

Pavel squinted nearsightedly as he skimmed the document.

The little girl tiptoed in, slipped over to the table, and took a blotter from it with her thin little hand.

"Thank you," Pavel said. "But I'm staying here."

"That's absurd."

"Maybe so."

"You have no right to luxuriate in idleness or in an amorous frolic with her mother. . . ."

"What reproaches!"

"Excuse me. But still I have to reproach you for a conscious idleness, an intellectual suicide."

"I'm not being idle."

"You're working? Where's your laboratory? Your books? Your assistants?"

"I don't need them."

"What is it you're working on?"

"Would you really like to know?"

"Of course. I want to know everything."

"I thought you already knew everything. Well, let's go. It's not far."

They went around behind a house on a path still slippery

wet from the recent rain. A barrel filled to the brim with rainwater stood across their path and he had to step in the grass. His pants became soaked immediately.

"Here it is," Pavel said, stopping on the edge of a small garden plot in back of the house.

Flowers were growing. They were huge, the size of a fist, white, pink, violet, and dark-red; coarse, juicy, sensual flowers. Somehow they reminded him of the flowers in pots on the windows of northern cities, cottony in their refined yet vulgar lavishness. Those flowers were offensive, but in their own way they were beautiful, as everything perfect is beautiful, when nothing can be added.

"What is this?" he asked. "Have you become a florist?"

"They're potatoes," Pavel said.

"I don't get it."

"I am raising potatoes for flowers."

"And the tubers?"

"Their tubers are small, green, and useless. But you have to admit that the flowers are extremely beautiful!"

"Yes. Huge flowers. What about carrots?"

"Carrots?"

"Are you raising them for flowers?"

"No," Pavel smiled.

"It's a symbol?"

"Why a symbol? Unfortunately, the cucumbers aren't in bloom any more. I'd like you to see them. You'd like them. I hope that next year they will bloom on water, like enormous water lilies."

The chauffeur was standing next to the car, holding the door open. Pavel stepped out onto the porch but went no further, as though fearful that he'd be pulled into the car and carried off.

"We'll see each other again." He did not want his voice to contain a threat but he could not help himself.

"I don't doubt it," Pavel said. "If you can wait a moment, I'll cut you a bouquet. Your wife would like it."

"Thanks. Next time."

The car set off, climbing out of a puddle. He did not turn around, although he knew that Pavel was still standing there, his hand on the doorknob. And watching him leave.

What a fool, what a bastard, he kept repeating to himself, trying to summon as much anger toward Pavel as he could manage—that way it would be easier not to think about anything when he gave Pavel's address to others, efficient but devoid of feeling.

"Potato flowers," he said aloud.

"What did you say?" the chauffeur asked.

He did not answer. Suddenly he was sorry he had not taken a bouquet for his wife. She would have laughed, found light, happy words.

Later, in another two hours, sitting in some kind of meeting, at the head of a long, boring table, he suddenly said, "Potato flowers."

And no one understood.

Gusliar Wonders

Introduction

It is sometimes asked why aliens, from outer space, when they select Earth as their destination, do not land in the Pacific Ocean, nor in the Pamir Mountains, nor in the Taklamakan Desert, nor, finally, in the city of Osaka or Konotro, but in the town of Great Gusliar. Why do other strange occurrences, the scientific explanation of which remains elusive, take place in Great Gusliar?

Innumerable scientists and amateur astronomers have asked themselves these questions, participants in the symposiums in Addis Ababa have spoken on the subject, and articles have been written for the op-ed page of the *Literary Gazette.*

Not long ago the academician Spichkin advanced a new hypothesis. Observing the trajectories of meteorological satellites circling the Earth, he came to the conclusion that the town of Great Gusliar stood on a bulge in the earth's surface, completely unnoticeable by Earth's inhabitants, but evident when seen from the neighboring stars. The bulge should not be confused with mountains, hills, or other geological formations, because no such thing is to be found anywhere near Gusliar.

The town of Great Gusliar is located on a plain. It is surrounded by *kolkhoz* fields and dense forests. The rivers flowing in the region are notable for their pure water and slow current. Floods occur in the spring and recede slowly, leaving brushwood and logs on the shores. In the winter there are snowdrifts that cut the town off from the neighboring populated areas. In the summers the temperatures are moderately hot, and thunderstorms are frequent. Autumns are mild, colorful. Toward the end of October cold rains begin. In 1876 the residents observed the northern lights and thirty years previously, a triple sun. The lowest recorded temperature was −48°C on January 18, 1923.

Previously, bears, wild goats, boars, raccoons, beaver, foxes, wolverines, and wolves were common and are found occasionally even today. In 1952 an attempt was made to introduce the buffalo-bison near Great Gusliar. They multiplied in Vorobyovsky Preserve, interbreeded naturally with elk, acquiring mighty horns and a calm, peaceloving nature in addition to their threatening appearance. The rivers and lake are rich in game. Not long ago *gambuziya* and the white *amur* were introduced into the Gus River. During the last few years, the Brazilian crayfish, a close relative of the lobster, has spread, no one knows how. Fishermen have learned to value their flavor. The local press has announced the appearance in the environs of the town of the tse-tse fly, but there are no known occurrences of sleeping sickness.

The population of Great Gusliar has reached 18,000. People of sixteen different nationalities live there. In the village of Moroshka there are four families of Kozhukhs. The Kozhukhs are a small forest people of the Ugro-Finnish group, speaking their own language, which has still not been fully analyzed linguistically. A Kozhukh alphabet based on the Latin alphabet was developed in 1925 by the Gusliar teacher Ivanov, who compiled a primer. Today only three Kozhukhs—Ivan Semyonov, Ivan Mudrik, and Alexandra Filippovna Malova—speak Kozhukh.

The history of Great Gusliar reaches back more than 750 years. The first mention is found in the Andrian Chronicles, where it is said that the Potemkin Prince Gavriil Nezlobivy "came and slaughtered" the unruly inhabitants of the town of Gusliar. That happened in 1222.

The town grew rapidly, being conveniently located at the

crossroads of trade routes leading to the Urals and Siberia as well as to the southern and western parts of Russia. The Mongol yoke spared the town, since the Tatar *baskaks*, frightened by the density and wildness of the northern forests, confined themselves to sending a list of the required tribute, which the inhabitants paid at rare intervals. The rivalry between Moscow and Novgorod for control of Great Gusliar, which arose in the fourteenth century, ended with the final victory of Moscow only in the mid-fifteenth century. During the rivalry the town was burned three times and pillaged twice. Once the Novgorod *druzhina* of the warlord Lepekha leveled the town. In the following years Gusliar suffered the plague and pestilence, floods and famines. Fires raged every year. After each epidemic and fire the town rebuilt and adorned itself with white-stoned churches that spread along the banks of the Gus River.

Of the explorers who set out to meet the rising sun, more than one-third were natives of Great Gusliar, which in the sixteenth century turned into a flourishing city, becoming the rival of Vologda, Ustyug, and Nizhny Novgorod. It is sufficient to mention Timofei Barkhatov, who discovered Alaska; Simon Trusov, who explored the Kamchatka River with a party of fifty cossacks; Fedka Merkartov, the first person to reach Novaya Zemlya; and the discoverers of the Kuriles, Chelyabinsk, California, and Antarctica. All of them returned in old age to their native town and built two-story houses on Torgovaya Street, Siny Lane, or Govyazhy Slope. It was in those years that Gusliar began to be called Great.

Incidentally, no unanimous opinion has been reached among scholars on the derivation of the name "Gusliar." On one hand, Professor Tretyakovsky in his monograph "The Conquest of the North" presents the view that the source of the word is *gusliar*, a person who plays the *gusli*, an ancient musical instrument, for the production of them was highly developed in the region. On the other hand, Ilonen and other foreign historians are inclined to the idea that the name derives from the Gus River, on the banks of which the town is located. A third view is that of Tikhonravova, which supposes that these heavily forested regions sheltered supporters of the Czech reformer Jan Hus, who fled from the oppression of the Hapsburgs. Finally, one must mention the view of Dranov, who derives the word "Gusliar" from the Kozhukh *khus-lya*, meaning "the rear leg of a large bear living on a mountain." Among the Kozhukhs, there exists even today a legend concerning the hero Dem, who killed a bear in this region and ate its rear leg.

In the late nineteenth century, the railroad bypassed Great Gusliar, and it ceased to play an important role in trade, becoming a mere stopping place on the Gus River.

During recent years, local industry has grown. There are a brewery and factories producing buttons and thumbtacks, as well as a sawmill, a dairy combine, and coopers' workshops. In the town are located a training school for river navigation, several high schools, three libraries, two movie theaters, a river workers' club, and a museum. Among the architectural monuments preserved by the state are the Spaso-Trofimovsky Monastery, the Church of Paraskeva Pyatnitsa (sixteenth century), and the Dmitrovsky Cathedral. The bazaar and several churches were torn down in 1930 when Explorer Square was created.

Great Gusliar is the center of the Great Gusliar District, where flax, rye, and buckwheat are grown. Animal husbandry and forestry are important. At the disposal of tourists who choose to visit the town during the summer is the Great Gusliar Hotel with the Gus Restaurant. In recent years a number of historical films have been shot in the town, for example, *Stenka Razin, Explorer Barkhatov, Sadko,* and *Ballad of a Hussar.*

The principal street, Pushkin Avenue, stretches along the river. On it are situated the department store, the bookstore, and the pet shop. One end of the avenue reaches a bridge over the Gryaznukha River, which divides the town into the old section and the suburbs. At the other end the avenue meets the town park, where there are an open-air stage, a target range, a merry-go-round, and a summer reading room.

Transportation to Vologda is by bus (six hours) or by airplane (one hour); to Arkhangelsk, by airplane (one and a half hours) or by steamer (through Ustyung and Kotlas, four days).

Aliens from outer space began visiting the town in 1967. Earlier traces of their appearance have not been found.

The Personal Touch

They were sitting in the yard, playing dominoes. It was summer, after a rainstorm, in fine weather. The clouds, having shaken off their water, floated overhead, luxurious and tranquil; the puddles dried up quickly; an invisible vapor had arisen from them. Soon it would be time to go have supper, and the game was becoming slightly tedious, so the time had come to chat about this and that.

"Somehow I feel tired today," Vasil Vasilevich said, sniffing the complex aromas flying down from the building's twelve kitchens.

"It's been hot," Valentin Kats agreed, moving his pieces. Then he asked his friends, "How about one more game?"

At that moment Kornely Udalov walked into the yard. He was sweaty, his blond hair curled, his pants dirty, his jacket over his shoulder. He was carrying a can of paint, in which a brush was moving back and forth.

"Our friend Kornely," Pogosyan said, "has become a painter?"

"Cut the kidding," Udalov said, casting a glance at his windows to see whether his wife Xenia was watching him. Then he set the can of paint down in the middle of the yard and took a seat on a bench.

"Something happened to me," he said. "Unbelievable."

"Something's always happening to you," Valentin said. "Anyone for another game?"

"So what happened?" Pogosyan asked.

Udalov, who wanted to tell his story very much, answered

immediately, "You know the road to Gryaznukha? The one to the resort?"

"Yes."

"That's where it all happened. There was no road there today."

"Where'd it run off to?"

"I don't know how to answer your question," Udalov said. "It is too soon for humanity to learn such secrets."

"Kornely, please don't play games," Vasil Vasilevich said, somewhat hurt. "Things are always happening to you. And you are always giving them a cosmic significance."

"That's precisely it: cosmic. Nothing less."

"I know," Grubin said out of an open window. He had obviously heard the whole conversation while he was busy with the tedious but creative task of carving "The Song of Prophetic Oleg" on a grain of rice. "I know—the Americans were bringing a rock back from the moon, dropped it halfway back, and it landed on Kornely's road."

"You're a cynic, Grubin," Udalov said with sadness.

It was clear to everyone that he really was eager to talk but could not quite make up his mind to begin. Beads of sweat appeared on his chubby face.

"You're a cynic, Grubin, and the most remarkable thing is that you almost guessed, although you can't imagine the full significance of such an event. I gave my word, almost my vow, that I would not publicize it."

"So don't publicize it," Grubin said.

"So I won't," Udalov said.

"Who needs your stories?" Grubin asked. Despite his rudeness, he was Udalov's best friend, and everyone knew it.

"So what happened with the road?" Valyo Kats asked. "Tell me quick, or my wife will call me in for supper."

"You won't believe it," Udalov said.

"We won't believe it," Grubin agreed from his window.

But Udalov had already decided to tell his story and seemed

not to hear Grubin's words. His eyes went cloudy and took on a vacant look, the kind the ancient tellers of tales had when they took their gusli out of their bags, turned their faces to the prince himself, and began to unfold a long, engrossing narrative, believable to his listeners but totally incredible to posterity.

"I set off for Gryaznukha on foot today," Udalov said. "I took the bus to the creamery, and from there on foot. In a month from now we'll have to rebuild the roof. So I was going to have a look."

"What happened to your business car, Kornely?" Grubin asked.

"The car went to Potma for a new generator. There's only one car for all of us. And I set off for the resort. What was the hurry, I ask you? What was the hurry, if the road went through a forest, at times right on the bank of the river, the birds were singing, there was no traffic and even no vacationers?"

"Is it true that the resort has been closed?" Vasil Vasilevich asked.

"Temporarily," Udalov said. "Temporarily the mud for the mud baths has dried up. We'll probably bring in some mineral water. Whatever we decide. It was then that I met them."

"Vacationers?"

"What vacationers? The people driving the Moskvich. An entire family. Tourists, most likely. Everything was fastened to the roof: tent, mattress, a baby carriage. That's why I didn't hitch a ride—there were already five people in the car."

"Why hitch a ride?"

"Why not? They'd drop me off at the resort."

"So they were headed toward you?"

"No, Valentin, you have it all mixed up. First, they passed me. And I didn't hitch a ride. Why rush? And then they came back. Toward me. He himself, the guy at the wheel, was all pale. The kids were crying. He leaned out of the window and waved to me to turn around and go back. A real weirdo, I thought. I still did not know what was awaiting me around the corner."

"Around the corner there was a cold corpse awaiting Kornely," Grubin said.

"Don't interrupt," Pogosyan said indignantly. "The man is telling a story, and you go and interrupt."

"Around the corner, a sign was awaiting me. 'Under construction'—you know the kind—a triangle with a man with a shovel. I was even surprised that there was any construction work going on without the knowledge of the construction office, where I work. Our town isn't that big, so there can't be any construction we don't know about. And I was also surprised because the sign was strange. Poorly done from the point of view of the artistic image. The worker had three legs and a messy appearance."

"Who makes our signs?"

"They're sent in from Vologda. That's police business. But that's not the point. Whether the sign is good or bad doesn't matter—but the man had three legs!"

"Graffiti artists," Lozhkin's wife said. She was already feeding her husband but had stuck her head out the window to hear an interesting story.

"That's what I thought," Udalov agreed. "And the people in the Moskvich bothered me, too. What had frightened them?"

"The graffiti artists," Lozhkin's wife repeated.

"The sign was standing there, dug into the ground, and from around a bend in the road I could hear the sound of clanging metal and all kinds of construction noise. I took another ten steps forward, and I have to admit that I took them very, very carefully. Then I saw it: Across the road was a barrier, a railroad-crossing gate. And on it, in black letters, was written: 'No Thoroughfare.' And right behind the gate there was this strange-looking bulldozer, and on the bulldozer was sitting—you'll never believe it—an alien, with four arms and three eyes."

"Come off it," Pogosyan said, not believing a word of it.

"Valentin, your dinner's getting cold," Kats's wife shouted down from a window.

"Wait a minute," Kats said. "I want to hear the end. Then I'll come."

"Just think!" Kats's wife yelled across the yard to Lozhkin's wife. "Valentin doesn't come running when he's called."

"On his head he was wearing a transparent helmet, the kind the cosmonauts have," Udalov continued, squinting his eyes in order to picture the scene more clearly. "Little wires were sticking out of the helmet, and he was wearing an orange suit! He saw me but pretended not to be surprised, turned off the engine, and jumped to the ground. I saw that he had a minimum of three legs, and a different shoe on each foot. I greeted him, because I was in a state of shock, and he said, 'Hello.' "

"Come off it!" Pogosyan said. " 'Hello' he says in his interplanetary language, but Kornely, sure thing, has studied it."

"Since childhood," Grubin said, going along with the joke. He had stopped his work and was not missing a word.

"He said it in our language," Udalov objected. "So then I answered with all the necessary responsibility, 'Who gave you authorization to perform this work?' "

"Of course," Grubin said. "We see a person with three legs, a guest from a distant star, and instead of saying 'Welcome' we immediately start bugging him: 'Who gave the authorization?' "

"I was frightened," Udalov said. "Otherwise I'd have said what I should have. But out of fright I seized the bull by the horns."

"Did he have horns, too?" Lozhkin's wife asked in amazement.

"He was speaking figuratively," Vasil Vasilevich said.

"I'm going," Pogosyan said. "Otherwise instead of beef for dinner I'll get bull."

But Pogosyan did not leave. He wanted someone to stop him, to say that it was all a joke, but no one did. Everyone knew that although Udalov had a highly developed imagination, and although he was a nervous person, he was still extremely truthful, and Xenia, his wife, would have taken his head off if he lied.

"I asked him," Udalov continued, "and he threw up his arms and said, 'It's terrible, a real mess.' "

"Were they big, the aliens?" Vasil Vasilevich asked.

"No, not very big—about the size of a third-grader," Udalov answered.

"That's what I thought," Vasil said. "Why should they be enormous?"

"I tried to crawl under the gate, and at first he wouldn't let me through, pointed to the sign, muttered that there was no thoroughfare. Well, I showed him that I was the head of the construction office in Great Gusliar, on the outskirts of which he was performing repair work of an unknown nature."

"Weren't you afraid?"

"I became afraid later," Udalov admitted. "But first off I felt indignant. They come with their bulldozer, won't let you through, scare people away, and the bulldozer wasn't even any of our makes. Then the alien became timid and said, 'Excuse me, but would you be good enough to follow me, you can speak to our leader.' "

Kats's wife stuck her body out the window up to her waist, and almost fell out. "Did you go?"

"Of course I went. I crawled under the gate, went around the bend, and there, beyond a little hill, I saw an amazing sight. The road there was totally destroyed for about thirty meters as though a giant hammer had struck it or an avalanche fell upon it. But I immediately realized what was going on—further down the slope lay their flying saucer, tilted to one side."

"What markings did the saucer have?" Pogosyan asked suspiciously.

"No markings," Udalov said. "They don't need any. The saucer was lying there, with a crowd of aliens around it. Some were fixing the saucer, others busy with the road. The technology, the equipment—it was remarkable how much stuff fit into that saucer."

Grubin crawled out of the window, feet first, and came closer.

"I asked them, 'A forced landing?' One of them—also with three legs—walks over to me from out of the crowd and answers, 'A lousy landing. A horrendous landing. I had to give the navigator two severe reprimands.' I asked, 'Why so stern?' And then he said—"

At that instant Udalov stopped speaking, for he felt, like Scheherazade, that his listeners were totally captivated by his tale.

Udalov turned toward his window and shouted, "Xenia, will dinner be ready soon?"

Xenia did not answer.

"You'll have time," Kats said. "Finish your science-fiction story first."

"To some it may be science fiction, and to others the real truth," Udalov said, and no one broke out laughing.

"Please go on," Vasil said. "It's getting cool."

"So I asked," Udalov continued after lighting a cigarette, " 'Why so stern?' And the head alien answered, 'What do you expect? Imagine yourself in our position. We fly to a strange planet. We have strict orders not to enter into contact but just to conduct visual observations. The natives,' he says, 'have to develop according to their own laws.' "

"Who does he mean, the natives?" Pogosyan asked.

"Us," Grubin answered for Udalov.

"We're not the natives," Pogosyan said. "That's insulting. What do you think, we run around naked?"

"Don't be insulted," Grubin said.

Meanwhile, Udalov continued, " 'Let's pick out,' the head alien says to me, 'a quiet spot just outside a small town—' "

"And who's the small town?" Pogosyan asked. "Is Great Gusliar a small town?"

" 'Let's pick a small, quiet town. We want to land nearby, to collect specimens of the plant life and take all kinds of pictures. And because of that bungling navigator we have an accident.' "

"He was right!" Lozhkin's wife said. "He was right to give the navigator a severe reprimand. If they let him into space, then he's supposed to work, and not goof off."

"Maybe he saw from up there how beautiful the country around Great Gusliar is," Kats's wife said, "and his hand trembled?"

"What about their precautionary measures? Were they in hermetic suits, or what?" Vasil asked.

"I don't know, I didn't ask," Udalov said. "If you're bored, you can leave, but don't butt in."

Finding himself the center of attention, Udalov became almost insolent, and his voice sounded metallic. His listeners shut up.

"All around us robots were humming, and machines, and cosmonauts. They were hurrying to keep their shame from being known to the inhabitants of Earth. The head alien shook his helmet, sighed in his own way, and said, 'How do you think it would be if the Galaxy learned that our ship destroyed a road on Earth, near Great Gusliar? Can you imagine how the Akarils from the planet Tsuk would laugh at us? How the ignobly spirited Tumses would meow in a fit of mockery? How the wise Yikiks would shake all their heads? Our reputation throughout the Galaxy would be ruined.' "

"No, they must have had precautionary measures, with total isolation," Vasil said.

"How did you manage to remember all those names, Kornely?" Grubin asked.

"They knew who they were dealing with," Kornely answered with dignity. " 'Imagine my position,' the alien says, and I of course, express my sympathy. Then another one comes up to us, in a striped jumpsuit, black all over, with his eyes apart, and babbles something in their lingo. I look all around, thinking that between the road and the saucer they'd be busy until night. Even with their technology. 'I don't know,' the head alien says, 'but I hope that fate has sent us an intelligent and kind native.' "

"He said 'native'?" Pogosyan asked.

"He did."

"I would have told him off," Pogosyan said. "Put him in his place. After all, you weren't naked."

"No, I was wearing a sport jacket," Udalov said. "Only I wasn't thinking about that. They talked to me as an equal. Why should I strain interplanetary relations for no good reason?"

"Right," Vasil said. "Otherwise they would have warned you, as soon as they saw you."

"Oh!" Kats's wife said. "How dangerous!"

"It was nothing," Udalov calmed her. "I immediately answered, 'If you have any request, the people of Earth and Great Gusliar in my person are ready to come to your assistance.' "

"Bravo!" Vasil exclaimed. "That's the way!"

"And then he told me that he had a request. The road they could repair, without leaving a trace, and they could put their saucer in Earth orbit. But they didn't have any paint."

"What?"

"Paint. Oil paint. The wood columns along the roadsides were splintered into matchsticks. And the new ones had to be painted white to prevent traffic accidents. He asked me, 'Bring us, brother-in-reason, a can of paint. We'll reward you in princely fashion.' I answered him, 'I don't need any reward, I'm always ready.' And he said that the Galaxy would never forget my modest services. Well, I ran back to town. . . ."

His listeners sat a minute in silence, pondering whether Udalov had finished his story or whether there would be a continuation. The sun was descending toward the river, the shadows were lengthening, a cool breeze stretched out from the forest. The Katses' dinner was burning, but they did not notice.

"Is that all?" Grubin asked finally.

"Almost," Udalov said. His holiday was almost over, as was his story. "I spent a whole hour looking for the paint. And the brush, too. The hardware store was closed, at the warehouse the watchman had gone off to have dinner, and so forth. Then I ran back to the aliens—you can't let people down. I ran back and there was no road sign. There was nothing. No saucer, no machines, no robots. Empty."

"And the road?"

"The road had been completely repaired."

"So you came straight home?"

"No," Udalov said. "First I kept my promise. I painted the posts."

"They were unpainted?"

"Yes, unpainted. Four of them. Brand new, but unpainted. And next to one of them was a note. Should I show you?"

"Of course."

"Look."

Udalov took a note, folded in quarters, out of his pocket. He unfolded it, flattened it out against the table. And read it aloud. The others bent over the table and read, repeating Udalov, word by word. The note was printed in black ink: "Thank you in advance for your help. The posts are at your disposal. Your help will not be forgotten. We request you not to spread the story of what happened here."

"No signature," Pogosyan said.

"And quite right not to have one," Vasil said. "Only you, Udalov, have not lived up to the trust, and you'll get a serious warning eventually."

"Why's that?" Udalov asked.

"They asked you not to spread the story, but you have. Do you know what you get for that?"

"You're completely wrong," Udalov said with hurt feelings. "They're fine ones to talk. I would have kept quiet, but they flew away, without leaving a trace. Maybe I would have liked to ask them some questions. Maybe I would have liked to ask their advice about the future. Maybe they could have expressed their gratitude by leaving just one of their bulldozers for our construction office, instead of a little note. Aren't I right?"

And everyone agreed that he was.

"I didn't even ask them for their address, what planet they're from. I didn't even find out what they would do if someone starts a nuclear war on Earth. Is that the way real cosmonauts act?"

And everyone agreed that real cosmonauts did not act that way.

Then everyone was silent for a while, digesting the seriousness of the event. Then Pogosyan asked, "Udalov, do you have any proof?"

"What kind of proof?"

"Proof that you met aliens today."

"What are you talking about?" Udalov became totally outraged. "The paint can, that is sitting in the middle of the yard for all to see. Full of paint. I got it from the warehouse today. On my personal account. Why would I buy paint? Why, I ask you? You know that I do supervisory work."

"He's right," Vasil said. "Why would he lie about the paint?"

"And tomorrow's Sunday," Udalov said. "Let's all go out to the road. You'll see the posts, freshly painted. And they're too smooth for our carpenters to have made them. Like imported furniture. And the paint is still fresh."

"Kor-ne-ly!" Xenia shouted from her window. She was not aware of what had happened, and therefore did not feel respect for Udalov: "What is it, do I have to heat your soup a third time?"

"Coming, Xenia, coming," Udalov answered. "See you tomorrow," he said to his friends and neighbors.

"Well, now," Vasil said after him. "Why shouldn't we believe the man? Of course, we'll believe it."

And everyone believed it. And they did not go to the road the next day, even though Udalov wanted them to. What was the sense of looking at the posts?

Now in Great Gusliar the people are awaiting a new arrival of cosmonauts. They expect that the arrival will be in their hometown, because relations have already been established. The personal touch. Almost friendship.

Who Can Say?

Loudspeakers roared over the town of Great Gusliar, playing cheerful music. The sun broke through the clouds. Pioneers in white shirts ran around all over the place. The townspeople flowed under the banners and slogans stretched across the streets. Buses full of tourists formed a line in the square, where earlier tradesmen's stalls had stood but which now had a canvas-wrapped monument to explorers. Today, on the town's 750th anniversary, the monument would be formally unveiled.

The residents of Building 16 were sitting in the yard around a table, rickety from long hours of domino playing. They were waiting for their wives to finish dolling themselves up, and chatting about things past and present.

Kornely Udalov, wearing a white shirt and dark-blue tie, his hair parted on a slant to conceal a bald spot, was disputing the opinions of Pogosyan that there were better places than Gusliar.

"For example, Erevan," Pogosyan was saying. "Two thousand years! Three thousand years! Five thousand years in the same place!"

"It's not a question of numbers," Udalov objected. "Ivan the Terrible almost moved the capital here from Moscow."

"He was a smart guy," Pogosyan persisted. "He changed his mind."

"The *oprichniki* stopped him."

"And were the *oprichniki* so dumb?"

"It's hard talking to you," Udalov said. "You're not very patriotic about your hometown."

Lozhkin, an old man in a black suit, his chest decked with medals, agreed with Udalov. He waved his hand in the air and said, "Our ancestors had their reasons for calling Gusliar great."

"They lived here, and they called it great. No one's called Erevan great. Why should they? Every last dog knows it," Pogosyan retorted.

The conversation degenerated into personalities and squabbling. Sasha Grubin, who had combed his hair and shaved for the occasion, listened to them, listened and then finally said, as though it had no relation to the conversation, "It would be great to go to sleep and wake up two hundred years later. And to see our Gusliar in the distant future."

The neighbors interrupted their argument, thought a moment, and agreed with Grubin.

"On the other hand," Udalov said, "Two hundred years into the past wouldn't be bad."

"Make it seven hundred," Vasil said. "You arrive in ancient times, and all around are people with spears and bows, and they pay taxes to the ancient city of Kiev."

"Or to the Mongol invaders," Lozhkin corrected.

"So it was the Mongols. There are bears around, deer, boars. The people brew their alcohol out of honey."

"All they'd have to do would be to give you a taste of their honey drink," Grubin objected. "They'd find you out right away."

"What?" Vasil said in surprise.

Everyone broke out laughing, and Lozhkin answered, "They'd know by your clothing. And your accent. They spoke a different language, Old Slavonic."

"So instead of honey, you'd get a sword across your neck," Grubin concluded.

"All right, all right," Vasil said, refusing to give up. "Do you think I'd go without preparation? First I'd go to the Academy of Sciences. Let me have, I'd say, a consultant on Old Slavonic. I'd read up, learn what I had to. I'd get the right clothes from a museum. Then there'd be no telling."

No one believed Vasil. The conversation lit on time travel. Someone had read about it in science fiction. Another person hadn't read anything, but had heard about it.

Suddenly Udalov had a fascinating idea.

"A few hundred years from now," he said, "such travel will be an everyday affair. After all, there are no limits to science. Tourists will come, scholars, mass migrations will arise. Life will be so interesting that we can't even imagine it. Let's say that schoolchildren have to learn about life in ancient Egypt. The teachers will push a button and they'll be visitors in the court of Cleopatra. OK, kids, learn about our difficult past."

"Most probably," Lozhkin said. "Only they'd have to observe traffic laws strictly. I read about what would happen if you broke them. Once in the Mesozoic Era someone crushed a butterfly, and as a result a different president was elected in America."

Everyone was silent. They were thinking. Then Grubin said, "No doubt about it. If the laws weren't observed, we would have met these visitors from the future more than once. No matter how you try to cover it up, nature will out. The education will be off, ignorance of some trifle that everyone else knows. How would a visitor know, for example, what place our soccer team is in?"

"Sixth," Pogosyan, Udalov, and Vasil answered in unison.

"See there," Grubin said happily. "No one will trip you up. But the visitor wouldn't know, because in a hundred years all the records will have been lost."

"But I don't know," Lozhkin said. "I don't even know who is in first place."

"Serdobol," Pogosyan, Udalov, and Vasil explained.

"But I don't know," Lozhkin persisted. "Does that make me a traveler in time?"

"Perhaps," said Pogosyan, looking at Lozhkin seriously. "You can't trust anyone in such matters."

"Don't worry, Lozhkin," Grubin interjected kindly. "We know you. If need be, we'll let the authorities know."

"If someone isn't one of us, it's Pogosyan's wife, Berta," Udalov said. "Yesterday she gave my son Maxim a spank. One of us wouldn't act that way."

"She had good reason," Pogosyan said. "He broke a window. The kid shouldn't act like a delinquent."

"If I met a visitor from the future," Grubin said, "I'd ask him two or three questions right off."

"You're not going to see any visitor," Pogosyan said. "What could interest any intelligent person in our town?"

"What an error!" Lozhkin exclaimed. "Today the whole country is interested in our town. On one hand, seven hundred fifty years. On the other, the unveiling of the monument, by which we give our glorious past its due. Visitors from all over. The broadcast about it on the radio from Moscow. If I were in our descendants' shoes, I'd sure arrange an excursion here."

"Kornely!" Xenia Udalova called from a window. "We're ready. Are you taking an overcoat?"

"No."

"Rain isn't predicted," Lozhkin said. "I read the newspaper. It says that the writer Putskhveriya has come for the festivities. A delegation has come from Kamchatka. A cosmonaut is expected, but which one hasn't been announced yet. Without counting the tourists."

"Just think," Pogosyan said scornfully, to get in the last word. Actually he was an enthusiastic supporter of Great Gusliar, but only his relatives in Erevan knew it.

Lozhkin's wife came out into the yard and asked, "Are you through loafing around? They'll start without us."

"Coming, my dove," Lozhkin answered. "We've been having a discussion here."

"Sure, sure," his wife said, disbelievingly.

They left the yard first, then the others followed. The neighbors soon forgot the conversation, except Udalov, whom the idea haunted. He was so struck by the possibility of meeting a visitor from the future on the street that he began to inspect people with suspicion. And he discovered in people strange traits, ones he had never noticed before and which might indicate foreignness, a masquerade.

Walking toward him were the pharmacist Savich and his wife, the director of the department store. One would think that Udalov had known Savich for ages, but today his bald spot shone unnaturally, and the way he was holding his wife's arm seemed awkward. Perhaps Savich had been sent? But Udalov immediately told himself no. For just one holiday it was hardly worth sending a resident inspector to Great Gusliar. And if Savich hadn't been substituted for, Udalov knew him for twenty years. With this in mind, Udalov said, "Hello."

"Hello," the Saviches answered.

Four gymnasts in blue suits went past. They were rushing to the parade. Udalov realized that the visitor from the future could hide among the gymnasts, and then it would be hard to find him. But he dismissed the idea. It would be complicated for people in the future to find gym suits. And all the real ones were kept careful track of.

With each step Udalov became more and more convinced: A visitor from the future was in Gusliar. And Udalov had to search him out and have a heart-to-heart talk. That was very important. Just think, no one before Udalov had walked down the street with the intention of finding a time traveler among the most ordinary people. And a new approach, even though simple, might have a discovery hidden within it.

"What's the matter, Kornely?" Xenia asked. "Why are you falling behind?"

Kornely looked with new eyes at Xenia and his children. He supposed he shouldn't really have any doubts about them. Everything was in order. But Udalov felt that a wall of strangeness was growing between him and his family. A man who has a noble goal before him is forced to leave behind day-to-day concerns and interests. Just to be on the safe side, Udalov asked his wife, "Xenia, you wouldn't happen to know what place our soccer team is in?"

"You're crazy," Xenia said with conviction.

"Sixth, Papa, but why?" his clever little son Maxim said.

"Bravo, my son," Kornely said and felt ashamed of his suspicions.

"Still, what's going on with you?" Xenia asked. "Watch where you're going or you'll trip."

On the edge of the square stood a kiosk with cold drinks and cigarettes. A newly thrown-together reviewing stand had been erected near the canvas-covered monument. Xenia held back when she saw Raissa Semyonovna, her doctor. Xenia wanted to talk about the last analysis in an unofficial setting. Raissa squinted behind her glasses but answered the questions because she was bound by the oath of Hippocrates. Udalov, while there was still time, bought a bottle of beer and sat down at a table with a blue plastic tablecloth. These little tables, carried outside from the dining room, formed an open-air café.

Two drivers from tourist buses were seated at a table. The drivers were cursing out a foreman at the 110th kilometer. Udalov offered them cigarettes and also cursed out the foreman, whom he had never seen. To keep up morale.

But only a small fraction of Udalov's consciousness was occupied with the conversation. His eyes were galloping over the square, leaping from one group of people to the next, because he could not afford to waste time. Miss the visitor today, and he'll never be caught.

In the aisle between the tables a middle-aged man sprang up. He was holding a bottle and a glass, moving uncertainly, unable to find a place to sit. Udalov felt a sharp stab in his heart. A sixth, seventh, and eighth sense ordered him: "Udalov, take it easy. That's him."

"Join us," one of the drivers said, as though guessing Udalov's thoughts.

"My heartfelt thanks," the man answered with a drawl and plopped down on the chair next to Udalov.

And right then a tiny, insignificant, almost unnoticeable detail caught Kornely's eye. The man, as he sat down, did not pull up his pants' legs, as every man who wants to keep the crease in his pants does. Kornely's ears perked up.

His glance fixed on the visitor's face. The face was just too ordinary. Neither smooth nor wrinkled. Like a mask. Under his arm the man had a worn black briefcase with a brass lock. The sleeves of a red sweater or jacket stuck out of the briefcase. The tourist's pants were on the short side, unironed, as though he had the wrong size. And between the tops of his high shoes and the cuffs of his pants checkered socks peeked out. The man's eyes were hidden by dark glasses.

The man might be Udalov's only chance. Kornely looked at his ordinary shaven cheeks and waited for the visitor to say something. You can't just go up to a person and ask, "What century are you from?"

The tourist drank his beer in small swallows and was silent.

"How's the beer?" the driver Kolya asked him.

"It's the Gusliar brand," Udalov added. "It's been famous since before the revolution."

"I know," the man said curtly and smiled shyly. "I've been meaning to try it for a long time."

"Where are you from?" the driver Kolya asked.

"Moscow," the man answered. "I came specially for the occasion."

That's right, Udalov thought. It would be dangerous for him to mention someplace near like Vologda. Witnesses might turn up. But Moscow is big.

"Why go to the bother of traveling?" the older driver asked. "Don't you people in Moscow have enough monuments of your own?"

Bravo! Udalov thought, he's playing right into my hands.

"There are monuments and there are monuments," the

man answered. "For many years I've been studying the history of the Russian North, the conquest of the Urds and Siberia. This monument says a lot. I've been waiting for the unveiling a long time. I just haven't been able to get away any sooner."

"If you had, you wouldn't have seen the monument."

But the time traveler was not to be caught so easily. He answered immediately, and almost without any accent, "I would have seen the monument earlier because it was supposed to have been set up many years ago. So that in my imagination it already existed."

"Enthusiasm is a good thing," the older driver said. "I'm going to get another beer. Our group is staying here for the night. So the foreman doesn't matter to us."

"Thanks, I shouldn't have any more beer," the visitor said, but he realized from the expression in the drivers' eyes that they meant business, so he took out a ten-ruble bill.

While he was still groping in his pocket for the bill, Udalov already knew what it would look like: brand new, without a single wrinkle. And if the paper was sent for analysis it would turn out to be prepared the day after tomorrow.

The driver, of course, did not take the money from the time traveler, but did bring a half-dozen bottles. When they were gone, the traveler had to go to the stand and get another four bottles.

"So how is it?" Udalov asked, when the man, staggering from the drinks, returned to the table. "The girl in the kiosk didn't notice, did she?"

"What was she supposed to notice?" the man asked, and fixed Udalov with a piercing glance. Udalov felt confused.

"Oh, nothing," he said. "Just kidding."

"So what was the joke?"

Those people from the future sure were touchy, Udalov thought to himself. He did not say anything out loud, but tried to joke his way out. "There's this joke," he said. "Two guys decide to make counterfeit money. They made a four-ruble note. They decided to go change it at a neighbor's. He gave them back two two-ruble bills."

No one laughed. Only the older driver asked: "Are there really four-ruble bills?"

"No," the time traveler answered firmly. "I know for a fact that the Soviet Treasury has not issued and is not now issuing notes in denominations of two or four rubles."

"To the health of the Ministry of Finance!" Kolya suggested. "Let it not confuse us further and pay us in twos."

"And new ones," Udalov added.

"New ones or old ones—we'll take either," Kolya answered.

"Oh, so that's what you were getting at," the man said. "I have a lot of new bills. Right before leaving I received a bonus."

He pulled a packet out of his pocket. About twenty bills, fresh and crisp.

"These are the ones I was given."

"Where?" Udalov asked quickly.

But the drivers butted in. "Why are you giving the guy a hard time?" Kolya asked. "Wherever they give out bonuses, that's where he got it. It's none of our business."

The visitor from the future looked at Udalov with hostility, and scowled. He did not like to be found out. That's OK, Udalov thought, we'll still drive you to the wall. We'll find arguments.

On the rostrum in front of the monument the town leaders and guests of honor appeared. Comrade Belov came to the microphone. The people began to listen.

"I'm going. Thank you," the visitor said.

"I'll go with you," Udalov said.

"I can manage without your company," the man answered, his glasses glittering. He stood and, sideways, like a crab, began to squeeze his way closer to the rostrum.

"Stop bugging him," Kolya said. "Let him have his fun."

"I have to," Udalov snapped. "He's not one of us."

And immediately regretted having let the cat out of the bag. The drivers' curiosity was piqued.

"Not one of us in what sense?" the older driver asked. "Look, friend, don't try to cover up—let us in on it."

"I have a suspicion," Udalov said and dove into the crowd after the visitor. He felt his head buzzing from the beer and wanted to stretch out on the grass, but he could not, because full exposure of the time traveler was only a step away.

"Kornely," Xenia shouted, spotting his bald spot in the crowd. "Where are you going?"

Fortunately, Comrade Belov waved his hand, the marching band struck up a tune, and the canvas fell to the ground, revealing the bronze figure of the explorer.

Udalov squeezed through the crowd, trying not to lose the direction in which the stubborn guest from the future had disappeared.

Suddenly Udalov bumped into the visitor's back. The visitor did not notice the arrival of his pursuer because he was busy jotting down notes in a small notebook. Udalov waited politely for the man to finish, since there was no place for him to run.

The speeches began, and the visitor put away his notebook in his briefcase. Udalov tapped him gently on the shoulder.

"You're here?" he said in surprise. "What do you want?"

"That you admit everything," Udalov said frankly.

"You amaze me," the visitor said and tried to make off into the crowd.

But Udalov grabbed him firmly by the lapel of his jacket.

"Listen," Udalov said, "You people must be humane and intelligent. So that once you've been caught, we should talk about things."

"What makes you think that we people are humane and intelligent?" the visitor said in surprise. "Where did you read that?"

"I am assuming it," Udalov answered. "Otherwise there is no reason to continue living in this world."

"A noble way of thinking," the visitor said. "But it does not apply to me. I am egotistical, and have lived the better part of my life quite uselessly. I love many but not my own wife. I assure you that that is the real truth."

"OK, OK. There are moral perverts everywhere. As exceptions," Udalov said. "I'd like to visit you."

"So come."

"So I will."

A pause set in. Udalov wanted to say something more, to demonstrate hospitality, to smooth over relations. "We here have some beautiful spots, too," he said. "The surrounding areas are just stunning. Forests, hills, hunting for grouse."

"Hunting is a cruel sport," the guest from the future said. "Animals have to be preserved, understood, not exterminated."

"Right," Udalov supported him, although the week before he had planned on going hunting but overslept, and the hunting party left without him. "I agree completely. But if you just take your fishing rod—"

"What's the difference?" the visitor said sternly. "Does a fish want to live?"

"Very much," Udalov said.

Another pause set in. Contact was not established. The man listened to the speeches distractedly and kept looking around, as though seeking a rarefied area in the crowd through which he could escape.

"But many fine people have been passionate hunters," Udalov finally found an answer. "Take Turgenev, for example. He's a writer of the last century, the author of *A Sportsman's Sketches*."

"I've read it," the visitor said. "But nonetheless, the cold-blooded murder of a living being is immoral."

"What's it with him—is he a religious nut?" a voice broke out behind Udalov.

Udalov turned around and saw the driver Kolya, who, overcome by curiosity and the desire to help Kornely hunt down a strange person, had pushed toward the rostrum and listened to the entire conversation.

The visitor flashed his glasses at Kolya and said with a hurt tone, "If you mean, do I have ideals, the answer is yes. If you mean the Christian God, the answer is no."

"He himself probably loves pork chops," Kolya said to Udalov, took out a cigarette, and lit up. "But he objects to animal husbandry."

Fighting two rivals at the same time was more than the time traveler could handle. He dodged away into the crowd, with an agility surprising for such an elderly man, slipping under a person's arm and zipping through the crowd, headed toward the edge of the square. Udalov was about to take off after him, but Kolya, with too much beer in him, puffed smoke in Korne-ly's face and demanded, "Don't try to get away from me, and don't chase the guy. Just tell me what it is with him. I feel it myself—he's not right, but I can't explain why."

"That's what it is—something personal," Udalov said, trying to avoid giving an answer.

"No, that's not enough," Kolya said. "Let's have it."

He held Udalov firmly by the lapels, and the people nearby began to stare. Udalov, fearing a scene, said, "Let's leave here."

"OK," Kolya agreed.

They made their way out of the crowd. The beer gurgled in their heads. The visitor was not to be seen. The chase after the man from the future had not succeeded. Although he might not have been a man from the future.

And Udalov, taking a cigarette from Kolya, told him frankly, from the soul, about his suspicions.

Kolya was not dumb. He caught on to the basic idea, although he regarded it critically. Like Pogosyan, he had objections: "Why come to Gusliar, even though it is a special occasion?"

"You don't understand a thing," Udalov said, leaning toward the driver's broad chest, which smelled slightly of gasoline.

"Even though you're my friend, you don't understand what a chance we let slip today. We would have learned everything from him."

Kolya looked at Udalov sympathetically, slapped on his octagonal Estonian cap, spit out his cigarette butt and said, "And you, my friend, don't get so upset. If necessary your buddy Kolya will take care of anybody you want. Did he put you down? He did, don't deny it. We'll find him and kick his ass. Just say the word. One word and we kick his ass. Let's go get the damned spy."

Old buddy Kolya was walking ahead with broad, unsteady steps. Udalov ran behind, muttering, "You didn't understand me right, Kolya. He didn't insult me. And you can't—"

"Don't give up," Kolya said. "He's a wanted man. Writing down secrets, doesn't eat meat. We'll find out what we need to know. Don't try to wriggle out of it."

The traveler from the future ran away toward the river, toward the big cathedral. There he had taken a seat on a green bench and was once again taking notes. From here the square wasn't visible; only a muffled roar and an occasional orator's word amplified through loudspeakers could be heard. The visitor felt safe. But the indirect route that Kolya and Udalov had taken led straight to the bench.

At the sight of his pursuers, the visitor shoved his notebook into his pocket, snatched up his briefcase, and was about to run off. But Kolya spotted him.

"Stop!" he yelled. "Hands up! Don't try to get away!"

"I wouldn't dream of it," the visitor answered with dignity. "If you need money, take what you need. I have modest needs."

He tried pulling out his new bills, but Udalov stopped him with a gesture.

"We're not thieves," Kolya said. "You haven't understood. You can't buy your way out of this one. We've got you. You've come to us from the future. Admit it."

Udalov glanced at Kolya reproachfully. Directness might ruin everything.

"That's not true," the visitor said. "You'll never prove it."

"We don't have to prove it," Kolya said. "We'll just check you out and find your phony identification papers."

"I don't have any ID with me," the visitor said. "I left them in the hotel."

"They don't carry identification," Udalov agreed. "It's actually quite logical. Maybe, they won't even have identification."

"Is that all?" the visitor asked. "Can I go now?"

"Admit it, and you can go," Kolya said.

"After all," Udalov said, "we're wasting time, you're wasting time. And we have only a scientific interest in you, nothing else."

"Precisely," Kolya agreed. "And you can't bribe us with your funny money."

The visitor frowned and thought hard. It was clear that he realized he was not going to get away and that it was best to confess. And then go his merry way.

"Well?" Udalov pressed. "What century are you from?"

The visitor inhaled deeply. Tears shone under his glasses.

And at that very moment two girls wearing shorts and colorful blouses appeared on the cathedral steps.

"Ah!" one of them said, not noticing the dramatic scene. "What remarkable seventeenth-century frescoes! What expressiveness!"

"And the tile stove? Did you see the tile stove, Nelly?"

"I saw it. Look, who's that down there?"

The girls ran down the steps and raced toward the man.

"Sergei Petrovich!" They tried outsquealing each other. "You were absolutely, totally right! The Day of Judgment is not structured canonically! There was a Gusliar school! Rappoport is put to shame!"

He summoned reinforcement by telepathy, Udalov thought. Now there are three of them, and only two of us. And maybe these girls aren't really girls but police.

"What luck!" the visitor exclaimed. "I had given up hope of seeing you!"

"Are they threatening you?" one of the girls asked suspiciously, searing Udalov with a glance.

"Not at all," Kolya said and pulled back Udalov by the sleeve.

"All of our group will be here soon," the girl said.

How many of them are there? Udalov thought. They might just liquidate me, if I turn out to be dangerous.

And in reality, as though hearing the girl's words, the others appeared in the cathedral door at that very moment, about ten of them, with cameras and notebooks, tall and short, young and old, and with them was Elena Sergeevna from the town museum.

Oh, trouble! Udalov thought, retreating submissively after Kolya.

"Oh, there you are, professor!" one of them shouted. "The history of art section is happy to greet its leader near these ancient walls."

"Sergei Petrovich! Sergei Petrovich!" voices exclaimed.

"Do you admire your professor?" Kolya asked with curiosity.

"And how," the girl said. "He's given us all a real education. The whole world knows him!"

Surrounded by his students and colleagues, the professor set off. He turned around and winked at Udalov, apparently relieved to get away from the nuts.

Udalov felt grateful to the professor. After all, he could have called the police. Kornely collapsed on the bench, his head sagging. Kolya sat down next to him, lit up a cigarette, and said, "No luck, buddy. Even though your idea was a great one."

"Forget it. Please, not a word to anyone."

"Don't worry—not me. I'll get behind the wheel and that'll be it. But what were you expecting? If he really was from the future?"

"That he would tell us about the wonderful future."

"Mmm, yes," Kolya said. "I'm going. You're a good guy, only you've got some mess inside your skull. Even in school they teach you that no such trips are possible. Remember!" He shoved something into Kornely's outside jacket pocket and walked away. He turned around, waved good-bye, and smiled warmly.

Udalov slowly returned to the square. One of his friends might have noticed the hunt for the professor. Very bad. Udalov groped in his pocket to find the driver's present. It was a little card, a calendar the size of a playing card, the kind prudent people carry in their wallets. On it, in gold letters was printed:

CALENDAR FOR 2075

On the other side of the card was a city with long houses, over which flying machines were soaring and the sun shining. The picture was three-dimensional, and microscopic leaves on the trees rustled in the wind of the future.

"Stop!" Udalov shouted into a deserted place. Then he said, "Eh, Kolya."

Under the picture an inscription appeared before his very eyes: "A good idea. You just misapplied it. Don't be sore."

Udalov never found him.

A Mine of Information

An alien appeared to Kornely Udalov in a dream.

"Listen, Kornely," the alien said. "We of the Galaxy know that you are favorably disposed toward cosmic friendship."

"Yes," Kornely agreed. "I believe in the possibility of contacts and as far as possible—"

"Hold on," the alien interrupted. "I'm very rushed for time."

The alien was surrounded by a blue aura, and it was hard to distinguish his form behind the glow. Kornely knew that the encounter was taking place in a dream but was in no hurry to wake up—he always liked chatting with a new person.

"We of the Galaxy have discussed matters," the alien continued, flying up closer and including Udalov within the limits of his glow, "and we have decided that you are suitable. You understand?"

"I do," Udalov said.

"And in gratitude for your past and future service we will give you a gift. Of cosmic significance. At the same time, I must warn you that this gift is a test of your entire planet, of humanity itself. If you are capable of coping with the present, that would mean that humanity has reached maturity. If not, you'll have to wait."

"But why did your choice fall on me?" Udalov asked out of modesty.

"I said, for your services. In addition, you are the very most average and ordinary person in Gusliar."

"Me?" Udalov asked, his pride somewhat injured.

"It's not important," the alien answered. "I'm in a hurry. Running out of energy. For the time I remain in telepathic contact with you, the lights on twenty-three planets have to be extinguished. So take the gift, and good-bye. If you can't cope with it, just say out loud, 'The game is over.' And everything will return to normal."

Udalov did not have time to answer, or even to reach out for the gift, before lightning flashed and Udalov awoke.

It was early morning. Rain was falling. Alongside him, Xenia was sleeping, breathing deeply. It's interesting, Udalov thought, did she hear our conversation? Somewhere in the distance an alarm clock rang out. Two-thirty—old man Lozhkin was getting up to do his exercises and feed his birds. Maybe it was just another dream? Maybe there had been no alien?

Udalov pulled his hands out from under the blankets. They were empty. No gift.

"Nonsense," Udalov said and went to sleep again.

He opened his eyes at seven-thirty. His son Maxim was getting ready for school. Xenia was clattering in the kitchen.

"Do your homework?" she asked her son. "Or did you stay out until dark playing ball with Sasha?"

"Didn't have any," answered Maxim, who resembled his father with his turned-up nose, wheat-colored hair, and tendency to excessive fantasizing.

"What do you mean, you didn't have any?" Xenia said anxiously. "I looked at your schedule. In history you have the Strelets rebellion."

"I know about it," Maxim said.

"Lord, if I could only check on it," Xenia said. "I'd drive you to school like a goat to pasture, but I have to go to work."

"Xenia, you woke me up," Udalov said. "I don't have to be at the office until eleven today. I told you yesterday."

"Get up anyway," Xenia answered. She had the habit of transferring her annoyance from one member of the family to another. "How many times have I asked you to fix the lock in the entry hall? One fine day they'll steal us all away, and you won't even notice. Your son hasn't done his homework again. He's going to get another C. He doesn't know anything about the Strelets rebellion."

"I may not know much, but I know more than you," Maxim answered rudely. "If I told you that Suvorov crushed it, you wouldn't even be surprised."

"I've really lost whatever I knew about history," Udalov confessed.

But then something clicked in his brain. It was as though an open textbook page appeared before his eyes. Udalov glanced over the page and said perfectly calmly, "They're teaching you wrong, son! If you have it that Suvorov crushed the Strelets rebellion. Especially if you consider that the Tsaritsa Sof'ya, Peter the Great's sister, was behind them, as well as Prince Golitsyn, her most important military leader. Suvorov, who was born only in 1730, could not have taken part in it."

Udalov gave his oration, then sat up on the edge of the bed, poked his feet into his slippers, and stood up. Maxim stood gazing in the doorway. Xenia glanced out of the kitchen, holding a lid in her hand, and asked, "Did you know that yourself or did you look it up somewhere?"

"I knew it," Udalov said. "I have a good memory. Hurry to school, Maxim, and in the future don't try to fool your dad. And Suvorov—"

"Come to the table," Xenia said, feeling kind. "Your kasha will get cold."

"I had an amazing dream," Udalov said, pouring milk into his kasha. "It seems this alien from space appears to me and says, 'For your progressive deeds, Comrade Kornely Udalov, please receive an unusual gift.'"

"You are going crazy with those aliens of yours, Kornely," Xenia said with pity. "And what was the gift?"

"That's the problem—I don't know. I woke up, and there was no gift."

"Precisely. Last night I dreamed, for example, about a tank. The neighbors were hanging on it. It must mean something too."

"It must," Udalov said, disillusioned. He was sorry about having such a rare dream.

"By the way," Xenia continued, "yesterday the electric bill came. Two rubles forty-two kopecks. I just can't believe how much energy the refrigerator eats up."

"Two forty-three," Udalov said automatically. "And for the alien to reach my mind, several planets had to go without energy."

"Two forty-two," Xenia said. "I saw the bill."

"No, two forty-three."

"Why have you decided to play a joke on me? As soon as I got the bill, I put it away in my box. When did you manage to rummage through it?"

"I haven't seen your bill." Udalov was honestly hurt. "It just seems to me that it's two forty-three."

"Wait a minute."

Xenia took out of the chest a painted box with a picture of a farm scene. The box had been a wedding gift from one of Udalov's fellow students. Xenia opened it and took out a blue piece of paper lying on top.

"Here it is," she said. "Just look!"

But she did not give him the bill, because she saw that on it was written, "Two rubles forty-three kopecks."

"You've been going through my things," she said with conviction.

"I didn't, I just guessed," Udalov answered.

"You've been going through my things. You're jealous. You're trying to find where I keep my letters."

"Who would want you?" Udalov said.

"Someone did—Kolya Semenikhin proposed to me."

"That Kolya of yours forgot about you twenty years ago."

"And why would he forget? Because I've spent the best

years of my life on you. I've given you everything in me that was fresh and unspoiled. Like a birch tree in its spring apparel. . . ."

Xenia drew her hands over her broad thighs and broke out crying.

"Aw," Udalov said, getting ready to rush to work. "Don't cry, there's no reason. . . ."

Udalov walked to work leisurely. Since he left the house earlier than anticipated, he chose the long route to the construction office—along the quay, past the cathedral, past the eighteenth-century house that had belonged to the Anuchin family of merchants, across the market square. The day was Septemberish, variegated, and merry.

On the way Udalov thought about the events that brought Peter the Great to power. He had never had time to think about it before—he'd always seemed to be too busy. But now he realized that he, unfortunately, knew very little, extremely little, only what was in a grade-school textbook. He really wanted to analyze the role of the *boyar* Shaklovity, but the textbook had very little information about it.

Ahead of Udalov children were rushing to school. Kornely overtook one little girl, looked at her thin, skinny little briefcase made of artificial leather, and said, "*Après le petit déjeuner, je vais à l'école.*"

Moreover, he pronounced the sentence with a more or less correct accent.

"What?" the girl asked, turning around. "Are you also studying the lesson?"

"I am," Udalov admitted. And blushed from the unintended lie. In school he had taken German, and then never studied languages again. And the strangest thing was not that he had said a French sentence and known that it was French. After all, he might have overheard the sentence somewhere and remembered it. The problem lay elsewhere: He knew the whole French textbook for eighth-graders. The whole thing, in its entirety, and could quote any page including the copyright information and the catalog number.

Later, thinking about these strange events, Udalov was surprised that he hadn't guessed that it was the gift from space. But he didn't. He was upset and walked on.

On a bench near a technical school, future river sailors were sitting and boning up on their trigonometry. Tangents, sines, and cosines surged into Udalov's mind, and then were mixed with comprehensive information concerning the preparation of baked goods—an extremely fat woman had stepped out of a nearby building, carrying a cookbook.

"Some business!" Udalov said to himself. "You never know what nonsense is going to pop into your head."

Near the entrance to the market square, a pile of white books lay on a rickety table. Next to it was something in a pink soap container. The white books' covers showed an ancient queen and was titled *The Secret of the Golden Tomb*. Many people stopped at the table on their way out of the market square and bought a copy, hoping that it was about spies. Misha Stendhal, a reporter for the local paper and an acquaintance of Udalov, had bought a copy, and after saying hello, asked, "What do you think?"

"I'm not interested in archaeology," Udalov announced loudly. "It's written in a boring style."

"Ladies and gentlemen!" the woman selling the books interrupted. "Buy the new novel about the secrets of Egypt. Who killed Nefertiti? The mystery of the old house on the banks of the Nile!"

"You see," Stendhal said preachily. "You don't read very much, Kornely."

"I read as much as I can," Udalov answered with dignity. "No less than others. And this work is specialized. For specialists."

"How could he know?" the bookseller asked. "We received the book just a few hours ago, during the night. And I've been standing here only a quarter of an hour. There are people who make up whatever comes into their minds just to spoil other people's moods."

"So!" Udalov burst out, losing his self-control. "Open that treasure of yours to page—say, page one hundred thirty. Do you have it? I'll begin with the eleventh line from the top."

Stendhal rustled the pages. A crowd of curiosity-seekers gathered.

" 'Here, to the north of the capital,' " Udalov recited, squinting his eyes, " 'were found ornaments with the names of other kings and queens; in a limited number, Amen-hotpe IV, and in a large quantity, Semoh-ke-pe, and in addition, his wife Anes-em-iyot. However, along with cartouches with Nefr-et—,' "

"Stop," Stendhal screamed out. "Are you doing magic tricks?"

"Misha," Udalov answered reproachfully. "You know me. Everybody in town knows me."

Udalov turned around for support from the people. A large crowd had gathered, holding the books open to page 130.

"Yes!" a bald man in a T-shirt said. "How about reading from page one-twenty. From the top. Maybe you memorized page one-thirty specially."

"Whatever you want," Udalov said. "Only that's not the point."

"Go ahead and read." The people started to find page 120.

"You ought to pay for the book—the cover is white, and if you get it dirty, who's going to buy it?" the bookseller asked, but no one paid any attention.

" 'Go,' " Udalov said. "That's the continuation from page one hundred nineteen. *'Go* for *Re. Kiya,* with the addition of the refrain "she lives!" ' "

"Correct, exactly correct!" The man in the T-shirt seemed ecstatic, took an apple out of the pocket of his riding breeches, and handed it to Udalov. "Eat it, don't be embarrassed! With your talents, you ought to be a professor."

"Thank you," Udalov said shyly. All of a sudden he imagined what he looked like to the others: The director of the town construction office stands near the entrance to the market and mutters something about ancient Egypt. He felt ashamed.

"Kornely," Stendhal said, catching up to the fleeing Udalov. "I have to talk to you."

From behind they heard the voice of the revived bookseller: "Buy the latest mystery about the secrets of sarcophagi! Who killed Nefertiti and her husband? Just in from Moscow!"

Stendhal did not manage to grab Udalov by the arm, since new events distracted him. A group of foreign tourists, relatively rare in Great Gusliar, came walking down the street, craning their necks in unison at the cupolas of the Church of Paraskeva Pyatnitsa. The group consisted mostly of elderly women with well-cared-for gray curls, in hats adorned with cotton and nylon flowers. These women's husbands, retirees from beyond the seas, were decked out with Polaroids and Canons and had cheerful appearances.

The tourists chattered with each other with great animation. Udalov ate his red apple and could not move from his spot, because he understood everything. Down to the very last word. He even knew each and every word in the English-Russian conversational dictionaries the tourists were carrying. They were talking among themselves with exclamation points.

"What a god-awful mess!"

"Magnificent barbarian architecture!"

"My God, how damp it is in this miserable little town!"

"It resembles the Taj Mahal!"

"Mrs. Henry, just look at that foreigner with the apple in his mouth. He's a riot! It's that Slavic directness!"

"What a mess! It's time to have breakfast, but where has the translator run off to?"

"This church would be impressive if it had the background of Notre Dame de Paris!"

"This is terrible! We pay good cash, but no translator!"

"Just look at the local with the apple in his mouth!"

At this point Udalov realized that the local was he himself.

Then he was seized by disgust, mixed with pity toward these people, so far from home, who had lost their translator and their breakfast. He stepped forward and said with a pleasant British accent, "Please, I'm an uncultured local, but apparently you should turn to the left, and you'll come out directly to the Great Gusliar Hotel."

"Ah!" Mrs. Henry exclaimed. "Excuse me, what did you say?"

"He made himself no less clear than President Nixon," her husband said. "Let's listen to him and go to the left. Thank you, sir."

The entire group followed Mrs. Henry, and only a single, short tourist, with curly hair, remained behind.

"Why are you standing here?" Udalov asked him in English. "Oh, yes, you're Puerto Rican and did not understand everything." He very casually began speaking in Spanish, repeating his instructions in the man's native language.

"Oh thank you, señor," the tourist exclaimed, "I don't always understand when people speak English as fast as you did," and rushed to catch up with the group.

Mrs. Henry, turning the corner, said to her husband, "There's no getting away from these GPU agents. I think I saw him near the National Hotel dressed in the uniform of a lieutenant general."

Udalov heard and smiled a bitter, condescending smile.

Finally Stendhal regained enough composure to open his mouth and ask, "Kornely, why haven't you ever said anything?"

"What's to say?" Udalov said. He threw up his hands and strode quickly toward his office, in order to think over what had happened and make a decision. His quick imagination already cast him as the head translator for Intourist. He would meet the plane at Sheremyotov Airport, and tall Africans would descend.

"Hello," Udalov would say in Swahili.

They would be followed by inhabitants of the Maldive Islands.

"Welcome," Udalov would say in their native language.

Japanese children carrying white cranes would run down the ramp.

"Greetings," Udalov would say to them in the language of the Land of the Rising Sun.

A big boss from the international section would run up to him. "Comrade Udalov," he would yell in a strained voice. "Here's your diplomatic passport. Catch the next plane. You're needed in Addis Ababa. An inscription in an incomprehensible language has been found. The United Nations is insisting on your help."

By this time Udalov's head was full of knowledge that had come to him during the two hours he had been awake. And he was already beginning to understand that his personal memory had nothing to do with it. The situation was far more complex. For some reason he had acquired the ability to instantaneously soak up any written information he was near. And to accomplish it, he did not have to open the book or glance at others' notebooks. He just had to be near. It was possible, for example, to put several textbooks near him, and within a second Udalov knew everything written in them, down to the last comma.

"A hell of a business," Udalov said. "What if my head bursts?"

Fortunately, at that moment Udalov passed a newsstand.

He absorbed the contents of all the newspapers and magazines, even the old ones lying on the floor. Including the issue of *Health* where it was said that the normal person uses perhaps one percent of his or her brain. The remaining cells lie without movement and goof off, using up food and vitamins to no good purpose.

"Aha," Udalov said and stopped in the middle of the street. "It's all clear. This is the gift. So it wasn't just a dream but a fantastic reality. Why, with my new powers, didn't I guess sooner? It's embarrassing."

And if the glowing alien had been telling the truth, you had to know how to cope with the gift. It had to be directed toward its use by humanity and to assist thereby the interstellar friendship and mutual understanding.

What was the next step for an intelligent man to take, who, if he wanted, could become an academician tomorrow? To go to the library? No, it was not worth it. There he'd absorb so much rubbish that even the free ninety-nine percent of his brain couldn't handle it. To hand himself over to medicine? He'd miss his freedom.

Meanwhile his legs, independent of any thought, had been carrying Udalov toward the office. When he reached the door, his hands opened the door by themselves, and his tongue greeted his coworkers by itself. And since Udalov's mind was occupied with incidental matters, he gave a confusing answer to the bookkeeper's question about third section. "The Academy of Sciences would know better." He then proceeded beyond the partition into his office.

There he sat on his chair, buried his elbows in a pile of reports, and still not aware of where he was, continued to meditate.

A diplomatic career was tempting. A black automobile, an expensive Volga at the entrance of the ambassador's residence, respectful foreigners with cocktails in their well-groomed hands and their secretaries wearing low necklines. He also considered the space program. "Only you, Professor Udalov, can tell us whether we should add a third stage to this rocket." All around are medaled cosmonauts waiting for his answer. After all, whether they fly to Mars or have to wait depends on Udalov's answer. Or he might solve the riddles of ancient civilization and learn whether there really was an Atlantis or whether it was just a figment of the imagination. That path led to the quiet scholar's study, and free trips to resorts for leading thinkers. And of course, the international congresses. . . .

"No," Udalov decided finally. "I won't hurry to have it published. It is not impossible that tomorrow everything will be gone and you'll end up playing the fool. During the dinner break I'll drop in the Technical School and absorb higher mathematics. It will never hurt. Then to the museum, and find out what they have on Peter the Great. That's the way I'll do it."

"You here to see me?" he asked, raising his head.

"We've been trying to get your attention for fifteen minutes, Mr. Udalov," a man with chocolate eyes, a boxer's nose, and a yellow imported briefcase said.

"Or even longer," a little old man supported him. The little old man was wearing glasses and the lenses were so thick that only the blue pupil, magnified ten times, could be seen, with all its veins.

"Ah, you've come," Udalov said. In that instant he learned the contents of the fat briefcases down to the last line: mostly reports, requests, and various forms used by the shop that supplied the office with hardware, locks, keys, and miscellaneous items.

The visitors sat down opposite Udalov, and the man with the boxer's nose said, "It's a fine day today, Mr. Udalov."

The day was rotten—windy, overcast, and gloomy. Thank God that at least the rain had stopped. Udalov tacitly agreed with his visitors and meanwhile studied all the papers in his pockets. And he realized that he could become the greatest government inspector of the contemporary age, a remarkable inspector, who in view of his knowledge of languages would be invited throughout the Soviet Union, the socialist world, and possibly even the West. And on his office door would be a modest nameplate: Militia Commissar of the First Rank, in Charge of the Special Section for Particularly Important Inspections, K. I. Udalov."

"Yes, the day isn't that bad," the little old man said, and the magnified veins in his lenses reddened noticeably. "And you, I hear, have some grievance against me. It's undeserved and unfair."

"So then," Udalov said mysteriously and drummed his fingers on the table.

"No, Mr. Udalov, you can't go on that way," the man with the boxer's nose said and shrugged his broad shoulders. "Our shop is working hard, fulfilling and overfulfilling the plan, providing your office with high-quality goods, without interruption, and in response we get no gratitude. I'm taking the matter to the town council."

"Take it to the Vologda if you want," Udalov said. The contents of one of the pieces of paper in the man's upper-right jacket pocket interested him very much. The erasure on the invoice had been done clumsily, it was clear to the naked eye.

"Why so hostile, Mr. Udalov?" the little old man asked. "We have all the records with us. We used the best metal for those hinges. We hired experienced craftsmen. Didn't sleep day or night. And was it all in vain? What about the quarterly bonus?

"What about the quarterly bonus?"

"Wait a moment," his companion interrupted him. "If you're dissatisfied, why go through official channels? Tell me, I tell Porfirich, and Porfirich will take care of it."

"I will," the little old man said. "Always amiably."

"The hinges bend in the wind," Udalov said. "The locks can be easily picked with a fork. Construction on the resort building has been stopped. And the materials you sold on the black market. Correct?"

"Not correct," Porfirich said with conviction.

"But the three thousand eight hundred dishonest rubles that you split?"

"What money?" the little old man asked indignantly. Beads of sweat appeared on his companion's forehead.

"How much?" he asked.

"Three thousand eight hundred. Even now all your criminal calculations are in your pants pocket. You wrote in pencil, 'Porfirich gets seven hundred twenty. Shurov—three hundred. Udalov if he proves troublesome, one hundred under the table.' Isn't that correct?"

The man with the chocolate eyes lost his presence of mind. He jumped up from his chair, and grabbed the pocket with his fat, trembling fingers.

"You betrayed me!" he said.

Porfirich did not get up from his chair. He turned pale. Even his eyes turned pale.

"Three thousand eight hundred? And I get seven hundred twenty? So . . . you'll get no mercy from the people, neither in this world, nor in the next," he said in a thin but stern voice.

"We'll write the statement for the police right now," Udalov said, striking while the iron was hot.

"I don't know anything," the man with the boxer's nose said, trying to chew up a piece of paper he had taken from his pocket. The note was on good thick paper and couldn't be chewed.

"It won't help," Udalov said. "In Porfirich's right jacket pocket there is an erased invoice for sheet metal."

"There is," Porfirich said. "I'd rather go to jail as an accomplice and have that snake locked up for a long time."

"Correct," Udalov said. "He's been leading you on for a long time."

"You wouldn't dare!" the shop director said, his mouth stuffed. "I'll complain!"

"Complain, complain!" Porfirich said revengefully.

"There's no escape for him," Udalov agreed. "In your briefcase you have irrefutable records."

Seeing that it was necessary to deliver the final blow and knock out his opponent, Udalov tried to remember what detectives in the movies always said in such cases. Words he had heard recently circled in his head. "Hands up!" No. Close, very close. Aha! And Udalov boomed out, in a terrifying tone: "The game is over! Sit down and write your statement. Sincere repentance is the only thing that can make your fate easier."

Lightning flashed. There was the scent of ozone. The shop director, pale as a sheet, plopped into a chair, took out a ballpoint pen and with Porfirich's help began to write a confession.

Udalov suddenly felt a terrible emptiness in his head. A primordial, absurd emptiness. He did not remember the contents of any of the papers in the visitors' briefcases. He forgot English and Spanish, and could not remember a single trigonometric function. He even forgot the precise rhythm of the poem he had read in the last issue of *The Spark*.

"But why?" he exclaimed. "Why?"

The visitors cast frightened glances at him and began writing their confession more quickly.

"You'll turn yourselves in to the police," Udalov ordered them, and, totally oblivious, raced for the exit.

A drizzle was sputtering again on the yellowed leaves. It was quiet and ordinary. And, with the clarity of distant thunder at night, the alien's words roared in Udalov's ears: "If you can't cope with it, say aloud, 'The game is over,' and everything will return to normal."

"But I didn't want to!" he pleaded, raising his arms to the sky. "It was a mistake. I can handle it! It was an accidental mistake."

Udalov returned home and until evening did not utter a single word. He refused to talk to Misha Stendhal who was waiting for him near his entrance. He did not eat his favorite dumpling soup. He lay on the couch and relived his blunder, which had not only closed the road to a diplomatic career but had deprived humanity of friendship with the advanced Galaxy.

And only during the evening, after drinking a few shots of vodka to calm himself down and saying a few words his family could not understand—"Maybe they'll figure it out and change their decision"—Udalov went over to his son's desk and asked him, "Where's your history book?"

"What for, Dad? We don't have history tomorrow. No homework."

"Stupid," his father answered. "I just want to read something about Peter the Great. And keep your trig book out. Live and learn. It's just plain embarrassing to live in the Galaxy with this ignorance of ours."

Help Needed

Kornely Udalov was sitting home alone, watching television. The weather was miserable: Rain, wind, wet leaves flying down the street—weather not fit for man nor beast. His wife Xenia took Maxim and went across the street to her friend's, but Udalov declined. The show was boring, and he was ready to turn it off and get to bed. But he was too lazy to turn it off. And when Udalov got a grip on himself and pushed the button, in the room there appeared a creature with three legs, red eyes, wearing eyeglasses.

"Hello," the being said with a strong accent. "Forgive mine pronunciation, I learn your language in hurry. Don't worry about my appearance. I may sit?"

"Please," Udalov said. "How is it outside, still drizzling?"

"I'm from space," the being said. "I flew in a force field, and no rain."

"What can I get you?" Udalov asked.

"I bother your eating?"

"No, I wasn't doing anything. Tell me about yourself. Would you like your tea?"

"For me it is a fast-acting poison. No thanks."

"That's OK, if it's harmful, you don't have to drink it."

"I die from tea in convulsion," the guest acknowledged.

"All right, we'll skip the tea."

The being folded all three legs underneath itself, pulled itself up into an armchair, and stretched out a paw with about forty little claws.

"Udalov," it said warmly. "We need help."

"All right," Udalov said. "Whatever we can do, we'll try. As long as I don't have to go outside."

"You'll have to go outside," the being said.

"Too bad."

"I ask your forgiveness, but first give us to listen," the being said and breathed out of his mouth a cloud of pink, foul-smelling smoke.

"A cold," it said. "It is very far trip. Three thousand light-years and eight hundred years round trip. Great misfortune. Krupiks die."

"Too bad," Udalov said. "They're relatives of yours?"

"I explain?" the being asked.

Udalov nodded, took a sheet of paper and a ballpoint pen so that he could take notes, if necessary.

"I have eight minute. My name is Fyva. I from one planet in distant constellation, your astronomers know, not you."

Udalov agreed.

"We long ago fly to you on Earth, take experiments, samples. Help some build pyramids Cheops, write *Mahabharata*, Indian epic poem. Act with great respect, not touch what not ours. One time we take your krupiks back to our planet."

"Hold on," Udalov interrupted. "Who are these krupiks?"

"I forget your word. Small, gray, has ears, sits under fir tree, hops. Krupiks."

"Rabbits?" Udalov asked.

"No," the being answered. "Rabbit I know, also hares, kangaroos. Different animal. Not very important. We try genetics, grow big one, new species. All planet have krupiks. Very important in economy. Krupiks die—we have economy crisis. Every day we eat krupik."

What are the krupiks? Udalov thought in annoyance. Maybe gerbils?

"No," the being said in response to Udalov's thought. "No gerbils. Many years pass, three days ago krupiks begin to get

sick. And die. All scientist do experiment, no means. Means
only you have, on Earth. This morning they call me and say,
'Fly, Fyva, save civilization.' I say understandable?"

"I understand," Udalov answered. "Only a question: When
did you say you flew to us?"

"Today. Eat breakfast. Then fly."

"And how far did you say you came?"

"Three thousand light-year."

"Nonsense," Udalov said. "Science does not admit such
speeds."

"If fly direct, no," the guest agreed. "Only there is another
principle: I fly in time."

"Well, tell me about it," Udalov requested. He was very
curious and was drawn to new things.

"One minute I told, very short. Too little time. We travel in
time. One instant, thousand years ago."

"So you'll land on your planet a thousand years ago."

"What naive! Do not dare read science-fiction book.
Science-fiction writer not know science, copy each other.
Does your Earth stand still?"

"No, it flies around the Sun."

"And the Sun?"

"It flies, too."

"There you are, you a simple director of construction office,
but you know. Writer Wells not know, writer Parnov not know.
What shame! You hop into tomorrow, hop one hour ahead—
no Earth beneath you—you in space already, and Earth flew
onward, from under you. Very simple. If I hop one hundred
years forward or back, Earth go very far in that time. And a
different planet or a star take its place. You jump—and is
different planet. Only have to calculate. Make very many calculations. A mistake, and it is currants."

"Curtains," Udalov corrected him. He enjoyed seeming
smarter than famous writers. "Can you also hop ahead?"

"No," the being answered. "Time is like ocean. What was,
is, what was not, still is not. You can hop into ocean, dive, and

jump out. You calculate very well—hop one hundred years back—one planet. Another fifty years in other direction, a different planet. Three times hop—then surface on ocean, and it is Earth. Only, very complicated. Every day cannot hop. Sometimes once in hundred years right combination. Sometimes three times in one hour. I have three minutes left. Or else I cannot go home."

"All right," Udalov said. "I get it. But the krupiks—maybe they're mice?"

"No, no mice," the visitor said. "Will you help?"

"Of course."

"In your town," the alien said, "is one means. Red flower. It grows on window of one old lady. Three Merkartov Street. Flower must pick and give me. I said thank you in name of all planet. Krupiks also live. Also thank you. You have one hour time. I fly back and taken flower."

"But why don't you just buy the flower?"

"Cannot, old lady very fright. Three legs on me. Not work. All hope is on you."

Right then the alien melted into the air, because his time was up. He had apparently begun his leaps in time to return home and report that he had established contact with Kornely Udalov and that Kornely had agreed to help.

Udalov rubbed his eyes, looked at the armchair one more time, where the alien had just been sitting. The cushion had a depression in the middle. It had not been a dream, and consequently he had to help his brothers in reason. But what were the krupiks? Foxes?

Udalov put on his raincoat, took his umbrella, and went outside. A furious wind and rain spattered him and the trees creaked. Black puddles lurked beneath his feet, and the way to Merkartov Street, even though it was not that far, ran away from the center of Great Gusliar.

While Udalov made his way to 3 Merkartov Street, he got soaking wet, his shoes slurped, and water ran down his neck. The house was small, with just two little windows facing the street, and a fence with a gate. But before entering the yard, Udalov knocked modestly on a lighted window. The curtain was moved aside, and a round pink old-lady's face came close to the window. Udalov smiled at it and went to the gate. He opened the wet cold hook and paused to listen. The house was quiet. In the neighbor's yard a dog was yapping desperately. Udalov went up to the rickety porch and walked up the three steps. The dog was fussing around the fence, barking in spasms, as though guarding both houses was a combined assignment.

Udalov pushed the door and it opened heavily, with a sigh and a screech.

"Anyone here?" Udalov asked politely and took a step into the darkness. At that very moment something heavy fell on his head and turned off his consciousness. His last thought was, "Krupiks must be squirrels."

Udalov came to in the kitchen. It was light. He was sitting on a bench, his back against the stove, which was still warm after having been used in the morning. In front of him stood a heavy man in pajamas and a quilted jacket. The man was holding a rolling pin. He had a red nose and sad eyes.

"Still, krupiks must be squirrels," Udalov thought, returning to reality. He felt the back of his head. There was an impressive bump.

"Please excuse me if anything is wrong," the man said. "Auntie Nyusha called me over to help her. I thought that the same guy was coming back, wearing dark glasses. He kept bothering her, knocking on the window, threatening her: 'Give me,' he said, 'the flower.' A foreigner, I think. A gangster. But he didn't get into the house. Auntie Nyusha scared him off, and called me over to help. At least there is a man in the house. I'm her neighbor."

Udalov, having driven the many-colored circles away from his eyes, now noticed an embarrassed old woman with rosy cheeks, standing to the side.

"I'm all alone here," she said. "It would be easy to rob me."

"True," Udalov said, and was flooded with anger at the somewhat less-than-truthful alien, who had not come straight to him after all. He had ruined everything. If he had only let Udalov know beforehand. Now his head was going to ache. He might even have a concussion. It happens, especially with rolling pins.

"Some water," Udalov said.

"Nyusha, get some water," the man said, putting the rolling pin on the table.

"And you, Innokenty, keep an eye on him," Nyusha said, as she went out to the entrance hall, where she began to rattle around with a cup as she emptied water.

"Please excuse her," the man said. "She lives all alone, and she's suspicious. I know that she has nothing that anyone could steal. But she thinks that her stuff is valuable."

Udalov squinted at the window. There stood the pot with flowers. One of the plants was sprinkled with red buds.

"Yes, that's it," the man said, noticing where Udalov was looking. "Those absolutely worthless flowers are the cause of all the confusion."

The old woman brought a cup of water. While Udalov drank, she inspected him from head to soaked foot. It was difficult to determine whether she was satisfied with the inspection. Her eyes still harbored suspicion.

"Why are you paying me a visit?" she asked Udalov. In different circumstances Udalov would have left the conversation until the next day. The time was not right to get the flower. But now, only a little more than half an hour remained until the alien's return. And fifteen minutes would be spent returning home.

"I was walking by," Udalov said. "I looked at the window and decided to stop in."

"Why?"

"Well, I'll be going now, Auntie Nyusha," Innokenty said.

"No, wait a while," she asked. "Don't leave me alone."

The man sighed, threw up his hands, as though apologizing to Udalov.

"You grow remarkable flowers," Udalov said.

"Again?" the old woman asked.

"Is it my fault that there should be such a coincidence?"

"Maybe it's your fault."

"My wife is a plant lover," Udalov said hastily. Time was passing. The alien was already hurrying back, passing by star clusters and flying around meteor streams. "Tomorrow is her birthday. So I decided that I would buy her something unusual. After all, we've lived together for sixteen years. Xenia is her name. Xenia Udalova. I work here, in Gusliar, I'm the director of the construction office."

"I've heard of you," the man said. "Auntie Nyusha, if you ever need building materials, he can help you."

"If it's within the limits of the law," Udalov said.

Auntie Nyusha warmed up. "Do you have slate?" she asked.

"We do," Udalov said, although there were problems with the slate.

"But the flower isn't for sale," Auntie Nyusha said. "Go over to my neighbor's. She has remarkable geraniums."

"I already have geraniums," Udalov said. "Three flowerpots."

"Why are you giving the guy a hard time?" the man said. "Sell him the flower. He won't forget it."

"I won't forget it," Udalov said. "Sell me the red flower. Whatever you want—I'll pay. And, after all, I did get hit over the head with a rolling pin. That's a kind of damage, and I could register a complaint."

"He has a right to," Innokenty said. "He must have a nice bump on his head."

"I do."

"After all, Auntie Nyusha, I was just doing what you asked. I was defending you." Innokenty wanted to go home as soon as possible.

Auntie Nyusha began her lamentation: "Well, I thought, I will die, but before my death I will enjoy looking at my flower. It's unique, there's isn't another one like it in the whole town. And besides, I'm planning on going to my daughter's. To Arkhangelsk. The road there is not cheap."

"I'll pay for your trip," Udalov said. "How much do you need?"

"A hundred rubles," the old woman said, and squinted her eyes. She was waiting to see what Udalov would say to such impudence.

"A hundred rubles is impossible," Udalov said.

"Auntie Nyusha, you ought to be ashamed," Innokenty said.

"I guess I'd better go straight to the emergency ward," Udalov said. "I'll get medical witness to the fact that I've received a beating."

"Thirty-five rubles, but not a kopeck less," the old woman said.

"Oy, Auntie Nyusha, that's suicide!"

"I have to go now," Udalov said.

"So how much will you give me?" the old woman asked quickly.

"Ten rubles."

"Ten rubles is not enough. The pot itself is worth ten rubles."

"You can keep the pot."

"I won't need it without the flower."

"Twelve rubles—I don't have any more money on me."

"And you won't go to the emergency ward?"

"I won't."

"And you'll get me slate?"

"I'll try."

Auntie Nyusha sighed and said, "Take it, and God be with you."

Udalov pulled the money out of his pocket—it was a good thing he had brought it along. He counted out two fives, a ruble bill and ninety kopeks in change. Auntie Nyusha made him promise to bring the ten kopecks the next day, and Udalov embraced the dusty, heavy flowerpot.

He went outside with Innokenty, who had wrapped himself in his quilted coat. He walked Udalov out to the gate, and opened it. The old woman closed the bolt on the front door with a slam.

"Listen," Innokenty said as a farewell. "You were lying about your wife. Why pay twelve rubles for a lousy flower? Tell me. I won't say anything."

"OK," Udalov said, pushing some leaves to the side so he could see where he was going. "You won't believe it anyway. There's this planet where the krupiks are dying. They can be cured only with this flower. So the beings there turned to me for help."

"Aha!" Innokenty said. "That sounds more like it."

And when Udalov had already walked off, splashing through puddles, he shouted: "But what are the krupiks?"

"I don't know," Udalov shouted back. "Gray, furry, sit under bushes, I was told."

"Must be rabbits."

"Perhaps," Udalov answered and hurried home, slipping on the clay and squeezing the heavy flowerpot tight to his chest.

The alien was waiting for him near his home, under a tree on the street. "Did you get it?" he asked, stepping out of the shadows. "Thanks to you in enormous size. Give it here. I could not go your house. Your wife there."

Udalov set the flowerpot on the ground. "Did you find out back home what krupiks are?" he asked.

"No, I did not have time," the alien answered. "What a tragedy. All hope on you and I."

He began quickly to pick the red buds.

"You're not taking the whole pot?"

"With the pot I would not force my way through space-time continuum. There is no possibility."

"If I had known, I would have picked them. But tell me, are krupiks squirrels?"

"No. I fly. Much thank. Know what? Our planet will erect very big statue of you. Three times as big. I already made photograph. You go through rain and storm, in hand you have red flower."

"Thank you," Udalov said. "One little detail, if you don't mind. As it turned out, I spent all my money on the flower, and tomorrow I have to pay my dues."

"What an embarrassment for our planet! Of course, I give you all money. Forget completely. Here, take it. Dollars. Three thousand dollars."

"Are you crazy?" Udalov objected. "What can I do with dollars? I need twelve rubles. Or, more exactly, eleven rubles ninety kopecks. If you think I paid too much—well, there was a big rush. A fair price would be four rubles at the most, with the flowerpot."

"A fair price is one hundred million of your rubles."

"I don't need much. If I could just have eight rubles."

"Take dollars," the alien fussed. "I no other money. In three years successful position of planets once again, and I will come give you rubles. But today take dollars."

Udalov wanted to refuse, but the alien shoved a packet of crisp bills into his hand and yelled: "Thank you! I bring photograph of monument on next visit."

And disappeared.

Udalov sighed and went home.

Xenia was waiting up for him. She greeted him with reproaches and would not let him take his coat off, demanding that he confess whom he had been seeing.

"I'm not seeing anyone," Udalov said, while thinking, But maybe krupiks are elephants, or leopards? I never found out what kind of tree they sit under.

"All I have to do is step out," Xenia complained, "and you disappear into thin air."

"Don't get excited," Udalov answered, still thinking about krupiks.

"What's that you're holding?" Xenia asked, looking at the packet of dollars.

"Just some dollars," Udalov said, and held out the money to her.

"That I should live so long!" Xenia said, and broke out crying.

Reason in Captivity

If you want to talk about bad luck, why then I was terribly, tragically unlucky. If you want to talk about good luck, why then, you can consider me incredibly lucky.

I was unlucky in that I realized by the second orbit that I would have to land. The engine, which had been giving me problems for a long time, gave out. There can be nothing worse than an engine that refuses to work when a good half the Galaxy separates you from home.

I was lucky, even fantastically lucky, in that the planet had an atmosphere suitable for breathing. And that inspired a hope that I could someday fix the engine, reenter space, and see my loved ones again.

The face of the planet had been terribly disfigured by cataclysms. Huge cracks split its crust, mountain ranges and peaks of unbelievable height lifted themselves above the atmosphere, and their summits were surrounded by the cold of space.

But I had no time to study calmly my temporary and perhaps even permanent refuge. The time for that would come. I was occupied by only one thing—to find a spot convenient for landing and as safe as possible. And I found it on the surface of an extensive plateau and decided that I would land there on my next orbit, but precisely at that moment the engine gave out entirely.

At the time I was flying over the dark side of the planet, over a mountainous plateau, an enormous one that rose above the planet's surface so high that to land there meant dooming oneself to a certain death—the atmosphere, or more accu-

rately, the remains of an atmosphere were restricted to shallow ravines and depressions. If I were to miss, I was dead.

At the last moment before the crash, the instruments showed that I was headed straight for a hollow. Like a meteor I flew over the lifeless mountainous country; the ship cut into the dense atmosphere. The portholes were covered by darkness, the descent slowed—and finally I was on the planet's surface. I was alive. I had suffered a crash. Was I alone, or was an alien reason following me? Ready to come to my aid? Or to sharpen the weapon that would kill me?

I clung to the porthole.

I turned on the biofeeders. The ship bristled with needles and tubes, the sensor's eyes and the radar's ears opened. My first acquaintanceship had begun.

By the time dawn came, weak-blue, timid, I had learned much about the hollow I had landed in. There was no intelligent life but unintelligent life seethed around me—dangerous and bloodthirsty. All the individuals in this world were in a state of war against each other; the strong devoured the weak, the weak lurked in wait for the still weaker.

But I could not sit around doing nothing. It was time to leave the safe walls of the ship and to meet the new world face-to-face. I armed myself with a blaster and opened the hatch. The atmosphere was stuffy, stagnant, but I could still breathe. I had to go around the ship's hull, climb up to the rockets, and check their condition. The instruments could be lying—the truth and nothing but the truth had been demanded of them for too long a time.

I moved slowly, trying to keep my back against the safe hull at all times. But I had not taken two steps before I had to stop. Out of the crumbling, treacherous soil appeared the round head of a large worm. I was about to raise my blaster, but the head immediately dove back in the ground, and in dumb amazement I spent a long time watching new segments of the pink body crawl out of the ground, raise themselves in an arch, and disappear beneath the ground again. The worm was *not all that big—maybe half my size, but I saw only a part of it, so it seemed infinitely long and terrifying.*

I have to get a grip on myself, I thought. If I give in to my nerves, I can end up in trouble. How did the giant worm really threaten me? It didn't even have a mouth.

A black shadow flashed over me. I recoiled back against the ship's cold metal. A huge flying beast, malevolent and elegant in the lightness of its movement, curved its body and threw itself at me from above. Its enormous mouth gaped, studded with sharp teeth, and its stinking breath rolled over me.

I managed to pull out my blaster and sank a charge into its gullet. Its heavy body knocked me off my feet, and I rolled over the ground. The long, greenish, spotted body of the flying dragon writhed on the ground. Convulsions ran along its body. I did not dare go near the monster. Trying to calm a belated trembling, I got up from the ground and immediately saw that the path back to the ship had been cut off. Another beast was approaching, slowly, as if it knew that nothing would stop it. A large number of segmented legs supported a dirty, green body. Its eyes protruded far from the body, waving slightly on the ends of stalks, and on each side of the eyes, clumsy but murderous claws reached out. The beast raised itself on its legs and opened its claws wider.

I did not want to mark my entry into this world with murders, with bloodshed—there was more than enough of it without me. I retreated. The beast rolled its eyes, trying to frighten me off, but did not attack. I attempted to circle round it and reach the safety of the ship. I could not get rid of an unpleasant feeling of danger behind me—it seemed that the attentive eyes of the hollow's inhabitants were following me every step.

Without taking my eyes off the beast, I took two more steps to the side and then right under my feet something flashed. A strange object made of white metal lay on the ground. And it was *made, for only the hands of an intelligent being could have imparted the form of a slightly pointed ellipse to the* metal. *The object was flat, and its surface was carefully worked. Only a being that had traveled far down the road of civilization could have mastered the art of metallurgy to that degree.*

I picked up the object. It was heavy, and I was sorry that I could hardly carry it back to the ship—on the path back there was still the beast waving its threatening claws, and I did not want to weigh myself down with an unnecessary burden when it might take all my skill to make my way to the ship.

At that very moment, an elongated object cast a shadow over me once again. I thought it was another dragon and looked upward. But it was not. I could have sworn that I was looking at an air ship, a flying ship. It was big, no smaller than my spaceship, and was moving slowly. It was difficult for me to determine how it was put into motion. The regularity of its forms, the immobility of the parts with respect to each other, completely excluded the possibility that it was a living being. It was possible that someone was looking for me—that someone had noticed my ship landing on the planet, and after a certain amount of time had passed, was searching for me. But with good or evil intentions?

The flying ship froze above me. The beast with the claws, sensing something wrong, began to back up slowly into some vegetation that had come quite close to the scene of the accident. I had not let go of the metal object that had first alerted me to the existence of rational life. The air ship hovered on the upper limits of the atmosphere. I raised the metal object to attract attention—let happen what may. Intelligent life, although we had never encountered any before on any planet anywhere, must be friendly.

The beings on the ship noticed me. A Jacob's ladder was lowered right next to me. On the end of it a device for holding objects gleamed. They were inviting me up to the ship. Well, I thought, I'll take a chance. I took the metallic object with me. It might have been lost by one of the inhabitants. A gesture of good will is always interpreted positively by any intelligent being. I took one last look at my orphaned ship, grabbed the Jacob's ladder and pulled on it three times, signaling to take me up to the ship. In answer to my signal the ladder began to ascend rapidly.

"Just look what took my lure," Kornely Udalov said, overcome with anger and joy, as he pulled in his line.

"Look again—you're just not curious," Alexander Grubin answered his friend. They had just gone out fishing at dawn on Lake Copenhagen. "Have you ever seen an octopus in our lake before?"

The last part of the trip up, the ladder was pulled in very fast. I realized that a little more and I would go flying out beyond the limits of the atmosphere. And my spacesuit was back on my ship! I might die. I tried jumping off the ladder— better to risk crashing against the ground than to die by suffocation, but a sharp piece of metal on the end of the ladder pierced my body. Another second and, losing consciousness, I flew into the emptiness of space. Enormous monsters—two of them—reached out for me with massive extremities.

"A jar," Grubin shouted to the confused Udalov. "A jar of water! The bucket! Don't you realize what a discovery we've made!"

"Maybe, octopuses do live here?" Udalov asked with doubt. "Maybe they're found rarely—they're very cautious?"

"How could it be, you ignoramus," Grubin shouted. "Octopuses live only in seas and oceans!"

"Quiet," Udalov said. "You'll scare all the fish away. What are we going to do now?"

"Forget about fishing!" Grubin carefully removed the octopus from the hook. "We'll be written up in a scientific journal."

"What do you think? Maybe the octopuses here are a protected species? They were put here to reproduce, and we're poaching?"

"That can't be," Grubin said. "Then there would have been an announcement. Have you seen any signs along the shore?"

"I saw some," Udalov said. "Don't light fires, save the forests."

"What do fires have to do with it? Did you see anything about octopuses?"

"I didn't see anything about octopuses. But I'm sure there could be a warning. We passed it by in the darkness."

"No," Grubin said, lowering the octopus into a pail of water that the doubting Udalov had put down. "If octopuses were being raised in our Lake Copenhagen, the whole town would know about it. And in addition, note that this octopus has ten legs and is relatively big. It's entirely possible that it is a species unknown to science. That's what I'm hoping."

"You want glory," Udalov said reproachfully. "Let's just hope we get off with a fine."

The octopus sank lifelessly to the bottom of the bucket. One of its tentacles still squeezed the lure Udalov had dropped overboard.

"Sasha," Udalov said. "Take the lure away from him."

"Why me?"

"Maybe it's poisonous."

"Poisonous to you but harmless to me?"

"Hook it with a stick. It would be a shame to lose the lure."

The edge of the sun appeared from behind the firs on shore, the birds started singing, the bucket gleamed silver. The octopus wiggled its tentacles, coming back to life.

"Great!" Grubin said. "I was very much afraid it had died."

"What's the big deal about it?" Udalov said with annoyance.

The lure was still in the bucket, and the fishing trip was in danger. No way Udalov could tell his wife Xenia that she would have to make do with half an octopus, maybe inedible or poisonous. No, and Grubin would not give up his half—he'd want to study the octopus and maybe even raise it in his aquarium.

"Give me the lure, like a buddy," Udalov said. "Maybe we can still catch something. It's a shame to go home empty-handed."

"You were born a fool and you'll die one," Grubin said. "We go back right away."

"Something's going to happen to your octopus?"

"It might die."

"What if it does? You can preserve it in alcohol."

But Grubin had already grabbed the oars and begun to row to shore.

"You can do whatever you want!" he said to Udalov decisively, "but I'm going to town."

I came to. The metal cylinder in which I was imprisoned was rocking back and forth slowly. The cylinder was open at the top, but the atmosphere ended at its top, and any escape attempt would be fatal. The cylinder's inside walls were smooth and cold.

I let myself get caught stupidly. I cannot forgive myself for being so trusting. The race inhabiting the planet turned out to be duplicitous and cruel. You cannot deny their intelligence— they build air ships and know how to work metal. But apparently the idea of interplanetary brotherhood has not found a path to their hearts. I carefully tapped the side of the cylinder. The sound was weak, and they might not hear it. I groped for my blaster. At least I would not give up my life without a fight.

The round head of one of my guards appeared over the edge of the cylinder. It was enormous. The head alone exceeded in size my whole body exclusive of my arms. His eyes blinked from time to time, and had bristly fur growing at their edges. His mouth was surrounded by a strip of red skin, and inside I could see flat, yellow teeth. Even in that terrible moment the scientist in me had not died. I made a remarkable discovery: It turned out that the being was in atmosphereless space, and I

*was ready to swear that it was not wearing a spacesuit. But
we know that there is no being more advanced than a bacteria
that can live outside the atmosphere.*

*The monster stared at me, and I raised two arms and waved
them in the universal gesture of peace and kindness.*

"He's threatening us," Udalov said. "Waving his tentacles. If it
weren't for the lure, I wouldn't have anything to do with him."

---

*The monster's mouth gaped threateningly and inside some
kind of red organ began moving. I thought that they might
drag me outside, but had pity and put me in the cylinder with
air. But perhaps they just wanted to prolong my suffering?*

*Over the top of the cylinder appeared a limb with five
malformed, poorly manipulable stumps. The stumps sunk into
the atmosphere, came closer to me. It wanted to smother me!
And I, like a naive fool, brought them the metal object to make
them happy. I pulled out my little blaster. The critical
moment, and possibly the final one, was approaching. Before
my mind's eye there flashed scenes of my childhood, the hours
of my first love, the ecstasy of my scientific work, the long
days in space.*

*The paw came nearer, and its claws were already touching
my defenseless body. I put a charge into the giant paw. The
atmosphere in the cylinder seethed.*

"The slimy bastard!" Udalov cried out. "Can't even strangle
it. It really gave me a shock, the little monster."

"I warned you," Grubin said, without stopping rowing
toward shore. "The animal is only protecting itself, like a bee,
when a fool like you steps on it."

"I suppose you'll say that mosquitoes are only protecting
themselves too."

"No, they feed on human blood."

"Maybe this thing feeds on human blood too."

"It's not impossible."

The boat hit the sandy bottom, and water splashed out of the bucket. The octopus squirmed.

"It's not impossible," Grubin repeated, jumping out and pulling the boat up on shore, toward the bushes. "But can we blame an animal for what nature has preordained? No, we cannot. Give me the bucket—but be careful, don't hurt it."

"A real smart one," Udalov answered, gathering his line. "I may stay a while, do a little more fishing."

"Afraid?"

"Yes. The bucket is steel. And steel is an excellent conductor of electricity—we learned that in school."

"Wrap the handle with something."

But Udalov was not listening anymore. He was walking away, along the shore and waving away Grubin's words with his free hand. Only at a comfortable distance did he turn around and shout, "When you throw that ugly monster out, take out the lure. The stores here don't have them, and I had to have somebody pick one up in Vologda."

Grubin touched a finger to the pail. There was no current. Udalov might have thought there was out of fear.

"You'll be sorry, Kornely," Grubin shouted to his friend. He put on his knapsack, put his fishing pole over his shoulder, picked the bucket up, and headed for the bus stop on the highway, trying not to splash the water and upset the animal.

This trip will haunt me in my nightmares, if I survive long enough to have nightmares. The cylinder rocked back and forth, the atmosphere swirled in turbulent currents, I had trouble breathing, and I had to grab onto the smooth slippery walls to keep from turning upside down. I felt dizzy. I was ready to ask for mercy—but who was there to ask?

My situation had grown worse. Not long ago I felt things could not be worse. But they were. First of all, because I could no longer find my way back to my spaceship, since my guard carried the cylinder over a lifeless plateau, with each step taking me further from the hollow, I turned on my internal

*compass-speedometer, and the device automatically cal-
culated the route we were following. I did it without
thinking—I did not believe that the information would ever be
of use to me.*

*All around it was growing light. The dark, hard formations
that had blocked out the sky disappeared. Then the jolting
stopped. We were waiting for something. The size of these
creatures was remarkable—apparently, life in a rarefied
atmosphere permits them to grow to such unbelievable size. If
I ever reach home, what a sensation my reports of this cruel
but intelligent race inhabiting the edge of space would cause.*

*An incomprehensible roar reached my ears through the
layer of air. The bottom of the cylinder vibrated. My guard
picked up the cylinder, and we went up into some kind of
vehicle. The jolting started again, even more terrible than
before.*

"What are you carrying?" a friend from the creamery asked.
"Did you catch that many fish? Let me have a look."

Grubin sat down in an empty seat, and set the bucket on his
knees, so that it would not be jolted as much.

"Please," he said.

The bus raced along the highway, and the pine trees
receded into the distance, but Grubin was afraid that it was
not going fast enough and that the octopus might die.

"I can't figure it out," his friend said. "What is it, Sasha?
Caught a mess of tadpoles?"

"No," Grubin answered. "An octopus."

"What?"

"I caught an octopus."

"Mm," his friend said. "They're rare."

He showed no further interest, which upset Grubin a little.

"Have you ever seen an octopus before?" Grubin asked.

The bus braked suddenly for a stop. Water splashed out of
the bucket, and the octopus squirmed, as though protesting.

"In pictures," his friend said. "But I've never happened to catch one."

"And you won't," Grubin said sharply.

"Why not? Today you did, tomorrow I might get lucky. Although I'm not that interested in fishing."

Enough to drive you crazy, Grubin thought. I caught an octopus and he's not surprised. As though octopuses were caught every day.

"Taking it home for the kids?" the man sitting next to Grubin asked. "Kids like animals. Not long ago I brought mine a starling. We bandaged his wing and he's still alive. A funny little bird."

"A starling!" Grubin said scornfully. "But I caught an octopus."

"Where?" asked the man sitting in front of Grubin.

"In our lake, in Copenhagen."

"Never heard of there being any octopus there," the man said.

"No one has," Grubin said.

"I saw an octopus once," a young man said. "And I've eaten it. In a fish store. It was frozen. Squid."

"They make a sauce out of it," the man in front agreed.

This ignorance is enough to drive you crazy, Grubin thought indignantly. If I was carrying a tiger cub and said that I'd caught it in the woods, would they be surprised?

The octopus folded and unfolded its tentacles. He did not like the jostling.

"I'd never bring children an octopus," an old woman behind Grubin said. "Maybe it's poisonous."

"No," Grubin said. "Only, it gives an electric shock."

"What's poisonous?" someone asked from the back of the bus.

"Some guy is carrying a poisonous snake on the bus," another man said.

"Not a snake—an octopus," Grubin corrected him loudly. "A very rare animal."

"Yeah, they bite like mad. Driver, stop the bus!"

"I have him in a bucket," Grubin said. "Don't be afraid."

"He's got a viper!"

People started moving away from Grubin. The driver turned around, and touched his foot to the brake.

"Who's making trouble?" he asked.

"Put him off the bus," the old woman who would never give kids an octopus said. "It will bite everybody."

"Mister, don't break the law," the driver said, pulling the bus over against the curb. "It is forbidden to carry explosives and the like."

"But it's a valuable and harmless animal," Grubin said. "Rare enough for a museum and it won't hurt anyone. Somebody has said that they've even eaten some."

But the young man denied it. "I've never eaten anything like that. Those aren't the ones they sell."

"Each moment of delay," Grubin shouted, "could cost the life of the only freshwater octopus in our area! Who will take responsibility?"

"I will," said the driver. "I have passengers."

And Grubin was put off the bus on the outskirts of Great Gusliar.

———————

It's a terrible thing to know that around you dramatic events are taking place but not to understand what is happening. The inhabitants made a ruckus, the jolting would stop, then start again, and my guard emitted loud sounds. Most likely, a heated argument was taking place between the members of the expedition that had been sent to capture me: Where I was from, what planet did I represent. And perhaps they were concerned that we had already invaded their planet, or supposed that I was doing reconnaissance in preparation for an invasion. And I had no means to tell them of the well-known peace-loving nature of my fellows.

My guard left the rumbling machine and carried the cylinder with me further. The sun was fragmented into spots of light on the surface of the atmosphere. My head was swimming. The atmosphere had become stale, and soon, unless they found a way to freshen it, I would die of suffocation. Death lay in wait for me on this planet at each and every step.

The sun was scorching, and each step raised a cloud of dust that seemed to follow Grubin. The water in the bucket had become turbid and gave off an unpleasant smell. Grubin set the bucket down and looked at the animal closely. It still seemed to be alive. Fortunately on the way home he found a well. The water in it was cold, and Grubin poured it into the bucket bit by bit to avoid giving the octopus a cold, since most octopuses are children of tropical seas.

Drenched with perspiration and short of breath from the heat, Grubin dragged himself into the yard of Building 16. The yard was empty. Even the inveterate domino players who spent Sunday from morning to night around the table under the lilac had disappeared because of the heat.

Grubin did not even stop by his apartment but went straight to the third floor to see old man Lozhkin, a naturalist and bird-lover who was famous throughout Gusliar.

Lozhkin was home. "Why the visit?" he asked sternly, because he considered Grubin a frivolous dilettante.

"Hello," Grubin said. "You wouldn't happen to have a spare aquarium, would you?"

"What do you want it for?"

"Look at this," Grubin said modestly. "I caught this thing. I don't know whether it is of interest."

Grubin was being shrewd. What Lozhkin said was important to him. Perhaps there was really a species of lake octopus.

Lozhkin unhurriedly got his glass case from the chest, took out his glasses, told Grubin to put the pail in the light, and began to study the animal. He studied it for a long time. He was silent. Grubin was burning with impatience but did not interfere.

Finally, Lozhkin sighed, threw up his sinewy hands,

scratched his bald spot, and said, "At a minimum, a new species."

"What?"

"A new species of octopus," Lozhkin said, not taking his eyes off the captive. "Or a genetic freak, a mutant. It has ten legs—see? You can leave it here with me. When I have time I'll read up on it in Brehm's textbook and give an exhaustive opinion."

"No, it's better if it stays with me," Grubin said. He had not been wrong—the animal was indeed rare. "But do they live around here ordinarily?"

"A few!" Lozhkin said. "Did you buy it in the pet store?"

"I caught it myself."

"Curious. Leave it here. I'll write to Moscow. At your place the cat will eat it."

"The cat won't eat it—it gives off an electric shock. It shocked Udalov."

"Even a nightingale could give Kornely a shock. That's no proof. But if you must, I'll give you an aquarium. For a while. And I'll write the letter to Moscow. They don't know you there, but many of them know me—I've already written a lot of letters."

If I had been keeping a diary, I would have written: "My condition is improving. If it weren't for the hunger that is beginning to torment me after the first shock I would say that I ended up in the hands of a scientist, perhaps even a specialist in contact with alien civilizations, or even a special commission on contacts. They moved me out of the dark cylinder and into a transparent cube filled with fresh atmosphere. A tube brought in air so I did not have to worry about breathing."

But I was not writing a diary. I looked around. Strange objects and devices filled the enormous chamber that surrounded my prison. Beneath me a fur-covered animal larger than myself roamed constantly. The animal would open its mouth and lick its teeth with a red tongue. The animal looked at my prison with longing. Two alternate conclusions seemed possible. My prison used to be its home, out of which it had been moved and to which it wanted to return, or—the less pleasant alternative—it was a guard assigned to watch over me. It too might be intelligent.

Two members of the local civilization occupied themselves with studying me and attempting to make contact. One of them carried me in the cylinder. The second one, apparently a major specialist, joined him only later, in the Science Center. Their mouths moved open and shut—that, apparently, is their method of exchanging information. Now it was my task to prove to them that I was superior to them in intellect, but without piquing their pride in the process. And I was hungry.

"What do octopuses eat?" Grubin asked Lozhkin, who had brought a volume of Brehm downstairs. "We don't want to starve it to death."

" 'The most widely distributed octopus, the common octopus (*Octopus vulgaris*), its body grayish in color, but changing to brown, red, or yellow when the animal is in a state of excitement, during which the entire skin on the back becomes covered with uneven, warty pimples.' "

"But is it carnivorous?"

"Yes," Lozhkin said. "Take a stick and try to get the octopus in a state of excitement, and we'll take a look at the pimples."

While Grubin looked for a stick, Lozhkin confirmed the fact that octopuses are predators and learned how they multiply. But it was too soon to talk about reproduction when only one individual had been caught.

"I'm not going to poke it hard," Grubin said, as he walked over with a stick.

"You don't have to. All we have to do is to see if its color changes."

"But it's not gray to begin with."

"That's not important."

Grubin stuck the stick into the aquarium and touched the octopus.

After lengthy consultation and the perusal of folios they brought a rod and introduced it into the atmosphere. The first attempt at contact. I even blushed from the unexpected pleasure. My bashfulness, legendary among my colleagues, even now played a joke on me. I took the end of the rod and tugged it three times. The rod was quickly removed. Did they understand or not?

"It changed color to red," Lozhkin said. "It all fits. Most likely it is not a new species but just a freak. Like a two-headed calf."

Grubin went into the kitchen and returned with a piece of meat. The cat ran after him, leaping up and down in the assumption that the meat was destined for him, the loyal friend.

The meat flew into the aquarium.

"Did you wash the meat?" Lozhkin asked.

"In cold water."

A piece of disgusting flesh, dripping with blood, fell toward me from above. What's happening? Is it an act of provocation? Or an attempt to feed me? I am hungry. But I'm not going to eat meat, since I am a dedicated vegetarian. I took the piece of meat and hurled it out of my jail.

"It's behaving temperamentally," Lozhkin said. "It must not be hungry. In Brehm it is stated very clearly that they are carnivorous. They love mussels, fish, and so on."

"It definitely didn't want the meat. It threw it right out of the aquarium."

The cat picked up the piece of meat and tore it to pieces, while nibbling on it, on the floor. The octopus fixed its senseless eyes on the cat.

"You'll have to run out for some fish," Lozhkin said to Grubin.

"I will. But first let's do some more experiments."

I tapped out the numbers from one to ten on the surface of my home. They did not respond. Then I began to show them my limbs one by one in turn. First one, then two, then three, then four. That did not make any impression either. I picked up some pebbles from the floor and began to knock with them against the wall. Finally, hoping that the rudiments of geometry would be comprehensible to any intelligent living being, I tried to scratch an equilateral triangle on the hard transparent wall.

"It's really wriggling around," Lozhkin said. "Can't take captivity. Like all beings."

"Look! There's a pebble in its tentacle. It could hurt itself!"

"It won't," Lozhkin said. "But still, I think it will be hard to transport alive. All the more so since it refuses food. Have to put it to sleep."

"Too bad." Grubin repeated his only argument. "All the same, it's a living being."

"Living, but brainless," Lozhkin stated categorically. "It has a primitive structure—it's included in the first volume of Brehm, where the simplest forms of life are covered. The invertebrates."

"Sasha, are you home?" Udalov asked, stepping into the room. "I'm not alone. I came with Misha Stendhal, from the newspaper."

"They say you caught an octopus in our lake—is it true?" Misha asked. "Is it alive?"

"It is," Grubin said. "Kornely, why didn't you keep on fishing?"

"The fishing was bad. It's too late in the season. They're not biting. Your octopus must have eaten up all the fish. If they reproduce, it's good-bye to fishing. It still hasn't died on you?"

"No," Lozhkin said. "We're studying it."

"A charming creature," Misha said. "How many tentacles does it have? That's sensational. The first octopus in the area. We'll feature it in the Sunday human-interest section. Who caught it?"

"We caught it together," Udalov said.

"So then, we'll start off with 'Fishermen in our town . . .' "

Stendhal jotted notes, Udalov explained, and Grubin went back to the aquarium. The octopus, clearly starving, squirmed, folding and unfolding its tentacles, raising its rounded head and rolling its senseless eyes.

My entire arsenal of communication techniques was exhausted. They did not understand. For some reason it had never occurred to me that contact could turn out to be such a complicated process. Here I was, an intelligent being, a famous professor standing before the eyes of members of another intelligent race. True, the environment we lived in was different, and yes, we did differ in size, and yes, our appearances were distinct. But how did I know that they were intelligent and make an attempt to enter into contact? They stubbornly persisted in not reacting to my signs, in tossing hunks of meat at me, and starving me to death.

Udalov's wife Xenia dropped by. She was amazed by the monster in the aquarium and said, "I've seen one like it. In the book *Gifts of the Sea*. It tells you how to cook them."

Stendhal ran back to his office. Grubin got ready to go to a store for fish to feed the captive. Xenia, feeling a little malicious, took the picture over to the aquarium and said, "See what happened to your brother?"

"Take it away," Grubin said.

I managed to scratch an equilateral triangle on the wall. They just have to notice it. I pointed to the triangle. In response one of those present opened an enormous book and showed me a picture. The picture represented a being that was similar to me anatomically. A knife was suspended over the creature.

Everything became clear to me.

I was not the first space traveler who had experienced an accident over the lifeless plateau. And what more could you expect from beings living in conditions so little suited for life? No, I could not blame them.

"OK, Kornely," Xenia said. "Take the hook, and let's go eat. We'll make do without the octopus."

Lozhkin remained alone. He read Brehm, got engrossed and read on about jellyfish and other sea dwellers. Grubin had run out for fish and had not returned. Lozhkin dozed off.

One of the monsters remained to guard me. The others dispersed. Apparently they were preparing for the feast. But I could not surrender to the enemy without a fight. No, and all the more because I could expect no mercy.

Have my attempts to make contact failed totally, leaving me no escape? That is shameful for an intelligent creature. To fight to the last breath, to the last charge in your blaster! That is the way!

I started thinking. I would save the last charge in the blaster for myself. I could not kill them—when I shot one of them it only caused mild pain. But my blaster might still be of use. But I would have to hurry.

I felt the walls and floor. The walls were made of a fragile material. The floor was different—metal, and the metal was soft. That gave me some hope.

I turned on my blaster full force and aimed it at the floor. The atmosphere seethed, burning me. An opening appeared in the floor. I disregarded the pain, and stuffed one of my ten limbs into the opening. Then I glanced at the guard. He was sleeping. Very good. I bored another hole in the floor, and again blocked it shut with a limb. I managed to bore six holes—that was enough. But then the main guard came back into the room. He was carrying something wrapped in a white material. He put it down next to my prison, and unwrapped it with a rustling sound. It was a piece of a being like the one who had attacked me back in the unlucky hollow. The guard tore off a piece and tossed it toward me.

"It won't eat—what can you do!" Grubin said.

Lozhkin woke up and said that he was going to write the letter to the Academy of Sciences and would come back later.

"And I have to go to work," Grubin said. "I'll try to get home early. Maybe I can find some mussels down by the river."

"Don't bother," Lozhkin said. "We'll transport it in alcohol."

I could hardly wait until all of them left, except the fur-covered sharp-toothed being that had gobbled up the meat. The being did not seem to be paying attention to me. I stuck six of my limbs through the holes. With the four remaining ones I held the upper edges by the opening at the top. I was ready for the difficult and most likely tragic journey.

My limbs rested on the elevation on which my prison was standing. I strained to stick them out as far as possible, raised myself within my prison, and once again became mobile. Having transformed my prison into a clumsy spacesuit of sorts, I walked to the edge of the elevation. Far below was the floor of the room. I would have to jump—there was no escaping it.

The fur-covered being rose to its feet when it noticed my movement and arched its back. I transferred my blaster to a free limb. I would try to cope with it.

The decisive moment! I pushed off with six limbs and leapt downward, trying not to lose my balance. My limbs came into contact with the room's hard floor. I was seized by an agonizing pain. With the utmost difficulty I stayed on my limbs. Grinding my jaws in pain, I fought against nausea and hurried toward the exit.

I did not have to use my blaster. Once he saw that I, together with the transparent house, had jumped from the elevation and was headed toward him, the guard raised his furry tail, and in a panic, emitting loud noises, ran out of the room. I felt a grin spread within me. Cruel creatures are always the most cowardly.

I was counting on surprise and on my good memory. The direction to the hollow, back to my ship, was known—if I could make it before the atmosphere ran out.

I walked down a long corridor and descended some steps that were taller than I in height. I reached a plain, surrounded on all sides by the monsters' dwellings. In one place there was a break between dwellings, so that is where I headed.

But I had not reached the halfway point when a loud shout reached me. I turned around. In one of those windows I saw the head of the being who had shown me the cruel picture. The being was shouting and pointing at me. Gasping from the stress, on limbs bending under the terrible weight, I limped on further.

"Oh my Lord!" Xenia shouted in a strained voice. "What is going on?"

"What's up?" Kornely asked, continuing to slurp his soup. He was used to the fact that his wife constantly exaggerated the significance and tragicality of events.

"Oy!" Xenia moaned. "It's running on six legs. Every man for himself!"

Udalov could not stand it. He walked over to the window, glanced outside, and his eyes met with an incredible sight. The aquarium was running across the yard, headed for the gate.

Some of the tentacles of the octopus stuck out beneath the aquarium; with others, he held the edges to keep the water from splashing out. The octopus was running with the speed of a three-year-old, and his eyes gleamed threateningly through the thickness of the water.

Udalov's mouth gaped.

Lozhkin stuck his head out of a window above Udalov, and the other residents joined him at their windows—both those who knew about the octopus and those who had not heard a thing. An unbelievable roar began; some were frightened, and others did not understand and began rooting the aquarium on.

In the gateway the aquarium almost collided with Stendhal, who had forgotten to write down information about the life of octopuses in their natural surroundings and was returning to Lozhkin's to have a look at Brehm.

At the sight of the running aquarium Stendhal flew upward, grabbed the lintel of the gate and hung there, his legs pulled up underneath him, even though he was not a cowardly person. The aquarium paused an instant under Stendhal, one of the tentacles appeared above the edge and a small bolt of lightning pierced Stendhal from behind.

The aquarium ran out the gate and headed down the street.

The population of Building 16 finally regained their senses and gave chase. Passersby on the street stopped, squeezed up against buildings, gasped or laughed, thinking that it was a child's prank.

The aquarium almost ended up under a bus, but it managed to brake in time. Then in its path stood the policeman Semyonov, and the aquarium tried to run around him. But that was not to be. Semyonov stood like a cliff. Then the aquarium, or more precisely the octopus, fired lightning at him. Semyonov withstood that attack. A crowd gathered from every direction.

I realized that I was done for when my path was blocked by one of them clothed in gray with shining buttons.

I darted to the side, and emptied my blaster into him. There was nowhere to go. It was all over. And the most terrible thing was that the blaster was totally discharged. I could not put a charge in my own head.

A crowd of monsters ran toward me from all directions. For them, it was amusing; for me, a tragedy.

Then I pulled my limbs out of the holes in the floor, and the atmosphere flowed out with a babble, and the dust around me turned dark. I decided that they would not take me alive.

Grubin reached the fleeing octopus when there was almost no water left in the aquarium. People were staring at it blankly, not realizing that the octopus was attempting to end its life by suicide.

"Water!" Grubin yelled. "Water, quick! It will die without water!"

"Water!" the policeman Semyonov yelled.

The octopus lay like a lifeless heap of slime on the punctured bottom of the aquarium.

Someone brought a pot of water, someone a pail, others just a cup or glass. Grubin picked out the cleanest pail he could find, and put the octopus in it gently. Then he picked up the aquarium with his other hand.

In that pose he was photographed by Misha Stendhal. And that photo later appeared in newspapers throughout the world.

I am writing these lines with a specially constructed pen on white sheets of plastic. I write in large letters so that Doctor Polosov, a very kind old gentleman, can read my notes without a microscope.

As soon as I finish my official conversation with Polosov and Masha—our secretary—Xenia Udalova will bring me cherries. Wonderful cherries grow in Great Gusliar, I cannot imagine how I will do without them when I go to Moscow. But my old friend Sasha Grubin has sworn that he'll bring several pounds with him. And I believe him—he is also a kind man. Not as well-educated as Doctor Polosov, but then Grubin never went to college. But somehow I'm going to help him get his doctorate. If only for discovering me.

Don't Make the Wizard Mad

No one believes in wizards anymore. You get the impression that they have died out, even in literature. On rare occasions you may still find a magician. But a magician is a poor substitute for a wizard—a TV performer with a bag of tricks but without real wizardry.

It is therefore not surprising that when the wizard came out of the forest and headed for Udalov, Udalov did not have the slightest inkling of something bad.

The wizard was dressed sloppily but, at the same time, rather pretentiously. He was wearing a tattered sheepskin coat, a rabbit-fur hat, and box-calf boots with the kind of clasps used on women's handbags.

"They biting?" the wizard asked.

Udalov glanced at the wizard, then concentrated on his bobber. They were biting okay, even though it was late autumn. The air was crisp, and the fallen leaves crunched underfoot.

The wizard bent over the pail, in which the perch were lying, sometimes quivering, and said, "I get half."

"Now what?" Udalov said, with a smile, and set the hook. This time it was a pickerel. It flopped over the withered grass, trying to dive back into the lake.

"Share it," the wizard said. "I am the master here. You have to split it with me."

"I've been coming here fishing for years," Udalov said as he tossed the pickerel into the pail, "and I've never seen any master. Here everyone is equal."

"I haven't been here that long," the wizard said, squatting down and sticking a finger into the pail. "I come from a different area. I'm basically peaceable, you understand?"

At that point Udalov took a good look at the wizard. He was dissatisfied with the wizard's appearance.

"What's it with you?" he asked. "Headed for a masquerade? Or escaped from a hospital?"

"Very rude," the wizard sighed. "I haven't run away from anywhere. Which is my half? You have six perch, three bluegills, and a pickerel. How do we split them?"

Udalov could tell that this guy was not kidding around. And it would have to be when there was no other fisherman around. Completely deserted. You could scream your head off. It was two miles to the nearest road, straight through the woods.

"Where do you live?" Udalov asked, almost politely.

"Under a log," the wizard answered. "When it gets cold, I'll take over an empty dacha. I'm not that demanding."

"So, you don't have your own house?"

The fishing was ruined, but all right, it was time to head home anyway. Udalov stood up, pulled in a second line, and began to roll up his tools of the fishing trade.

"I'm not supposed to have my own house, because I'm a wizard, a free being," the wizard began but noticing that Udalov was leaving, became angry. "So you want to leave? Taking it upon yourself to go against me? But nobody, and I mean nobody, goes against me. In the old days people would fall to the ground just looking at me, pleading with me to take something, and to spare them."

"There are no wizards. That's a superstition."

"To some it may be a superstition—to others it is a sad reality."

"So why should anyone fear you?"

The lines were rolled up. Udalov hopped along, to stretch his legs. It was cold. A wind was beginning to blow. A cloud was creeping out from behind the forest—rain was coming, maybe snow.

"It's pretty clear why they feared me," the wizard said. "I could put the evil eye on them."

"In what sense?"

Udalov did not care for the wizard's eyes, impudent eyes, terrifying eyes.

"In the most literal," the wizard said. "I can put the evil eye on you. On your cow. On your goat, and on your fowl."

"I don't keep any animals," Udalov said, picking up the pail and tossing the lines over his shoulder. "How could I if I live in town? So good-bye."

Udalov walked quickly along the forest path, but the wizard kept up with him. He buzzed around like a horsefly, disappearing behind the trees, reappearing on the path, talking all the while. In another case Udalov would have shared his fish with the man—he wasn't greedy—but this was a matter of principle. If you're threatened, you can't surrender. And there were so many good-for-nothings these days.

"So, you refuse? You don't respect my will?" the wizard grumbled.

"You've got it."

"You mean I have to take steps?"

"You have to."

"I'll set the evil eye upon you! I'm warning you for the last time."

"What kind of evil eye?"

"I can do a mange. Or a fever."

"It's disgusting to listen to you. Medicines have been invented for all that."

"Just give me two perch."

"Don't bother asking!"

"Stop!" the wizard ran ahead and blocked the path. "I warned you for the last time."

"Get out of my way, I'll miss the bus because of you, get home late, and show up for work tomorrow without enough sleep."

"You go to work?" The wizard seemed surprised. "And go fishing too?"

"Why not?" Udalov pushed the wizard aside and walked on. "Life without variety would be terrible. You could die that way. If I just went to work and came home to my wife, without any bother, I'd probably die of melancholy. A person needs variety. Without it a person's not a person, just a nonentity."

The wizard walked alongside, nodding in agreement. Udalov even felt that the wizard was about to admit that he too had a hobby—collecting butterflies or beetles. But instead the wizard started giggling, but there was something unsettling in that giggle.

"I've got it," the wizard said. "Your hour of death has come, Kornely Udalov. I know what spell to cast."

"Tell me." Udalov was very confident.

"Take a look."

The wizard pulled a clump of hair out of his gray beard, plucked a yellow leaf from a tree, began to squeeze it all together, reciting in an ancient tongue, and dancing. The sight was unpleasant and painful, but Udalov waited, as though he could not leave a seizure victim in the forest. But he got bored waiting, and waved his hand as though to say "Stay if you want" and walked on. Wails rushed to overtake him, and then it was silent. Udalov had just about decided that the wizard had decided to leave him in peace when rapid steps resounded from behind him.

"That is all!" the wizard shouted. "You are now enchanted, comrade Udalov. Your life will have no variety. That is the spell I am casting upon you. Your life will go in a monotonous round, day after day, week after week. And it will repeat itself exactly. You will not break out of the vicious circle until you die and you will pray to me to release you from the terrible captivity, but I will only laugh in your face and ask, 'Do you remember the fish?' "

And the wizard melted into the darkening air. As though he had fused with the aspen trunks. A rotten, damp heaviness descended on the forest. Udalov shook his head to drive away memory of the wizard and hurried to the bus stop. There, standing under the kiosk and listening to the patter of fine rain, he was amazed that the wizard had learned his name somewhere. After all, Udalov had not introduced himself.

Udalov thought about the wizard when he was on the bus, but as soon as he got home he forgot entirely.

In the morning his wife shook him. "Kornely, are you planning on sleeping through to lunch?"

Then she went over to their son's bed and asked, "Maxim, do you want to be late for school?"

And then: plop-plop—the eggs into the frying pan; rrip-rrip—the knife through the loaf of bread; blub-blub—the milk out of the bottle; eee-eee-ooo—the teapot begins boiling.

Udalov forced himself to get up, his head fuzzy from all the fresh air he had had the day before. This morning there was a meeting. Once again the schedule was in danger.

"Maxim," he asked. "Are you ever going to finish with the bathroom?"

In the bus on his way to work, he noticed familiar faces. In the office there was an appearance of efficiency. Udalov greeted the appropriate persons, went to his office, sat down behind his desk, and inspected its surface with suspicion, as though a scorpion might be hiding there. There was no scorpion. Udalov sighed, and the workday began.

When Udalov returned home, soup was bubbling on the burner. Xenia was ironing, and Maxim was doing homework. Through the window he could see the dregs of autumn—it was as dark as Hades. The table at which they had played dominoes during the summer glittered under the streetlight, and icy spray dripped onto it from the bare bushes. Fall. An empty time.

The week went by imperceptibly. Day by day. On Sunday

Udalov did not go fishing—they weren't biting. They went visiting, to Antonina's, a relative of Xenia; they sat around, watched TV, drank tea, and returned home. Monday morning Udalov was awakened by his wife's voice: "Kornely, are you planning on sleeping through to lunch?"

Then she went over to Maxim's bed and asked, "Maxim, do you want to be late for school?"

And then: plop-plop—the eggs into the frying pan; rrip-rrip—the knife through the loaf of bread; blub-blub—the milk out of the bottle; eee-eee-ooo—the teapot begins boiling.

Udalov forced himself to get up, his head fuzzy, and this morning, there was a conference. And work, work, work.

"Maxim!" he shouted. "Are you going to be in the bathroom forever?"

It was as though Udalov was playing a tape for his inner ear—where had he heard that before?

In the office everyone was bustling, and they were having an argument in the corridor. Udalov went to his office, sat down and looked suspiciously at the top of his desk, as though a scorpion might be hiding there. There was no scorpion. Udalov sighed and began preparing some papers for the conference.

On Sunday Udalov wanted to go fishing, but the weather was terrible, snow mixed with rain. So after dinner he went down to a neighbor's, chatted a while, and watched TV.

Monday morning Udalov was awakened by a strange premonition. He lay there with his eyes closed and waited. It came: "Kornely, are you planning on sleeping through to lunch?"

"Hold on!" Udalov leaped to his feet. "Who taught you that? Don't you know any other words?"

But his wife did not seem to hear. She walked over to their son's bed and said, "Maxim, are you going to school today?"

And then: plop-plop—the eggs into the frying pan. . . .

Udalov shoved his legs into his pants, hurrying to get out of the house. But he had no luck. He caught himself in a nervous exclamation: "Maxim, will you be out—" and stopped in midsentence.

He came to out on the street. Where was he going? To work. Why?

The office was in an uproar. Everyone was getting ready for the conference on the monthly figures. But one look at the worn surface of his desk was enough for an unknown force to seize him and carry him out into the street. For some reason, he ran over to the fish store, and after a short wait in line, bought a pike, a six-pounder. He wrapped the pike in newspaper and headed for the bus stop.

A wet snow was falling heavily, melting on the ground and trees. The forest was silent. Udalov listened carefully to what was happening.

"Hey," Udalov said irresolutely.

The wizard stepped out from behind a tree and said, "You brought a pike? Pike has a lot of bones."

"That's what a pike is like," Udalov said in annoyance. "It's not like bluegills."

"Bluegills are better," the wizard said. He felt the pike's tail, which was hanging out of the newspaper. "Is it frozen?"

"Yes, but recently."

"And was it baked?" The wizard accepted the pike like a young father receiving a baby at a hospital nursery.

"I can't take it any more," Udalov said.

The wizard looked up at the gray sky, and then said thoughtfully, "I'm in a good mood today. But why should I be sorry for you? You deserved your punishment."

"I brought you a pike. Over six pounds."

"OK, then. Hold the pike."

The wizard handed Udalov the pike and began to gesture with his hands. Kornely felt sick to heart. Suppose it was a joke?

"That's all," the wizard said, reaching out for the fish.

"You're free, Udalov. During the summer we split the perch fifty-fifty."

"You've got it," Udalov said, realizing now why he had come.

The wizard threw the pike over his shoulder, like a rifle, and stepped into the bushes.

"Hold on," Udalov said. "What if—"

But his words were entangled in the wet branches, and he realized that there was no one in the forest.

Udalov sluggishly made his way back to the bus stop. He shook his head and told himself that even if the guy was a wizard, he was still a repulsive person, an extortionist. On the way home he was so worn-out and old-looking that a girl tried to let him have a seat on the bus.

He went to bed in fear, and awaited morning in fear, in his dreams conducting senseless and embittered conversations with the wizard. The closer morning came, the less he believed in deliverance.

But everything worked out.

In the morning Xenia cooked oatmeal. Maxim was sick with the mumps and stayed home from school, and Udalov himself had to go on a business trip to Vologda for ten days.

Wunderbaby

"Why so late? Stop by the Shchegols' again?" With his entire body Nikolai Lozhkin played the abandoned, neglected, and hungry husband.

"What could I do?" his wife sighed as she hurried into the kitchen to put the teapot on the stove. "I had to help. They don't have any other relatives in town, and today is their union meeting. Boris is a member of the committee, and Klara had to be there too. So who would stay with little Leonardo?"

"Of course you had to. It's all right to be charitable once, twice, even three times, but—"

"Why didn't you eat the piroshkis? I left them on the kitchen table for you."

"I didn't feel like it."

Dasha Lozhkin set the table expertly while talking excitedly, since she felt guilty toward her husband. "And little Leonardo is such a happy baby. So cute—he smiles all the time. Come to the table. The tea is ready. Today he saw me and babbled, 'Gam-ma, gam-ma.'"

"How old is he?"

"Just three months."

"You're exaggerating. Who ever heard of a three-month-old baby talking?"

"I was surprised myself. I said to Klara, 'Did you hear that?' But Klara said—well, that I was losing my wits in my old age."

"Is that what she said?"

"Yes."

"Look, my dear, don't go over there any more. Cut off relations completely. My word is law, and if people like the Shchegols think they can insult you—"

"Take it easy, Nikolai, and have a piroshki—you like them with cabbage. She was just excited, in a big hurry."

"So, you said the baby called you Grandma?"

"He's very advanced for his age. Today Klara put on her sweater inside out. And he winked at me, as if to say, Look, Dasha, see how funny!"

Lozhkin choked on his tea. "What next!"

"You don't believe me? Go over and see for yourself. It's only two blocks."

"I will," Lozhkin said. "Tomorrow."

"Tomorrow I'm not going. Let's make it Thursday."

On Thursday, Lozhkin, chuckling mistrustfully, as though he was doing his wife a great favor, set off for the Shchegols'.

The Shchegols, distant relatives of his wife, were getting ready to go to the movies.

"We were afraid you'd let us down, Auntie Dasha," Klara said as soon as she saw them. She was the kind of person who knew how to accept favors, and enjoyed doing it.

"Today Nikolai will stay with little Leonardo," Dasha said. "I have a lot of work to do at home."

"Nikolai, do you have any experience coping with infants?" Boris Shchegol asked as he tied his tie.

"I put three of them through college," Lozhkin answered, offended. "Our little birds have left the nest."

"College is no argument," Shchegol said. "Klara, help me with my tie. We're late. A high-school education was enough for me. And we don't live any worse off than all those engineers of yours. But a little baby is a real problem. Since you're staying, take a look at this book, *Your Child*. You probably haven't heard about the scientific approach."

Lozhkin did not listen to the end of the monologue. He

watched the baby, who was lying in his crib behind wooden bars. The baby was inspecting his rattle, turning it in his hands, as though he understood what was what.

"Goo-goo," Lozhkin said. "Goo-goo-goo."

"Goo-goo," the baby said, as though he were exchanging greetings.

"So he does understand!" Lozhkin exclaimed. It was one thing to hear about it from his wife, another to hear for himself.

"Boris, the show starts in ten minutes," Klara said. "Nikolai, here's the baby's sugar water. The diapers are on the dresser."

"I'm going, too," Dasha said.

And Nikolai Lozhkin was left absolutely alone with the baby.

He stood next to the crib, admiring the baby. Then, unexpectedly for himself, without expecting an answer, he asked, "Should I read you a story?"

"Goo-goo," the baby answered.

"And what should I read to you?"

"Silber skates," the baby said. "Gamma read me."

The baby reached out toward the shelves, showing Lozhkin where to find the book.

"How about 'Little Red Riding Hood'?" Lozhkin suggested, but the baby shook his head no and set his rattle aside.

Lozhkin read for more than an hour, got tired, and absent-mindedly drank up the baby's sugar water. The baby did not wet his diaper once, did not whine, did not sleep, but listened intently, occasionally interrupting his uncle with pertinent questions: "What are skates? What is Holland? What is Amsterdam?"

Lozhkin satisfied the baby's curiosity as well as he could, charmed more and more by the baby's open, sparkling personality.

By the time his parents came home from the movies, the baby and Lozhkin were fast friends. Saying good-bye, Leonardo waved to his uncle and babbled, "Come thoon, come tomowwow."

His parents were tired and did not pay any attention to their tyke's cooing.

From that day on Lozhkin tried to take his wife's place as often as possible, becoming the baby's nursemaid. The Shchegols did not object. They were young, active, and liked skating and skiing, taking trips, going to the movies or to visit friends.

Within two months Leonardo had learned to sit up in his crib, and his tongue was now fully under his control. His vocabulary had grown significantly. And he often voiced regret that his still-too-weak legs would not carry him outside where he could see the places that interested him so much.

Occasionally Lozhkin would take Leonardo for a ride in his baby carriage. The baby would twist and turn his head and constantly ask questions: Why does snow fall, what was that dog doing near the hydrant, why don't women have whiskers, where do babies come from, and so on. Lozhkin did his best. When they returned home, they would start reading, or Lozhkin would tell the youngster stories about his life, about people he had met, about various unusual places and events.

Once Leonardo asked his uncle, "Ask Mama Klara to let me learn how to read. I'm already five months old. At my age Leo Tolstoy was probably writing stories already."

"I don't think it will work," Lozhkin said, "but I'll try."

He went into the kitchen where Klara, who had just returned from a friend's, was preparing cheese fritters for the following morning.

"Klara," he said chummily, "what are we going to do about Leonardo?"

"Why? Is he sick? Is his forehead hot?"

Klara was a good mother. She loved her son, worried about him, and even rocked him to sleep, which he did not really like, since it distracted him from his thoughts.

"His forehead is cool," Lozhkin said. "Only he and I were wondering whether it wasn't time to start reading."

"The old ones are as bad as the young ones," Klara scoffed. "You and your crazy ideas. Why don't you go home, Uncle Nikolai? But could you stop in tomorrow? I'd like to stay late at work. And don't forget to stop off at the store for milk."

Klara did not breastfeed Leonardo, and he was just as happy. He would have felt embarrassed.

Once his parents took Leonardo to a doctor for a routine checkup. Nothing was found. Lozhkin had advised the youngster to keep his mouth shut, just in case. Leonardo followed his advice and remained silent. However, he became fascinated with medicine. The doctor's office with all its equipment made a vivid impression.

"You know, uncle," he said after returning home, "I'd like to become a doctor. It's a noble calling. I know that I will have to study a lot, but that does not intimidate me."

Leonardo soon learned to read. Lozhkin gave him a little flashlight so he could read underneath his blanket when his parents were sleeping.

At this point in our story, the reader will have a quite natural question: How could Leonardo's parents have failed to notice their baby's exceptional abilities? How could it happen that it was a stranger who would say to his wife, "I see a sign of fate in the fact that the baby is named Leonardo. The world has waited half a millennium for the next universal genius, and now he has come." How could the parents remain convinced that their little Leonardo was an ordinary child?

It is indeed remarkable—but true.

Here, for example, is what happened on the day Leonardo turned nine months old. Boris Shchegol brought him a new rattle as a present. The baby at that time was sitting in his crib and listening to Lozhkin read from Montaigne's *Essays*.

"Look at the nice toy," Boris said. As usual, he was in a hurry and did not intend to stay long, but Leonardo, to his great misfortune, said, "This toy somehow reminds me of a spatial model of the solar system."

His father lost his temper. "Nikolai, what kind of nonsense

have you been reading to my son? And he's repeating it. As though we didn't have any good children's books. About the little red hen, for example. I bought it myself. What have you done with it?"

Lozhkin did not answer, because Leonardo had torn it up to make paper airplanes: He wanted to explore the possibilities of gliding flight.

The infuriated Shchegol took the book of Montaigne's *Essays* away from Lozhkin and left the room.

Or another example. A few days later there was an incident with Klara. She carried a plate of strained soup into Leonardo's bedroom, but there was no place to put it down. She had to knock several medical journals and dictionaries off the table to make room.

"What are you babbling about?" she asked Lozhkin amiably.

"We're studying Swedish," Lozhkin confessed. Usually he and Leonardo preferred not to let the parents in on their studies, but now the evidence of the crime was right there.

"Well then, study away," Klara said, her mind elsewhere.

Leonardo shrugged his shoulders, as if to say to Lozhkin "Don't mind her."

A few minutes later they overheard Klara talking with a friend of hers in the next room: "My little guy . . . I was just in his room, and he was chattering away in a make-believe language. Like a little bird."

"Does he talk already?"

"He will soon. He's very advanced for his age. But for now he chatters in his own language. What is remarkable is that there is this old man who comes over to help out, and he understands."

"Old people often return to childhood," her friend said.

Leonardo put his plump little hand on Lozhkin's, which was trembling with anger, and whispered, "Be patient, uncle, what can you do? I really do love my parents. They are nice, kind people. But I get so tired of them. If you only knew!"

Klara and her friend entered the bedroom. As soon as Klara's friend caught sight of the baby, she started to quiver and repeated over and over, "Oh, how cute he is!"

Then she said, "Say 'ma-ma.' "

"Ma-ma," Leonardo answered obediently.

"He really is remarkable! What an intelligent baby!"

At this point the youngster got bored with wasting his time on idle chatter and turned to Lozhkin. "Shall we continue with the Swedish, colleague?"

The women did not make out what he said. They started talking about clothes and left the room.

When Leonardo learned to walk a little, he and Lozhkin made a hiding place under a floorboard, where Lozhkin could hide new journals and books. Leonardo was writing his first article, on enzymes. In order not to arouse his parents' suspicions, he dictated it to Lozhkin, who typed it up and sent it to a journal. Unfortunately, it was to be the last of the baby's accomplishments.

Sometime during his second year Leonardo, quite unexpectedly for Lozhkin, began to grow cool toward the natural sciences and began to consume books on philosophical issues in unbelievable quantities. Incidentally, his child's imagination was greatly impressed with Freud.

"What's going on with you?" Lozhkin asked, puzzled. "You are forgetting your destiny—to become a new Leonardo da Vinci, and to enrich humanity with remarkable discoveries. You are forgetting that you are the *homo futurus*."

"I grant that what you say may be true," the baby agreed submissively. "But I must say that I find myself confronted with an almost insoluable dilemma. In addition to my duty to humanity, I feel no less an obligation to my parents. To them I am a freak. Their healthy instinct for self-preservation protects them against the idea that I am an exception. They want everything to be normal—maybe a little better. They want to be proud of me, but within limits comprehensible to their friends. Recognizing this, I am forced to conceal what I am. And every day this grows harder."

"Just try to talk to them one more time."

"It won't work. They don't want to understand."

The next day, when Lozhkin arrived at the Shchegols' with a volume of Spinoza he had obtained with great difficulty, he saw the little guy sitting at the table next to his father. His dad was enthusiastically teaching him to read, syllable by syllable. Leonardo repeated after him, "Ma-ma gave Ma-sha a dol-ly."

"He's learning!" Boris exclaimed triumphantly. "He's not even three, and he's reading! No one at work will believe it!"

Lozhkin could not contain himself. "It just isn't right!" he growled. "Your child is expending so much energy appearing to be what you want that he is turning into a genius at hypocrisy, instead of a universal genius."

"Uncle, no!" Leonardo pleaded.

"Because of you, he's given up his scientific studies."

"What scientific studies?" Boris asked in amazement. "Are you putting me on?"

"No, I'm not. Haven't you noticed that for months your apartment has been littered with books and journals you can't understand a word of? I'm going to write to the Academy of Sciences and have them send special teachers."

"So you're going to send in a complaint?" Boris stood up. "You people are great at writing complaint letters. But when it comes to taking care of the child, where are you?"

"I won't allow it."

"You won't allow it! Get out of my house! Don't you dare hurt my child."

"But he's a *wunderkind*!"

"Watch out who you're calling names. You're senile!"

Lozhkin put his hand over his heart, and Boris realized he

had gone too far. He said almost guiltily, "I beg you, Nikolai, please don't interfere in our family life. Leonardo is a normal kid, and I'm proud of it."

"Please don't, uncle," Leonardo said.

"But Boris, you too will be famous. As the parents of a genius. As the discoverer, so to speak. Imagine that your child was a future world champion in gymnastics. Wouldn't you want him to have special training?"

"That would be different," Boris objected.

At that moment Lozhkin suspected that Boris had caught on but fought the idea off.

"Today we learn some alphabet," Leonardo said to Lozhkin. "Daddy is happy. That is more important to me than all the enzymes in the world."

His voice was firm.

"Listen Boris, to what he's saying," Lozhkin persisted. "How would an ordinary child know about enzymes?"

"Some nonsense he picked up from you." Boris snapped. "And, thank God, he'll forget it soon."

"I will forget it, Daddy," Leonardo promised.

Another three years passed.

Leonardo would soon be starting school. He learned to read fairly well and to write without making too many mistakes. Lozhkin had stopped going to the Shchegols'. Once he met Leonardo on the street. He was about to hug him when the boy stopped him with a wave of the hand and said, "Wait until college, uncle. It's not over yet."

"It was over years ago," Lozhkin answered bitterly.